**She wo**
which she h[...]
she descended and stepped, as she suspected, directly into the beginnings of the garden. Statues of various gods loomed whitely in the twilight. The tinkle of running water alerted her of the nearness of a small frog pond. She knew her way from there and walked confidently forward. She almost screamed when an arm reached out and encircled her waist.

"Shhh…little one. It is only I, Richard, your Noble Rescuer." He laughed softly and rubbed his face gently in her hair as he held her close. She twisted around to look up into his eyes but could not read his thoughts in the dim light. He released her and caught her hand, pulling her gently with him around the hedge and back to that private floral bower, borrowed once more from their host.

At his urging, she settled on a white garden bench which nestled against a flowering vine. Heady night fragrances enveloped her as she looked up into the handsome face of her friend. He gazed back at her but then paced a step or two back.

"I have things to say, sweetness. Please do not be upset when I use words I know are improper. Let us be two different people for tonight. What say you?" He stepped closer, but still did not join her on the bench.

Elisabeth waited for what she knew not. She was content to be this close to one for whom she had such feelings.

*To Marcia with my best Wishes! Enjoy! Emma Lane*

# Tutored
# by a Duke

## by

## Emma Lane

**Tutored by a Duke**

Cover Art by *Debbie Taylor*

The Wild Rose Press, Inc.
PO Box 708
Adams Basin, NY 14410-0708
Visit us at www.thewildrosepress.com

Publishing History
First Tea Rose Edition, 2016
Print ISBN 978-1-5092-0635-3
Digital ISBN 978-1-5092-0636-0

Published in the United States of America

# Dedication

Thanks to my daughter, Susan,
and my granddaughter, Emily,
for all their help.

## Chapter One

"Jamie, could you put a little more enthusiasm into it? You might as well be eating a green caterpillar for the look on your face. Am I so terrible to kiss?" Miss Elisabeth Barrows flung her hands up in the air, pulling away from him on the red leather sofa, where she had been poised and eager for her lessons. Her yellow-sprigged, muslin day dress was like a splash of sunshine in the book-laden room filled with dark furniture, but her face was a study in disappointment.

"Lizzie, this is not a game. You go too far. If your mother...or anyone comes into the room, I will never attain the title of a baronetcy because I will be a dead man." James Wilkerson slid away from his friend who sat with a frown on her face, golden curls springing away from the tightly coiled braids on top her head. This lovely creature had been his next-door neighbor and best mate all through their growing-up years, and a champion one she was, too. Only recently had she turned into a young woman, an impossible creature.

"I am already eighteen years old," she said with a pleading voice. "I am to go into society soon, and besides that, the ball is in a fortnight. What will they think of me if I know nothing about the ways of men? What kind of friend are you to refuse to teach me?"

Was she about to burst into tears? No, he just could not. There were many things he would do for Elisabeth, but kiss her he would not. Even if his father hadn't sat him down and lectured regarding the appropriate respect due a proper young lady, he still could not bring himself to answer her request.

He stood and walked to the window, longing to be away, riding into that peaceful landscape, anywhere but in the library being harangued.

"Lizzie," he began, and then paused. He turned to face her and shook his head. How to explain without crossing the line with a female? Sometimes he had no idea how to handle this hoyden of a friend. If her mother had any inkling what she was up to…but he would never betray her. He remembered the pact they made, a conspiracy against their parents at an early age, and he would no more spill her secrets than he would…well something or other important. But this was disconcerting to say the least. He was in no way qualified to demonstrate the finer arts of romance to her than would be her pet spaniel.

"It's a difficult thing to explain," he continued, understanding how very silly and awkward he sounded, but he plugged on. "Kissing between a male and female is not about being friends or, or…a certain technique. Oh, I don't mean the peck on the cheek kind of kissing. You seem to want a romantic kiss, and I tell you it just can't happen between friends." He felt his face warming, and he couldn't stop squirming. This was not a proper topic for a young unmarried girl, and he was too well aware of it.

"Oh, pshaw. You just aren't putting enough heart into it. Let's try again, shall we?"

Jamie tried but failed to restrain his amusement at the sight of his friend sitting on the sofa with her eyes squinted tightly closed, her lips pursed, and her hands clasped tightly in front of her, as if she were praying. The pose wasn't inspiring him to do the task assigned even if he could summon up the courage to try it again. Certainly he was not against kissing a pretty girl, only Lizzie was not just any girl. She was his friend—more like a sister, if he had one, which he had not.

This lovely chit of a girl was a handful, a bit of a baggage, even if she was on her way to turning into a diamond of the first water. He couldn't erase all the growing-up years between the two of them.

A vivid memory popped into his mind of Elizabeth almost running him through with a sharpened branch when they played at pirates in the home woods. She insisted he wear a black patch over one eye, and it obstructed his vision. She laughed at him, but it was the truth for all that. How old had they been? He was on a break from school—it must have been—only five years ago? Gad, how had he allowed her to talk him into that? What to do with her? She was a force to be reckoned with when she was in full pursuit of something she wanted.

"You don't understand, Lizzie. Kissing is a thing for grown-up couples usually after they are engaged, not something you can do as a parlor game. Well, some people do play games like that, but it's not for a gentleman's daughter, believe me," he said sternly.

"You are wrong, Jamie. These days all sorts of women play at kissing. I heard the girls at school talking about it. There was a rumor that Sal Mansel did it with a footman—and more than once, I tell you." She flounced on the couch and turned her face away.

"I have a great idea. How about I engage my

3

friend, Burt, to teach you? He'll be arriving for the ball in a few days, and you don't know him. He'll have more success than I, I assure you. Plus, if he gets out of hand, I can strangle him with no trouble."

"I'm sure I don't know what the fuss is about. So far, it has no appeal to me. Your lips are wet," she said as she wiped her mouth with the back of her hand. "How Sal could do that with a servant behind her father's barn is a mystery to me. At least I asked someone I know to teach me. Do you want me to find a servant who…?" Her usually low-pitched, pleasant voice flew up another octave, and she practically squeaked in her haste to tease him into compliance.

"No! You will not. Oh, you are pretending again, aren't you? Aw, don't be mad at me, Lizzie. Let's go for a ride while the weather is still nice, shall we?" He reached for her hand and pulled her up. She did not resist and even greeted his suggestion with enthusiasm.

"I wanted to try that sweet mare with the blaze down her face. The old duke told my mother we were welcome to any ride that suited us. Wait for me. I will change so fast you will hardly realize I am gone." The two left the room together with Lizzie chatting about her potential mount.

Chapter Two

Richard Hawlester, the present Duke of Roderick, stood and walked to the window, taking a quiet pride in the pastoral view. Hidden from the young couple by the wings on the red leather armchair, he had been engrossed in a novel. The prominent side wings kept uncomfortable drafts from the vulnerable neck of the person occupying the seat, but the side panels effectively screened him from view. Perhaps he should not have eavesdropped with such avid interest, and he would not have, but Miss Elisabeth Barrow's voice intrigued him. He had not yet been introduced to her, and it was certain her mother would not allow her to guess she was under consideration to become the next Duchess of Roderick. The young women were not to be informed; he insisted when he issued the invitations to his house party and the subsequent ball. She was not the only potential candidate for the job.

Chuckles involuntarily bubbled up as he remembered the earnestness of the young woman determined to experience the first nibbles of romance. So very young and eager to try out her feminine powers on the opposite sex. Beware, men! Someone soon would, no doubt, fall under her sweet, tempting spell. As matter of interest, it was her older sister who was invited, with the younger one along for the visit. Not yet out, but a force with which to reckon in due time.

Almost, it made him melancholy for his own lost youth. What fun it would have been to have the teaching of this spirited young lady!

He moved away and leaned against the long oak table set in the middle of the room. This was no doubt an insane idea his mother had suggested he execute. Yes, he needed a wife. He knew he was getting older and should already have gotten his heir. He had no ready excuse. It was his duty, after all, to see to the succession.

"Just couldn't see getting leg-shackled to one of that giggling bunch of silly women," he said aloud to the empty room. He couldn't abide facing another Season standing up with simpering debs or fending off their pushy mothers at Almack's, so he finally agreed to this dreadful house party. He pulled the bell for his butler. "There must be in all of this land a suitable bride for me. Quiet, biddable, and easy on the eyes. Oh, and must not giggle. " He turned as the man came into the room.

"Oh, there you are, Dooley. Will you inform the stables to have my black ready in half an hour? I think I'll take the air for a while." He left the room and ran lightly upstairs to change his dress. Later, mounting from a block, he had to mind his business, as his stallion was eager for exercise. He allowed the beast to shake out the fidgets for a while, until they were both breathless, but later paused in the shade of a lone oak on the top of a small hill and surveyed the valley below. A movement caught his eye, and he recognized the pair recently practicing kissing in his library. With a spurt of laughter, he wondered if they were more competent at riding than kissing.

He held his breath and watched the two as they sped down the hill. They jumped recklessly over a hedgerow blocking their paths.

Miss Elisabeth Barrows, flashing a crimson riding habit and some sort of ridiculous matching hat, clung to her horse as she sailed over the obstacle, as if she were Diana the Huntress. How she could maintain such a perfect seat on that death trap of a sidesaddle was beyond him. Surely her mother was ignorant of her dangerous behavior. With the sound of a distant whoop, the two disappeared down a bridle path that curved away from his sight. Was the little mischief seeker in the lead? He rather thought she was. The white-faced mare had a pleasant gait and a bit of speed on her as well. Perhaps the mare recognized competence and matched her efforts to it. His attention remained fixed as he waited for further glimpses of the two mad riders.

It was the timbre of her voice that intrigued him. What was there about that husky tone that caught and firmly held his attention? She was too young. What had he been like at eighteen? Possibly, he had been more reckless than either of the pair of kissing friends. He laughed aloud again as he thought of the interplay between them.

Grew up together, did they? It never worked out as parents thought it would. Jamie? He thought he had been introduced to that young man. Would that be the heir to Rowlings' Manor, the Baron George Wilkerson? Damnation. He was closer to the father's age than to the young son, James. Good family, solid English stock and a very nice property. Parents could not be blamed for encouraging a match for their daughter with that young man. But he was too young to wed, and Miss Mischief

7

was too eager to try her wings. If the parents were patient, the match might yet come about, but he rather thought James would rebel.

Richard raised his hand as he spotted another rider trotting up the hill to greet him.

"You found the tack just as you needed?" Richard asked, eyeing the stirrup on his friend's saddle.

"I did, and I thank you for the wisdom of an old groom who figured it all out for me," Captain Mark Estermire said, as he gentled his mount that reached to take a nip from the black stallion. "It took a bit of maneuvering to jostle me into the saddle, but we managed." He laughed without real mirth. "I've endeavored to keep my seat so far."

Richard hoped his face would not reflect the delight that rose within him. His friend, crippled in that dreadful war, was astride again. Never did he think to see the day after one glimpse of the horrible wound that all but paralyzed his friend's lower leg. Mark Estermire had struggled for many weeks, convalescing in a back room he insisted on using, as it was on a lower level and eliminated stairs for the most part. How he had managed to stay sane was a miracle, as far as Richard was concerned. He had such admiration for his friend's courage.

"You'll be surprised when I tell you that more and more of the feeling has returned. Old Doc Rawlings mentioned the possibility, but I confess I thought he was only trying to cheer me. What do you think? Is my seat grotesque? I can feel parts of the stirrup, and my grip on the saddle seems intact. I'm seriously out of tune with my muscles, however." He flexed his shoulders and had to quickly tend his mount that shied away from the brute of a black Richard favored. Richard joined his friend's laughter.

"Progress, indeed. You'll be stealing a waltz before your recovery is complete. By the way, will you join us for supper tonight?" He held up his hand to continue with his question. "I know you hide your limp, but do you hide you? I could seriously use your support. M' mother has overwhelmed me with eligible milk-and-water English misses. I fight my desire to flee every night. I do not possess the gift for conversing with a stranger that you have in abundance." They turned their horses down the hill and toward the gray stone manor set invitingly on the crest of the next rise. Grazing sheep filled one side, and healthy crops of small farms dotted the other.

When Mark did not immediately answer, Richard glanced quickly at the expression on his friend's face. "How about a picnic at the pond tomorrow afternoon? Jack can drive you within a foot of the benches there. Once settled, you need not move until everyone has left. What do you think?"

Mark turned to him with a slow smile lighting his face. "You tempt me. I confess I would not mind conversing with a bevy of pretty young misses. Think you my wounds render me disgusting...or could I play the injured hero home from the war?"

Richard laughed aloud, delighted when Mark joined him with his own burst of mirth. They turned at the noise of two riders coming fast behind them.

Richard could see Miss Mischief leading James by a head. They streaked by, heading for the stables, with both riders crouched low on their mount's necks. As they neared the path by the pond, a rabbit darted in front of the horses, and the mare with the white blaze reared in fright, coming to an abrupt halt. Elisabeth, who most likely had boasted she knew of no horse that could unseat her, sailed over her mount's head and splashed a noisy landing. To his relief, Richard saw her spring up amidst the water lilies, sputtering and flapping her arms in an attempt to wade ashore. He hastened to the water's edge.

James was already slogging out to reach his young friend by the time Richard and Mark arrived. The duke dismounted and stood on the shore, ready to relieve James of his sopping wet burden. She was clinging to her friend's neck and sputtering water when Richard reached over and took her into his arms. He cradled her to his chest regretting not at all how quickly his riding coat became drenched with the pond water.

Elisabeth looked up at him in surprise. "I assure you it was not the fault of my beautiful, sweet Blaze," she said quickly. "There was a hare! He ran...achoo!" She sneezed and bumped her head on Richard's shoulder. "Beg pardon, sir. Thank you for the rescue, but I think I might walk. I am not injured, I think. How is my horse?" She craned her head to see her mount standing, still atremble, with James holding onto the bridle and speaking to the horse in a soothing voice.

"You are very wet and a very lucky young lady. Thank goodness there was a soft landing for you, but we must get you to dry clothes immediately." He boosted her in front of his black and mounted quickly behind her where he pulled her securely against his chest.

"James, Mark here will ride with you to dry clothes; we want no chills." He signaled, and his mount surged forward. Richard's chin was tickled by wet curls, and he turned his eyes downward. A small lily pad rested atop a row of unwinding braids. His chest rumbled with suppressed mirth. She glanced back at him but asked no questions. The air was soft, and wisps of curls were soon drying. He detected a faint fragrance of roses mixed with, perhaps, pond water. They made their way directly toward the steps of the palatial, old manor house.

"Is this your favorite mount? It is a very fine animal. You know we are allowed to choose any that appeals to us. My mother said the old duke was amiable with his guests' wishes. I love that one—I call her Blaze—what tossed me into the pond. It wasn't her fault," she said quickly. She glanced back at him again and caught him smiling.

"Amusing, was it, to see me flying through the air? I assure you...no, you are correct. It was funny." She released a gurgle of laughter that made him catch his breath and tightened his arms to pull her closer. What was it about this chit that had him so intrigued?

He called out to a gardener working in his mother's roses. "Go inside and summon Miss Elisabeth's maid," he ordered, still holding onto his prize. She squirmed and looked back at him, when he did not immediately release her.

"Do you think I am injured? I assure you, I am able to walk. It was a shock when I hit that cold water, but I do not think I am wounded." As she squirmed again, he reluctantly allowed her to slide down his leg and booted foot to escape his embrace.

"Do go directly inside and order up a hot bath. You must warm up as quickly as you can." He dismounted and handed the reins to the gardener who had reappeared with two maids in tow. He walked beside Elisabeth as she trailed water onto the black-and-white marble tiles of the spacious foyer. From the height of three stairs, she turned back and grinned at him.

"I thank you, my rescuer, and release you to find other maidens in need of immediate aid. I am certain our host will praise you for your careful attention to his guests; only please do not relate to anyone that I was racing with Jamie?" she pleaded with her hands clasped and folded beneath her chin.

He stood looking up, amused, as she whirled and ran lightly up the stairs, the train of a sodden riding habit thrown over one arm. He entered his library and closed the door, peeling off his own now soggy riding coat. Standing near the fire always kept burning to keep his books dry, he pulled on his chin thoughtfully. What now?

*Are you falling for a reckless child, a chit newly emergent from the schoolroom with no idea who you actually are? She thought her horse more interesting than you.* He chuckled. Now why did that amuse him? It was a refreshing change from the giggling and flirting young women interested only in his title. He had a suspicion lovely Miss Elisabeth might evaluate him based strictly on the quality of his cattle. Thanks goodness he had always insisted on the best, and his stables were large and accommodating. What would she say when she realized the old duke was the same as the man who gave her a ride on an enormous black stallion?

Chapter Three

"Good sir!" Richard entered the wood where he could hear a faint cry. "Is someone there?" he called out. He stood in the dappled shade of the wood with his head cocked, listening, with nothing but the rustle of a slight breeze through the trees to excite his hearing. Then there was another call which seemed closer this time.

"Who is there?" he called again. He walked carefully through the well-groomed grove toward an enormous oak nestled in a clearing near a burbling stream. He remembered it well, a favorite haunt of his boyhood. Its many-branched trunk held the remnants of an ancient tree house—not his generation, but perhaps the one before him. Now he could see a small boot dangling from a branch several feet above. He shook his head in amusement. Some present day child had overestimated his ability to climb to greater heights.

"Are you going to stand there and leave me stuck up here?" Richard was jolted in a slight shock of surprise. His pulse beat a rapid tempo, and he made a conscious effort to still his shallow breathing. Elisabeth Barrows was the last person he expected to find dangling from the old oak. On the other hand, who better to climb that old tree than a sprite who desired to practice kissing? He should not have been surprised.

"What's the matter, Miss Elisabeth? Are you afraid

13

of the height? Are you hurt?" He placed his boot on the bottom branch and reached for the one above. Within seconds he reached her side and wrapped one arm snugly around her. He had, the evening before, made it his business to identify her family name. "I have you safe now."

Her curls tickled his cheek, and he restrained himself from snuggling closer, but when he tugged, he realized the problem. She could not move from her perch. He turned to gaze directly into her eyes and thought perhaps he made a mistake.

"My foot is stuck. That's why I couldn't get down. I tried to pull my boot free, but there's a hole in the tree, and my foot slipped into it. I don't think I'm hurt, just stuck. Can you reach down there and pull it free?"

He let go of her and balanced on a lower branch. Now he could see a cavity which she had inadvertently broken into. Her foot was firmly wedged. He tugged but stopped when she whimpered.

"I'm sorry. Let me try another angle. Can you wriggle it a bit? You will pardon me for my bad manners, Miss Elisabeth. I must try and pull on your leg for a minute to reposition it." He brushed her skirts aside and wrapped his hand around her slender ankle.

"Hold on tight now while I shift your foot a bit. Let me know if it hurts, won't you? Don't try to be brave." He slipped the half boot a bit to one side and then gave a sharp tug. Elisabeth yelled but then started laughing, as she clung to the branch and kicked her foot free. She uttered another half scream when a small owl flew out of the hole where once her boot had rested.

Richard couldn't help it. He roared in laughter. "You have surely disturbed the wildlife around here,

Miss Elisabeth. May I inquire why you are roosting bird-like in this tree?" He put his arm back where it wanted to go, and this time, when he tugged, she moved with him.

"I promise I am not injured, Noble Hero. You have once again come to my rescue. How may I repay you?" She wriggled free as they approached the last limb from the ground. Richard reluctantly let her go, thinking, and a bit startled at his thoughts, that he knew perfectly well how she might repay him.

"Your safety is all I require in thanks. There is a promise you could make me, however." He blinked as she turned crystal blue eyes trustingly up to his.

"Anything," she pledged. "I owe my life to you. I might have died up there all alone in that cruel tree." She gave a mock shudder and stifled a chuckle, but he caught the glimpse of a dimple winking in one cheek.

"That, interestingly enough, is exactly the promise I mean to exact as my reward. Should you wander about without an escort, Miss Elisabeth? Where is your friend, James?"

"Oh, him," she scoffed. "He must go off with other gentlemen to catch fish in a stream, perhaps the same one as that." She pointed to the grass-covered banks behind them. "I vow that water looks so cooling. I must have been stuck in that tree for hours. I really do appreciate your help." She walked over and dipped her hands in the clear water and then splashed it on her face. Afterward, she sank down in the deep grass, rested her hands on her knees, and then bobbed her head up at him.

"Would you be discreet, my rescuer? Please do not tell my mother I left the house without a maid. She was busy with my sister, and I did want to be outside with the sun shining so brightly."

He eased his long limbs into a seat near her in the lush grasses. "Would you confide in me about your busy mother? Who is your sister? There are so many guests here." He reached and plucked a wild daisy from the cluster growing near and handed it to her. She took it, staring absently off into the distance.

"I understand. You would not credit it, but I have not been introduced to our host, and we have been here for four days, although he has a very nice mother," she added.

Richard thought he detected a note of envy in her voice. She twirled the daisy in her fingers, caressing her cheek with it. Had the wicked monster taken hold of him and colored him green as well—of a flower?

"Your busy mother?" He pressed.

She looked up at him with interest this time, tilting her head as she examined him. "You are discreet, are you not? I have avoided a scolding about my dip into the lily pond. I deduce you are a friend who can keep a secret." She grinned with a mischievous twinkle, and he readied himself for the appearance of the dimples. He was not disappointed but was surprised to see the right cheek remained smooth. Miss Elisabeth Barrows, daughter of a gentleman, owned only one kiss of a fairy in her left cheek. He tried but knew he was failing to contain the smile that widened his lips.

"I amuse you, my rescuer? I am a trial to my parents and my oh-so-perfect sister." Her smile wavered.

"You are not happy, I see," he said, restraining with some difficulty his urge to take her in his arms.

"Can you tell me how I may be of some assistance?" He leaned forward and pulled a fragment from her shoulder, perhaps a piece of bark from the cruel tree, which would keep her clasped in its arms. Certainly he understood the desire.

"I am a sad case. Is your name a secret? I like you best as my Noble Hero, but you must be here as a guest of the old duke. What may I call you, sir?"

"Richard, little one. Could you call me Richard? I have not seen you at breakfast. Were you ill from your swim in the lily pond? I fear you became chilled in spite of our haste to get you to dry clothing." He allowed his gaze to drift at will from the top of her honey-colored, sun-streaked braids still in the process of striving for escape, to the small excuse of a nose, and lingered on the kissable lips. He watched her pull the petals from the wild daisy one at a time. She seemed distracted and unaware of her actions, but he filled in the gap with his thoughts, *she loves me, she loves me not.* She balled up the center and threw it into the grass so he could not decide the outcome. Had he lost his mind? If not completely, a partial loss for certain.

"No, not ill. You must not think I am craven or delicate in my senses. No, my mother strongly suggested I stay and have my meals in my room. I was instructed to read two chapters of *The Manners of a Lady* and be ready to report what I have learned to my sister by tonight. I am a sad disgrace to my entire family." She hung her head and clasped her hands.

"Not you," he exclaimed softly. "What behavior could prompt such strict punishment?" He stretched out his long legs and managed to wind up closer to Elisabeth. He reached for her chin and tilted it upward, then took his finger to the tiny tear sparkling on her cheek.

"I will confess all to you, my Noble Hero. I do not appreciate fine needlework. I know I shock you, but 'tis true. My sainted mother caught me out-of-doors reading a frivolous novel when she thought I had been hemming a lace tucker. It was a fine day, my Rescuer. How could I be expected to remain quietly inside and destroy my eyes with needlework?" The duke, no stranger to subterfuge, raised his eyebrows skeptically. Elisabeth laughed and threw up her hands in surrender.

"Caught. I cannot fool you, can I, Richard? I found a...well, I suppose it wasn't quite proper for an unmarried female, but it *was* in the library." She wrinkled up her insignificant nose. He leaned closer to examine a particular freckle perched just above the one dimple. "Who could know what it contained?"

"Did it have a red leather cover with gold insets?" he asked, feeling the hair raise on the back of his neck. He sat up and held his breath.

"Yes! Do you know it? It had very interesting illustrations, but my mother took it away before I could see much. She was very upset."

"Quite proper. You are too young for that sort of literature, my friend. There are many admirable storybooks there, but for that one. See you find those. I'm afraid I'm in sympathy with your parent this time." He ached for the dispirited expression that grew on her pretty face, even as he longed to kiss the pout from those delectable lips.

"However, it is sad for you to miss a nice day. Perhaps you could convince your parent to allow you to read in the garden. There are many comfortable benches to be found there. By the by, how is it you are outside today?" He thought he knew.

"Oh, please, I could not bear it another minute. Please do not tell…" She stopped when he raised his hand.

"I am sworn to secrecy, but you must try to stay out of mischief if you want to leave that bedroom, little friend of mine." He pulled her to her feet, holding her hands longer than necessary before he reluctantly allowed them to slip away. They strolled in companionable silence back through the greenwood. He glanced down frequently to admire how the dappled shade played upon her sunny curls and wondered at his fascination with this young girl. The why of it he knew not. He did a mental shrug and made a decision to play it out. It was the most interesting time he had found the whole week of this disastrous house party. At least he didn't feel like a title instead of a flesh and blood man. "Noble Hero" was the only title he preferred these days. He grinned.

"I must leave you now, Elisabeth. Will you take pity on your parent and return to your room? I fear she may be out searching for you as we speak. No doubt she will be so relieved you are safely found and unhurt, she will take pity on you and allow you a bit more freedom." He reached for her hand and kissed it, watching her eyes widen. She immediately lowered thick eyelashes to rest on sun-kissed cheeks. He counted three diminutive freckles sprinkled across that poor excuse of a tiny nose—would that he could place a kiss just there.

"Goodbye, my friend," he said, as he turned away toward the stables. He glanced over his shoulder, but she had finally started her slow walk toward the large wooden front doors of the manor. He sympathized with her. It was a very fine day to be outside.

Inside the barn, he found Mark discussing a change in his tack with Jack, the groom. In the last three days while Richard looked to no avail for a glimpse of Elisabeth, Mark made astounding strides in his ability to navigate the grounds. His gait, though still arduous and slow, was rapidly improving. His spirits, of deep concern to his friend, seemed to rise with each hard-won victory over the vicious wound he had endured.

"Well met, Roderick, my mate," Mark hailed when he spotted his host. "Have you been out surveying everything you see as your own? You have foregone your dangerous stallion for a walk? Has he gone lame?" He turned to walk with Richard out of the stables and into the bright sunlight. Their gait was slow as Mark leaned heavily on his cane, but his progress was far superior to even that of the last week.

"I surveyed my property on foot and was rewarded by another rescue." He gave a laugh that had Mark staring at him. "Ah, you want explanation, do you? I wonder if I will give it to you. In truth, I am in sad need of consultation. Do you think you would remain a friend to one who had totally lost his senses? You wonder if I am jesting, but I assure you I am in complete earnest. Shall we take a rest in the garden and I will confess all?" They chose a seat in the far corner of the garden where Richard thought they might be granted a moment of privacy from his houseguests.

Mark turned to him with raised eyebrows. "Tell all, Fair Duke. What sad occurrence has turned you insane, lost your mind, readied you to be clamped in irons?

Was it some poison from an herb? I overheard two attendants talk about ample supplies in your enormous stillroom. Perhaps you have disappointed some lady and she has…?"

"Nothing so exotic, my friend, for it seems I have been felled by a single arrow."

"An arrow? Which incompetent has sent his weapon so far from the target that you are impaled?" He inspected his friend all over with alarm, looking for any obvious injury. Richard greeted this inquiry with crinkled eyes and a shout of laughter.

"Not that sort of arrow, Mark. This is a much more deadly type, and I'm afraid there is no cure." He watched the expression on his friend's face change from worried to puzzlement to amusement merging into downright laughter.

"Oh, you find my state hilarious, do you?" He cocked one eyebrow with a grimace. "Beware the cupid's arrow for you, my friend. It strikes without warning."

## Chapter Four

"Lizzie, there you are. Mother has been asking for you this hour since. Where have you been, you naughty girl?" Without replying, Elisabeth stared blankly at her sister, walked past her and flopped onto her bed.

"Sophie? Can we chat for a bit? I will apologize to Mother shortly, I promise."

Sophia sat down at her dresser in the room they shared, and began to fuss with her curls. Elisabeth took a deep breath as she admired the perfection that was her older sister. Her gown was unwrinkled, her slippers immaculate, and her hair, a rich chestnut, was without a sign of the wispy curls always springing from her own head. Sophia's complexion was perfect. She had never gone outside without her bonnet and would be horrified that her sister, who owned to a few freckles across her nose, frequently did. Elisabeth could not feel jealousy of a sister, who she knew was gratified to be considered a possible choice for duchess. All the guests knew why they had been invited by the Duke of Roderick and the dowager duchess, even as they pretended it to be a secret.

"What is it? Have you lost another race to Jamie? You know very well, it is forbidden to ride in that hoyden manner that you do. Some day you will go too far and break your neck." She turned to look at her sister and immediately was concerned.

"Lizzie? What is the matter, dear?" She reached her sister's side and put an arm around her. A lone tear rolled down Elisabeth's cheek, but she shook her head.

"I do not know what the matter with me is, Sister. Did you...have you had...I feel so very strange. I imagine it must be nerves over my come-out. How long do you think we will stay here, do you think?" She sat up and wiped her eyes with balled up fists.

"Forgive me. I'm just being a silly chit of a girl. Lately, I have had the oddest thoughts and over a stranger at that. Did that ever happen to you?" She turned sad eyes to her sister, wondering why she said something as silly as all that. Elisabeth thought perhaps she was sickening for something.

"You are ill, Lizzie? What has happened to make you so sad?" Sophia asked with a perplexed expression on her gentle face. "What stranger have you encountered?"

Elisabeth smoothed her hair and plastered a pleasant expression on her face. How weird she should have confided in her sister about feelings toward a stranger. It was this visit at the Duke of Roderick's house. Were they cattle to be examined and herded out of the group? Picked for what? Wide hips to give him lots of heirs? Oh, she certainly knew about all that. She might not have experience in kissing, but she knew where babies came from—perhaps she was not yet straight on exactly how they got there, but never mind.

"Forgive me, no one at all, Sister. Mother waits for me, I know. Thank you for listening." She rose and prepared to leave the room.

"But I did nothing. I do not understand..." Sophia shook her head, but Elisabeth left the room without speaking. Perhaps she was sickening for something, for she felt both warm and chilly, but the vision of a tall man with black curls danced through her mind, and she felt her spirits lighten. She did not understand these strange new feelings, but they were not always uncomfortable.

****

Next day dawned fair and warm. Elisabeth's mother relented and sanctioned both sisters to attend the picnic on the wide side lawn which ended at the lily pond, with which Elisabeth had already become closely acquainted. Thank goodness she had brought more than one riding habit with her. She feared her favorite red one was a lost cause. Her maid scolded about the hat that Elisabeth had never retrieved from the pond. How embarrassing should it float to the surface and be recognized by her mother.

Dining *al fresco* had been arranged earlier in the week for the entertainment of the duke's guests, but rain had postponed it. Sophia tied a large green bow at the back of Elisabeth's sprigged muslin. Both young ladies donned large straw hats decorated with silk flowers. Sophia, mindful of her creamy complexion, tied a bow underneath her chin securing it firmly. Today there was only a caressing zephyr gently tumbling the leaves of the trees, but she wasn't taking any chances of losing precious protection from the sun. Her younger sister, mindful of pleasing her mother, tied hers just as securely.

They arrived outside to the scene of a dozen or more young ladies dressed in light summer frocks with wide straw hats shading their faces. Many also carried ruffled parasols which matched their ensembles. A game played with a stick and ball absorbed a half dozen of the young men who had been invited as escorts. Elisabeth spotted Jamie when he yelled a triumph. It was some sort of win, she supposed. A white tent with a red flag flying from its top was erected on the lawn where servants ran to and fro carrying food from the duke's kitchens.

Elisabeth joined another younger sister who was resting on a blanket near the shrubbery. Sophia's walk was graceful as she joined other potential candidates for duchess. She seemed almost to glide across the newly mown grass. Her mother watched with a slight smile from a chair placed in a cluster for the chaperones.

The young lady named Sarah pointed out a handsome young man and giggled to Elisabeth, who was searching the crowd for her Noble Hero. Neither of the girls was considered old enough to be out in company, but it was a private party and their mothers hovered close by. Elisabeth had taken a vow to be on her very best behavior to impress her ever-watchful parent. She was extremely tired of *The Manners of a Young Lady* book. Never could she abide staying inside for long. Even now, she longed to be off on her favorite mare from the old duke's stable, but she could not persuade Jamie to forgo the picnic in preference for a ride. She had some suspicion he had a flirt among the older young ladies.

Sarah suggested they stroll the garden and Elisabeth agreed, eager for any activity. Formal in some areas, more natural in others, the garden was large and rambling. They stayed on the paths mindful of the thin soles of their slippers. Lavender grew on one side heady with fragrance and tumbling into the walkways. The exquisite scent followed them as their gowns brushed against the profuse blossoms. Elisabeth leaned over to pluck a stem or two and crushed it between her fingers. They greeted a young man escorting Sarah's sister and turned back to walk the paths with them.

Around one corner Elisabeth spotted her friend, Richard, who surreptitiously beckoned to her. Her spirits lifted, and she stifled a gurgle of laughter. It was obvious Richard had something more in mind, and she was excited to join him.

"Oh no, a rip in my flounce," she said, thinking up a ruse on the spot and holding onto her skirt. "You go on, and I'll join you after I get my maid to pin it up." With that, she rounded the corner and ducked out of sight, laughing as Richard tucked her into a private corner of the garden.

"Noble Rescuer, you do not enjoy dining *al fresco*? What mischief will you tempt me with instead?"

He held out his hand, and she allowed him to clasp hers. It felt warm and solid to be held so. Elisabeth thought briefly that her behavior might be improper, but she dismissed it. The sun was shining brightly on this perfect day. What could be wrong to be in the presence of a friend?

"Will you miss the company, little one?" he asked, leading her into a section of the garden she had not yet discovered. They walked underneath an arbor and seemed to be in a private outdoor room. It was paved with gray stepping-stones. Large urns filled with cascading flowers surrounded a small table set with two chairs. Butterflies flitted throughout the garden in gay profusion, and a sweet fragrance of some white blossom teased her nose. A small umbrella shaded the intimate scene. A fat cabbage rosebush in full bloom formed a screen, leaving the tableau entirely private from curious stares.

Elisabeth looked with wonder at the scene, and then tilted her head at Richard who stood quietly watching her. "Should I ask how you managed to arrange this?"

He shook his head and smiled. He directed her to seat herself, which she did, but maintained a suspicious grin.

"I have it. You are a special favorite of the old duke's, are you not? This is his private place, and you have usurped it for your own purposes. Should I be afraid? No, a rescuer could not mean mischief to me. Are we to skip the picnic and have a private one of our own then?" She laughed when a servant carrying a huge tray appeared as if by magic and arranged it on their table. She clapped her hands with approval when he whisked away the cover and two roasted chickens tempted their appetites. This was followed by a bowl of fresh peaches. Richard used a knife and carved their fowl handing her a plate filled with succulent, choice pieces. He poured a glass of lemonade from a pitcher left for them.

Elisabeth's appetite was not shy, and she made good work of the delicious food. After they demolished the roasted fowl, Richard peeled a ripe peach and handed a bite to her. She opened her mouth wide like a baby bird and tucked it away with her tongue, laughing as the sweet juice dribbled down her chin. She lifted her face for his handkerchief, as he leaned toward her and tenderly wiped the juice away. She tilted her chin to see into his eyes, which seemed to be alight with amusement, and wondered at the quiver in her heart. The sudden feeling was both amazing and frightening at the same time.

"Wasn't it you, my friend, who made me promise to behave for my mother? I fear this tryst is not going to meet with her approval, although I confess I find it an excellent idea." She opened her mouth for another bite of the delicious fresh fruit.

"You are pleased with our retreat from the many houseguests then?" he asked, wiping his hands on the cloth placed beside his plate. A soft wind ruffled his hair.

"It's exciting to slip away from the crowd," she confessed. "I am not entirely comfortable dining with a gentleman unknown to my mother. Only because you are my rescuer do I trust you do not intend to damage my reputation. You do not, do you, Richard?" she asked, her head tilted to one side, gazing up into green eyes dotted with golden flecks. A complacent smile gave his face an appeal that had her catching her breath.

He placed his forefinger on her cheek. "Pretty Elisabeth, you must believe I could never mean you harm. I consider you a very special person." He looked up as a servant entered their private bower and whisked away all the platters, leaving as silently as he appeared.

"This has been a pleasure soon to end. I must leave you now, little one. Can you find your way back to your friends?" They both stood and he reached for her hands.

"Soon, you and I must have a private conversation. I have important news to relate to you, but I have obligations elsewhere for the moment." He kissed first one wrist and then the other, turned, and disappeared behind a large blooming shrub. Elisabeth stood mesmerized with flutters in her stomach, watching the leaves of the shrub still trembling with the disturbance of the recently departed Rescuer.

"How am I to handle this adventure?" she murmured aloud, as she wandered among the paths dreamily reviewing the recent events. "I suspect I am falling in love with my Noble Rescuer. His name is Richard and I have no idea who he really is, or if he is known to my parent. How is this happening to me? This must be the sort of thing my mother warned me against." She turned around a high hedge and rejoined her friend, who was sitting on a blanket with several other young people.

"Have you missed the picnic?" Sarah asked. "It was most delicious, I vow!"

"Had flutters in my middle," Elisabeth returned truthfully. "I am not peckish, but I thank you." She gazed across the lawn and saw Richard in conversation with a group of the older gentlemen.

"Is he not handsome? I wonder who he will choose for his duchess," Sarah said holding her hands underneath her chin and giggling.

"I wonder he thinks to marry this late in life," Elisabeth mused, staring at the gentleman conversing with Richard. The older man—she would not call him exactly handsome—stood with his gray hair blowing in the breeze, patting his rotund stomach. As they watched, Richard reached over and clapped him on the shoulder. She could hear their laughter from where she sat. It must be the Duke of Roderick, their host, and Richard was thanking him for the use of his servants and private garden room. She looked over at her mother, who was still sitting in a cluster of chaperones.

Impulsively, she jumped up and ran to her side.

\*\*\*\*

"Elisabeth, are you well?" she asked as her youngest daughter slid to her knees beside her mother's chair. She rested her head in her mother's lap as if she were six years old and took comfort at the nearness. For some reason she felt as if she were floating loose upon the world and wished she had an anchor to secure her safety.

"Yes, Mommy, I am just a bit tired today. May I be excused to take a refreshing nap?" With her mother's nod, Elisabeth ran for the doorway and up the stairs to enter her bedroom. Seldom was she alone in the room she shared with Sophia, and now she was pleased to enjoy some privacy.

What did this all mean? Every time she met Richard, her feelings for him grew stronger. He seemed to accept her as she was without scolding her for what she was not. That fact alone endeared him to her, never mind how very handsome...*Best not to think of that too much.*

Soon she would be going home and immediately afterward removed to their London townhouse for the Season. She would face the hectic social schedule and her presentation to the *beau monde.* Her mother was still preparing her for the rules she was expected to follow at the parties, soirées, and other activities planned for the younger crowd. Tears rolled down her cheeks, and Elisabeth rubbed them away with her fists.

Her mother worried her youngest daughter would not take. Elisabeth knew she was a problem for her parent, and when she thought of it, she despaired. Never could she live up to the standard set by her older sister.

She had no idea why she thought so differently from other young women, why she preferred riding to needlework, why the sun invited her outside where she raised her face to welcome it, in spite of the fear of freckles. She was a hoyden. Certainly in comparison to her perfectly-behaved sister, she was a minx. Thinking depressing thoughts, Elisabeth fell sound asleep.

Chapter Five

Richard watched from the corner of his eye his little love kneel beside her mother's chair and lay her head in her parent's lap. Would this be the end of their delicious privacy? How would Elisabeth explain their relationship to her parent? Amused, he imagined Elisabeth's mother's shocked reaction. He would immediately be expected to announce his engagement to her younger daughter rather than the eldest.

Poor little one. She had no idea he was her host. How that could happen, he could only surmise. Elisabeth Barrows, he knew, paid little attention to protocol or titles. Her father had been a gentleman farmer who owned vast lands and had deep pockets. Their family was older than several titled generations and enjoyed the deference and respect of most. His mother and the Dowager Barrows had been fast friends when they attended the finishing school for young ladies. Sophia, the eldest daughter, was an excellent candidate to serve as his duchess. He found her manners pleasing, her beauty enticing. Rumor had it he could expect a very generous dowry if he selected this worthy gentlewoman. Almost he had.

And then insanity hit in the appearance of a headstrong little spitfire with golden braids and one dimple in a peach-colored cheek, a sprinkle of freckles across an impossibly small nose, a little hoyden who pressed her childhood friend to teach her how to kiss. He laughed out loud thinking of that initial conversation between Elisabeth and her friend, James. Truth be told, he was lost from that very moment, and he hadn't even set eyes on her directly. Her husky voice impaled his heart, and it seemed a permanent wound. How could he explain it to friends or his parent? He didn't understand it himself.

"How goes the action, Richard? Picked out the lucky winner yet?" Mark asked as he limped into view. Richard winced at the vulgarity of the remark. He turned in annoyance away from his friend. How had he lost perspective? He must pick a bride. What was he playing at with this precocious child with the infectious chuckle? *Just one more day with her, and then I will sober up and get on with it.*

"Are you up for a ride, Captain?" he asked, turning his eyes toward the stables. "I think we might safely leave our guests at this point, don't you? The picnic is over and Mother must take charge of their entertainment for the rest of the day."

That evening, he requested a maid to take a note to Elisabeth's room.

Chapter Six

Elisabeth turned the note over and over in her hand, finally tucking it into a pocket of her gown. What did it mean? It was signed only with the initial R, but she knew who had sent it. Should she do as the note suggested and meet him in the garden after dark? How many rules had she broken in the last week? Did she want to spend her life memorizing dull books on the proper conduct of young ladies? She grimaced and shrugged her shoulders.

Certainly she would meet him. A pulse throbbed in her neck, and she acknowledged her excitement with a half chuckle. It must be Richard. Aside from Jamie, she wasn't closely . acquainted with any of the other gentlemen present. How to manage the deed was her only consideration. Perhaps she was sickening for something. A headache? She felt her forehead in case it was true. The oddest feelings were roiling around in her middle, as if she had dined on butterflies. She felt warm all over. A fever? How horrid if she would really be catching a disease.

She planned to stay in her room until all had gone downstairs. Sophia did not come back upstairs until quite late anyway. Would her mother become upset? Surely not. Her primary consideration was for Sophia's future, hopefully as a duchess. It was probably unfair for her to take advantage of her mother's distraction as she shepherded her eldest daughter toward marriage to a duke.

Elisabeth thought about that for a moment. What kind of life would it be as mistress of one's own household? Could she choose to ride every day instead of the hated needlework? How exciting the thought, but would the old duke frown on such uninhibited behavior? Would he demand his wifely duties? Of course, he would. It was said he determined to set up his nursery and get himself an heir.

How could he accomplish the deed—oh, she knew all about it, even before she came upon that leather bound book—with his enormous belly with which to contend? It was a fearful thought. She pitied her sister and any of the other candidates for the position. Perhaps the freedom of marriage was worth it. Never would she permit that dull book of manners to inhabit a library where she was mistress. She suppressed the thought of how wonderful it would be to be married to Richard. He did not approve of her reading the red leather book, but he would never force her to mind her manners. She was certain of it. The best thing about her new friend— well, aside from disapproving of the red book—was how he accepted her just the way he found her. Not once did he scold her for climbing a tree, never mind getting stuck in it. Richard as her husband? She felt her face wreath in wide smiles.

She must put marriage to Richard out of her mind. How likely was that? Her family would leave this man's enormous manor house in two days after the ball tomorrow night. The announcement of the old duke's engagement to some one of the debs was expected at the party, probably just before a late supper.

Immediately the next day, they would be packed to travel first for home and then to London to settle in for the Season. She would ask Richard if he would be in Town soon.

Perhaps he did not...how little she really knew about him. How could her feelings have gotten so out of hand when the man was a virtual stranger to her? She smiled at Sophia as her sister came quietly into the room and greeted her.

"Will you be pleased if the duke announces for you, Sister?" she asked.

"He will not," Sophia returned emphatically. Elisabeth was surprised, but not shocked. That belly...

"I thought you were set on the title. What made you change your mind? It was that giant stomach wasn't it? I could not understand how he could manage an heir, but I thought being addressed as 'duchess' pleased you."

"Lizzie, I fear my sentiments have been stolen by another." She sat on the bed and hid her face in her hands. Elisabeth stood shocked. Her perfect sister had contracted an impossible attraction?

"Do I know this gentleman, Sister? A groom perhaps? What could make you so sad that you cry? Perhaps it will pass," Elisabeth said and put an arm around her tenderly. Sophia looked up and laughed.

"No, Lizzie. What an imagination you have. I've not even been riding since we've been here. You must know I would never—why would you think groom?"

Elisabeth laughed in relief. Some of those grooms were handsome lads, but she hoped her sister knew how improper—but who was she to say what was and was not improper?

"Am I to know the name of the lucky man? I wonder if our host knows you are out of the running because some handsome young man has captured your attention. He is truly caught in parson's mousetrap if you have set your eyes on him. What is his name?" Elisabeth persisted.

"You know him. At least you have noticed him as he limps when he walks. He was wounded in the war. His name is Captain Mark Estermire, but he will not think of marriage to anyone." She burst into tears, threw herself on the pillows, and proceeded to sob her heart out.

Elisabeth sat stunned. Her perfect sister collapsed in tears over a wounded captain in the army? She knew the man, a friend of Richard's, and one who witnessed her dip in the lily pond. He struggled to walk but seemed to be making remarkable progress in the last week. A handsome fellow with a genial smile, he was seen to enjoy the company of several of the young ladies. How had her sister become attached and how so quickly?

A tiny hint of suspicion crossed her mind as she stared at her weeping sibling. Could Sophia have a secret life similar to her own? It was almost impossible to believe, but then how did a romance develop so quickly and no one knew about it? Never mind. She would not pry.

"Sister, dry your tears and tell me why the captain cannot marry. Does he already have a wife and family?" She reached over and hugged her sister, who sat up with swollen eyes, still hiccupping, fat tears rolling down her porcelain cheeks.

"N-no-no. He thinks his wound makes him unfit.

He can no longer be in the army and...oh, I'm not certain of it all. I think it has to do with d-d-dancing.

"He loves me, he told me so, but he thinks he is not worthy of me," Sophia said as she choked back her sobs. She blew her nose elegantly. Her sibling could always maintain her manners in spite of her unhappiness. Elisabeth hugged her sister, thinking rapidly how she might facilitate this unexpected romance. Perhaps she could find out more from Richard when she met him later.

"All is not lost as yet, Sophia. Dry your tears and ready yourself to go downstairs. Be at your best and show him what he's in danger of losing." She cajoled and petted her sister until the tears disappeared. Finally, Sophia smiled and stood to repair the ravages of her swollen eyes.

"No man can resist you for long, Sister. Just you hold out hope he will soon come to his senses and be ready to tell him no for a while when he does. He deserves to worry for how he has upset you." She reached to pat an errant curl on her sister's usually tidy head.

As Sophia readied herself to join the guests downstairs, Elisabeth begged off joining the others for the headache she confessed to having all day. Sophia exclaimed at her selfishness but agreed to leave her sister in quiet in hopes of a quick recovery. Alone, Elisabeth felt a rapid pulse of excitement.

"What does one wear to a secret assignation?" she wondered, smoothing her gown. When her maid entered the room, Elisabeth dismissed her with the same excuse of a headache. She actually made ready to put her head on her pillow until the maid left. She laughed quietly to herself and felt somewhat guilty. It was almost impossible to stay still with her heart thumping hard in her chest. After waiting for what seemed to be hours but was in reality mere minutes, she sat up and smoothed her hair, despairing of the wisps of curls that always escaped her efforts to tame them.

The guests were gathered in the front parlor, but she peeked carefully out the door just in case. She would make her way by the back stairs, which she hoped would lead her to the garden. Quickly she descended and stepped, as she suspected, directly into the beginnings of the garden. Statues of various gods loomed whitely in the twilight. The tinkle of running water alerted her of the nearness of a small frog pond. She knew her way from there and walked confidently forward. She almost screamed when an arm reached out and encircled her waist.

"Shhh…little one. It is only I, Richard, your Noble Rescuer." He laughed softly and rubbed his face gently in her hair as he held her close. She twisted around to look up into his eyes but could not read his thoughts in the dim light. He released her and caught her hand, pulling her gently with him around the hedge and back to that private floral bower, borrowed once more from their host.

At his urging, she settled on a white garden bench which nestled against a flowering vine. Heady night fragrances enveloped her as she looked up into the handsome face of her friend. He gazed back at her but then paced a step or two back.

"I have things to say, sweetness. Please do not be upset when I use words I know are improper. Let us be two different people for tonight. What say you?" He stepped closer, but still did not join her on the bench.

Elisabeth waited for what she knew not. She was content to be this close to one for whom she had such feelings. She nodded. Why did she trust him so implicitly? She only knew she did. Perhaps it was because she enjoyed an enchanted night in a magic room with a handsome man who called her pet names. This was not real life, but she could not give up the thought that magic existed, especially for those who were in love. Surrounding her was a fairy garden which glowed with moonlight under the watchful eyes of stone guardians. Perhaps they came to life when the sunlight faded?

She inhaled sharply and clasped her hands together in her lap when he settled himself on the bench, their shoulders touching. His unique scent wrapped around her, causing her head to spin with excitement. As he turned toward her, he reached out with his arm, first touching her shoulder with his hand, and then folding around it. She did not stop herself from leaning toward him, although briefly she did try. The prickling of her conscience was like a buzzing, annoying gnat she could easily dismiss. Elisabeth was mesmerized by an intoxicating spell she never wanted to end. Richard leaned closer pulling her gently forward.

"Richard?" she whispered tentatively, not certain whether she wanted him to move away or come closer. "Richard?" She put her hand on his chest and pushed him gently. His hand was on her neck, and then he caressed her bare shoulder. Bare? How did that happen? She felt her stomach give a lurch, and her heart threatened to leave her body. Who knew a man's hand on her shoulder would trigger so profound a reaction as this? Now she knew what sin felt like, and why so many rules were written concerning it.

"Elisabeth? Will you object strenuously if I kiss you? I so dearly would like to. What do you think?" He continued to caress her shoulder but pulled her toward him inch by inch. A thought crossed her mind that she should resist. Who was this man who wanted to…his lips touched hers as if a butterfly had landed there, just a whisper of a touch. She was not absolutely certain he had kissed her. She could feel his breath, a hint of a cigar, on her cheek before his lips descended and hovered over hers once more.

"Sweet one? Elisabeth?" he said, and she could hear amusement in his voice.

She opened her eyes and stared directly into his. He was smiling. Was he laughing at her? He reached and held her hand, swallowing it in his roughened large one. He squeezed it and placed it where it rested on his chest, then pulled it to his lips where he kissed the tip of her fingers.

"Elisabeth, would you like for me to kiss you?" he asked, his voice low and seductive. He kissed her hand once more…in the middle of her palm. She felt the slight roughness of his whiskers when he rubbed her hand against his cheek, but his lips were soft.

"Yes, no…yes. I fear it is not proper behavior for a young lady like me. Richard, Noble Rescuer, will it harm my reputation? I confess I'm a bit unsettled about all this. It makes me feel odd." She chattered away and he smiled once more.

"I would never let anything harm you. I want only wonderful things to come to you, little one." He moved both arms around her until she rested against his broad chest.

At first she stiffened, uncomfortable in the unfamiliar closeness to a man, but she ventured to rest her head on his chest. He was hard with muscles. She felt jolted with sensations she knew not how to name, where to put them, how to use them. This was all so very strange and new to her. She could hear his heart beating almost as rapidly as her own. Could he be filled with the same excitement as...oh, dear. His hand was tipping her chin up and his lips were descending. She had her eyes wide open, not wanting to miss anything this time.

The kiss was tentative. He rested his lips against hers until she relaxed her mouth. Then he nibbled. He pressed his mouth more firmly against hers, and Elisabeth almost gasped aloud. The sensation was nothing like she had ever dreamed it would be. Soft lips sliding over hers seemed to be asking a question, but what? A tongue pressed against her firmly closed mouth while he nibbled and teased her lips. She inhaled sharply and opened her mouth.

It seemed this was the answer to his quest all along, she thought, as his tongue slipped inside her shocked lips. He probed between them while she tasted him with her own tongue. Tingling from her middle to other parts of her body alarmed her with its intensity, and she pulled abruptly away.

"Richard!" she whispered urgently. "This must stop," she whispered into his neck. He tucked her close to him and moved her gently back and forth against his chest. The tingling was like a loud clamoring inside her head, but now that the kiss had ended she felt bereft. She wanted more; she wanted his kisses to never stop.

Part of her wanted to run, but another part wanted to melt her entire body into his and never be parted from him. He hugged her to him and sighed.

"Elisabeth Barrows, you do not like my kisses?" he asked, pulling away to look down into her eyes. An expression she could not discern came over his face as he gazed at her, and she felt her senses grow weak.

"I d-do, l-like them. I try very hard not to because I feel very wicked. But you know how wonderful kisses are, don't you?" She patted his neck cloth, which had somehow become—how odd!—wrinkled. "That was my very first one, well, I had a sort of one with Jamie, but it was nowhere like—" She stopped. It was difficult to talk when his lips were covering her own. This time she relaxed and let the exquisite sensations envelope her entire being, as they rippled over her body like a waterfall of exquisite delight.

How could a person stay still with these feelings overcoming their sensibilities? She wanted, indeed needed, to press even closer to him. She wriggled until her chest rested firmly against him and she heard him groan. She jerked away, fearful she had somehow injured him. He pulled her close again.

"Richard?" she said, as his lips slid down her throat, trailing kisses.

"Ummm?" he answered with his mouth on her bare shoulder, his hands gliding against her shoulders, which were now bare to the night. Richard's lips came back to her mouth and seemed content to nibble while his hands—what were his hands doing to her gown? She pulled abruptly away, feeling as if she were just awakening.

"Richard!"

He smiled. "You are correct, of course. I am a beast. Will you forgive me, Elisabeth? I intended only to enjoy a goodbye kiss with you. I quite forgot myself." He leaned over to kiss her lightly and stood up.

"You are leaving?" she asked, dismayed. What did all this mean? He could kiss her and then just walk away? She wanted him close again.

"I must. I have been called away by the Ministry. I am leaving first thing tomorrow morning." He reached over and touched her cheek. "It has been a pleasure to know you, sweet Elisabeth. You are going to make some man a lively mate. If I were not so old...will you remember me fondly?"

Elisabeth recovered her dignity long enough to stand and hold out her hand. "Have a safe trip, Richard who-ever-you-are. It has been quite an adventure I have had in your company." He took her hand, turned it and kissed her wrist where the pulse beat rapidly. "I will ever be thankful to you for my rescues." She pulled her hand away and ran from the fragrant bower in the outdoor room.

Holding in her tears, she found the stairs and flew up, hoping against hope not to meet anyone. Gaining the safety of her room, she sat down on the edge of the bed in shock. Behind her surprise, her tears threatened to fall, but she could not let go long enough to seek their relief.

How could he? Was this what happened when a man kissed a woman? They fled her company? Jamie had tried to warn her. Why had she not listened? She scrubbed her hand across her lips, trying to erase the feelings Richard's kiss had invoked. Why had she thought them delightful? She had been careless of her reputation. Why then did she expect him to be other than the same? Would he tell everyone how easily he had tricked her into meeting him on the sly? Her face burned at the thought.

The tears rolled down her cheeks as she dressed for bed. She crawled between the covers, but pictures of the two of them kissing—his lips warm and seeking over hers, their hearts beating in unison—kept running through her mind, the scene playing over and over. Shame replaced the excitement. Were all men as cruel as Richard, the man she thought her friend? Suddenly, she understood her mother's concern and all the admonishments she had endured because of her constant rule breaking.

Sophia came quietly into the room. "I'm awake, Sister. Is everything all right with you?" Elisabeth asked, hoping someone had a happy future.

"It's over, Lizzie. He is leaving for Town in the morning, something to do with government business. He is eager to serve as a diplomat until he can rejoin his regiment."

Elisabeth drew in a sharp breath. It seemed the two men were to depart together. She sat up in bed and held out her arms to her sister. While Sophia sobbed and she soothed, Elisabeth stared straight ahead, feeling a coldness settle. Never again, she repeated over and over to herself, comforting her breaking heart. Never again would she be taken in by a smiling stranger.

## Chapter Seven

After it was announced the duke had been called away, organized chaos reigned as the house party broke up. Although the guests were encouraged to remain, most felt the need to return home. The purpose of the visit was no longer valid. Mothers would waste no more time lounging in the country when their marriage-aged daughters were not yet promised. Carriages were called for and servants bumped into each other in their attempts to answer all the immediate demands. Large trunks soon appeared stacked and ready to go at the foot of the stairs.

Upstairs, the Duchess Roderick sat sipping tea and enjoying a cozy last visit in her private drawing room with Helen Barrows, her close friend since finishing school.

"Almost our plan worked," she said and both women laughed, comfortable in their conspiracy.

"We tried. Are you still surprised at the pairing of our children? Who knew he would prefer the lively younger one and she him? I suspect Sophia's heart has not remained intact either. How do you feel about that?"

"Certainly, she is not the one for your Richard," Helen said. "It remains to be seen if she will find a new love. Society will soon present many opportunities if either of my daughters choose to select anew. How long do you suspect your son and his friend will be gone?"

"There is no way of guessing. I could strangle Lord Victorial for calling him away at just that point. I shall have a few sharp words to say to him, I can assure you."

"Nothing you could have done about it. When your country calls…I can hear the refrain now, but I do agree with you. The timing was at a critical point in our plot to be interrupted," Helen said with a frown.

The duchess smiled as she reminisced. "It was amusing to watch them. Do you suppose some day they will guess we know everything that goes on in our households?" She sipped her tea and chose a tiny apricot tart to nibble.

"Perhaps, but I hope we are both bouncing grandchildren on our knees when it happens," Helen said. They chuckled at their cleverness and the naiveté of their children.

"Will you remove to town soon? I must settle my girls before the Little Season starts." They stood to say their goodbyes.

"In a fortnight or so. I vow I must recover from all the excitement. I grow weary and long for peace, my good friend. But I will be there to lend you support as you launch your youngest. She is a fascinating combination of the two of you. You must miss him every day. I know I miss His Grace more than I ever imagined I would."

Helen Barrows laughed. "You were so set on marrying that younger son who wore the cavalry's uniform. Not a chance your father would have permitted it, but he was a handsome devil. Or was it that suspicious count from…what nationality was he?"

"Oh, pshaw. Who remembers? I had my eye on the duke. I just wanted a little excitement before I settled down. Listen, Helen. I don't think we must sink in discouragement just yet. I will write to you a plan." She gave her friend a quick hug and a pat on the shoulder.

"Just so. I refuse to dictate to my children who they marry, but I never promised not to manipulate." Their laughter rang through the halls as they joined the exiting throng of the guests of His Grace, the Duke of Roderick.

## Chapter Eight

*Two years later*

Couples already forming squares for a country dance gathered in the middle of the spacious ballroom while the violinists tuned their instruments. Two impressive chandeliers sparkled with what seemed like hundreds of crystal drops. The candles glowed and accented the huge, long mirrors on one side of the room, which doubled the vision of the gathered crowd. Misses Sophia and Elisabeth Barrows entered on the arms of their friend, James Wilkerson. He was handsome in his dress but almost unable to turn his head with the restrictions of his fashionable high collar.

Sophia was splendid in a pastel pink gown with tiny cap sleeves and seed pearl embroidery on the low-cut bodice. Long white gloves covered her arms past the elbow while a white silk shawl with tassels draped from her arms. Her rich chestnut curls were pulled high above her swan-like neck with two curls left to dangle on each porcelain cheek.

Heeding Elisabeth's advice, she had added two pink feathers in the coil of her hair with sparkling pins, while her pink pearl necklace dangled low around her neck. Matching earbobs glowed like lures, catching the light with her every movement. She was immediately besieged by three young men for the next dance. She used a new idea, a card tied to her wrist to record her promises, leaving each man determined to be the sole recipient of her favors. Each time, she had to return to a table set up to record the name in ink with a small sharpened feather. It was a bit of a nuisance. Sophia smiled benignly and noncommittally on them all, and wondered if this small card idea would catch on in popularity. She doubted it.

Elisabeth Barrows wore ice blue. Sun-streaked, blonde curls cut short, ending low on her neck, were a new creation of her hairdresser. Before she trimmed Elisabeth's unruly ringlets, the lady tried several styles but despaired of taming them in any other way. To the amusement of her family, Elisabeth's new look had gained some popularity with young debs attempting to copy the effect with curling irons. Whether the style flattered or not, she couldn't say, but she thought it an easier way to dress her unruly curls, which formerly had given her the appearance of a fuzzy baby chick, according to her friend Jamie.

Nestled in Elisabeth's curls was a tiny tiara that glittered in icy splendor reflecting the candlelight. Dainty earbobs of pearl and diamond chips that matched her necklace moved with every nod of her head and enhanced the ice blue of her gown. A single diamond pendant nestled low, almost disappearing into her décolletage. Her gown had the appearance of simplicity, as two sheer layers of muslin gathered at the high waist cascaded from a single aqua silk rose tucked beneath her bosom. The under gown was an embroidered white silk. Her shoulders were almost bare except for tiny puffed sleeves that held the gown in place. When she moved, Elisabeth could feel the softness of the material and was pleased with the notion that she was not dancing but floating. Her sister exclaimed it made her look like an angel. Her mother demurred, not happy with even the tiny diamond sparkle from her earbobs and the very nearly bare shoulders. She frowned at the diamond pendant.

"You are too young to be draping diamonds on your person, Daughter. You will be thought fast," she protested. Elisabeth reached over and hugged her harassed parent who did her duty by her daughters, but who had grown weary with the two of them refusing to choose mates even after two seasons had passed.

"My godmother thought it appropriate, Mother, or she would not have presented them to me on my last birthday. I feel very special when I wear them. Do they not make this dress more beautiful?" She twirled and caused her mother to laugh.

"It is a private ball, so I suppose you can slip it by. You are especially nice in that gown. Was that another of your own designs?" she asked. Elisabeth had unexpectedly shown a talent for creating new and startling fashions which, she noticed with surprise, were soon copied by other young debs.

"It is, but I am allowing Madam Cherie to claim it for her own, and she is very gracious with the cost of sewing my gown. Do you disapprove, my dearest mother?" She leaned forward and bestowed a quick kiss on her parent's soft cheek. Elisabeth remained cognizant of her pledge to herself not to break rules. Once she realized society's customs were for her protection and not to keep her from enjoying herself, she was careful to obey them to the letter. She shook her head. What a naïve young lady she had been.

"Not as long as it remains a secret. You do not want to have your vouchers to Almack's taken away by being known to dabble in trade, do you? Those ladies who sponsor the social club are strict arbiters of what is expected of a young debutante." Her mother moved closer and touched her on the cheek fondly.

"You are aware how swiftly rule breakers are censured and never receive invitations to attend the dances again. It does not matter that the hall is dim and the punch and late supper dismal. The young ladies who disobey will lose their bid to enter with good grace the *bon ton* in the upper levels of society. You surely do not desire that? Elisabeth?" She busied herself rearranging the folds of her own gown.

"No," Elisabeth answered succinctly. She had learned her lesson about breaking rules. It was a painful experience, and she was not likely to forget it any time soon. Her unwelcome thoughts made her pulse increase with anxiety, and she made a determined effort to turn them away.

Later, standing with her sister in the sophisticated ballroom, she was approached by Matthew Diver-Jones, an ambitious young secretary who hoped for an appointment as attaché to an ambassador. He had been born a second or third son of a baron, Elisabeth wasn't certain which, but knew him as an amusing escort. He immediately begged her permission for the next dance. When he was amused, his wide grin was his best feature, and a slight stutter only made him more endearing.

"I s-say, Miss Elisabeth. Think you are a magic fairy tonight. Wand? Wave it over Lyndon there and turn him into toad, what s-say?" He grinned broadly.

His friend and first cousin, Lyndon Peron, protested vigorously.

"Toad! Turn me into a warrior with a broadsword. Help me lop off heads here and there," he rejoined, swinging his arm in demonstration toward Matthew.

Elisabeth broke into an open laugh when Lyndon nipped in front of his cousin, tucked her hand into his arm and walked triumphantly away while Mr. Diver-Jones protested loudly. Fearing her mother would become upset with the noisy commotion created by her good friends, she had turned to shush Mr. Peron when she stopped still. Richard, tall and handsome, stood in the doorway watching her with a serious expression on his exceptionally tanned features.

She gripped Lyndon's arm in a desperate attempt to regain her senses and fought the dizziness that threatened to disgrace her. She would not give him the satisfaction! Her stomach lurched but steadied. Lyndon looked curiously down at her. "Ship shape, Miss Elisabeth? Need to take the air, do you?"

She shook her head and continued toward the set just forming, taking her place near her sister. She must not allow this man to disturb her life. Although he was a big mistake, she had to thank him for teaching her the lessons of the *beau monde*. Never again would she fall into the trap of believing the words of a smiling stranger. Or—and this was a critical rule—never let herself be talked into dining alone in the company of a man unknown to her parent. She glanced over at Sophia and observed a panicked expression on her usually serene features. Her sister's cheeks were flushing bright red. *What to do?*

"My gown has a tear," Elisabeth exclaimed holding

her skirt with her hand. "Forgive me, Mr. Peron. Sophia, would you accompany me to the receiving room? I need your assistance." She clutched her sister's arm and hurried from the ballroom without a backward glance. They reached the room set aside for ladies to repair any unlucky ensemble problems. Fortunately, it was empty. Sophia collapsed on a blue velvet chaise in tears, holding her hands in front of her face.

"You saw Captain Estermire, didn't you?" Elisabeth guessed. Her sister nodded her head vigorously. "Try and hold your feelings in check. We will leave shortly. Sit here and I will find Mother. Hold it, Sophia. We will soon be away." She gave her a tight hug and patted her on the shoulder. "You'll do, Sister. You must contain yourself if we are to scrape through this."

She ducked out of the room and found her way to the row of chairs set against the wall for chaperones and relatives. Her mother looked up in surprise when she leaned over to whisper in her ear but nodded and rose immediately. They gathered their wraps and, curtseying to their hostess and murmuring excuses, made for the door. Elisabeth tucked Sophia's shawl tightly around her head and shoulders, partially covering her face, took her firmly by the arm, and joined their parent. They exited the town house as the footman called for a hackney. Their carriage would not return for hours yet.

"What is the matter? Are you sickening for something, Sophia?" their parent asked. Elisabeth could clearly hear the concern in her voice.

"Just a headache, Mother. It will go away soon as I can be in my bed in the dark." Sophia had all but a slight quiver in her bottom lip under control. Elisabeth thought they might manage to make it to privacy if only her sister could contain her tears. Her mother must not discover the truth about these silly attachments from the past. The facts would not place either of her daughters in very good light.

"I'm certain it's not serious, Mother," Elisabeth hurried to assure her. "You know how easily we recover. By tomorrow, Sophia will be in health again."

"It's just as well. I saw what was to be served for a late supper. I cannot believe how that Margaret Attabostore—well, she used to be called by that name before she managed to trap that silly baronet in her coils. They say she made her way right into his bedroom—never mind about that—what was I saying? Oh, yes, she stints on the refreshments. She was like that in school. Always in the funds, but never spending a pound she wasn't forced to. And did you see that headdress? When did you ever think there would be a bird that big and so tall to lose his feathers to such a one as Margaret? I thought for sure she would catch fire when she walked underneath the chandelier." She twittered like a teenager, and Elisabeth forced a chuckle to join her.

Sophia sat silent in the corner with her hands clenched tightly in her lap. Horses' hooves striking the cobble-stoned street echoed hollow night sounds outside the carriage as all three ladies returned to their private thoughts. Elisabeth stared at Sophia hoping against hope she would not succumb to hysteria in front of their mother. It would be a wonder if she did not as well, she thought wryly. With a sigh of relief she heard the driver signal their arrival back home.

After the sisters said their goodnights to their

mother, who spent several minutes advising Sophia on various efficacies for headaches, they hurried to dismiss their maid. Elisabeth removed her sparkling diamonds, sighing over how pleased she had been wearing them, believing she was in good form for the ball. Sadly, she removed her ice blue gown, wondering if she would ever wear it again without thinking of this night.

Elisabeth stiffened her resolve not to allow the unexpected appearance of the rogue she knew as Richard to upset her. How was she to convince her sister it would be wise to achieve the same with the captain? Sophia, tears streaming freely down her face, reached to hold her sister's hands.

"The worse part, Lizzie. You know the worse part? My heart was quite pierced. I never dreamed he could be so wicked. He was dancing in the square next to us. Remember what I related to you? He was not worthy to be my life's partner, although he loved me. He said that to me! That man swore he could never dance a waltz and couldn't bear to see me on the floor with anyone else. There he was forming up a square with that dreadful Susan Tillburry." Sophia stalked around the room trailing her night-rail, her agitation palpable as she clenched her fists and tightened her jaw.

Seldom had Elisabeth seen her exhibit so much emotion, but she was pleased to see anger replace sadness. Her sister would need all her courage in the coming days if Mark Estermire had come back to town. She decided she would finally confide some of her unfortunate history to her sister. She also needed all the courage she could muster.

"Sister, do stop pacing. You're wearing a hole in the carpet." She reached out and drew her sister to sit beside her on the bed. "I have something to tell you. I too have suffered from forming affection for the wrong person. I was even enticed to meet him in the garden on the night before he and Mark left the house party. I was too ashamed to tell you about it when you told me Mark had left. He is Mark's closest friend, you see. I know him as Richard, but I'm even reluctant to admit to you, I don't even know his last name or anything else about him. He kissed me in the garden!

"Oh, Sophia, I not only allowed him liberties, but welcomed them. Can you imagine? The next thing I knew he was telling me he was leaving the next morning. I was so very ashamed and shocked to learn the manners of a gentleman. I more think of him as a rake, I can tell you. I still am embarrassed, but I assure you I have learned my lesson."

"Mark's close mate?" Sophia asked incredulously. "Lizzie, are you sure? What does he look like?"

"Nothing special. Tall, dark hair, enticing smile, not as old as the duke. Maybe about the same age as his friend Mark. Why do you ask?" Sophia was staring at her with a strange expression.

"How did you come to be acquainted with this man, Elisabeth?" Sophia stood up and walked toward the fireplace wringing her hands again.

"I raced the horse with the white blaze with Jamie. A hare popped out of the shrubbery and startled it. I sailed over her head and landed in the lily pond. Richard was there with Mark and took me on his black stallion to change my riding habit into dry clothes. The hat even now lives its life in the middle of the lily pond. Never fear, the horse suffered no harm." She gazed at the violets in the pretty wallpaper as she remembered, forgetting for a moment what followed next.

"Elisabeth, when were you introduced to the Duke of Roderick? Did Mother take you to meet him and his mother?" Sophia's voice had changed to almost a squeak. Elisabeth stared at her and wondered if her sister were indeed sickening for a cold.

"Certainly. I met her when we arrived. I don't think I ever came face to face with the duke, but I saw him several times from a distance. How anyone could wish to marry him is beyond me. That fat belly was beside enough. What is the problem, Sister? What's troubling you? Were you sorry you weren't chosen? I don't think anyone was singled out. The Regent called him back to town on some errand before any announcement could be made. Remember?" She stared at her sibling who was making a strange gurgling noise in her throat and holding her hands against her cheeks. Was she having the vapors?

"Elisabeth, do you know what the duke's name is?" She came and sat on the bed beside her sister. Sophia was staring intently at her. What was this interrogation about? What did the old duke have to do with Richard and Mark?

"I'm sure I don't know. Should I? It's not as if I had occasion to call him by name. It was you mother wanted him to marry—I never paid him much attention." She jumped when Sophia uttered a small squeak.

"Are you aware that Captain Mark Estermire is a particular friend of the Duke of Roderick?" Sophia asked. Elisabeth began to have a sinking feeling in the pit of her stomach. She wasn't certain what her sister was suggesting, but it sounded as if it were nothing good.

"He must have many friends, do you think? Tell me what is troubling you, Sophia, please."

"Do not be upset, Lizzie, but I think the man you met in the garden was Richard Hawlester, the Duke of Roderick." She reached her hand out and gripped her sibling's arm. Elisabeth stared at her with a numb feeling spreading over her entire body. Her face grew warm, then hot. Disbelief settled her feelings, and she allowed a chuckle to escape. It was a joke. Richard could not be the duke; he would have explained it to her. He might have been a rake to kiss her in the garden, but she didn't believe he would have pretended to be someone else.

"No, you're wrong. Roderick is an old man with a fat middle. I saw him chatting with Richard the day of the picnic. I had luncheon with Richard in a private bower that day, a special retreat of the duke's…loaned to him. It was so very beautiful…oh, dear." She sat wordless, staring at the flickering of the candle in its stand on the dresser. The room took on a dim oddness. For a moment she thought she might lose consciousness.

How could he do this to her? He was her Noble Rescuer—her thoughts jumbled in her head—he kissed me and then left me. The Duke of Roderick? *Not a fat old man? He tricked me. I hate him. I loved him. How could I be so naïve? How he must have enjoyed the joke at my expense!* Her anger flared and her face burned with humiliation.

"So, it was Richard Hawlester that met me that night in the garden. I let him kiss me, Sophia. I expect he thought me a mere child playing at games. He, no doubt, believed I was attempting to entrap him by allowing him to kiss me. I had no idea who he really was. He left with Mark the very next morning, did he not? The duke did not ask anyone for their hand in marriage. He just left." She felt life leave her and what remained was a dull throb where her heart used to be.

"I'm sorry. You are no doubt correct. Had you given him all your affection at that point? I did the same with Mark. There were no kisses between us, although I confess I regret there were not." Sophia leaned her head on her sister's shoulder. "Oh, Sister, I am so tired. Shall we climb in bed and hope the morning brings us wisdom? Now that the two of them are in town, we shall need a plan to follow."

Elisabeth nodded and they pulled the covers over their shoulders. Soon she could hear Sophia's even breathing and rejoiced her sister could sleep. Perhaps the tears had exhausted her. *Would that they could come to me.* She stared into the darkness long into the night, trying to forget remembered sweetness when the duke had tutored her in love.

## Chapter Nine

Subdued sisters met at the table to break their fast. Their mother never made her toilet before noon after a late night out. Whether they had actually experienced late hours would hold no consideration with their parent as the fond siblings knew and were grateful for it this particular morning. Both suffered from the effects of too much emotion and not enough sleep.

"Do you ride with Mr. Diver-Jones today, Elisabeth?" Sophia asked, propping on one hand. Perhaps she was miserable, but she presented a picture of female perfection in peach-sprigged muslin, her hair pulled high and tied with peach ribbons which allowed thick, rich-colored locks to cascade down her back.

Her sister marveled at Sophia's attractiveness but without envy. Their own mother was a great beauty in her youth and was amused when, after her period of mourning for her beloved husband, she was besieged by several offers. She ignored them all. Elisabeth more closely resembled her father's side of the family. He, too, had loved to ride.

"How do you feel about staying home without me for a while?" Elisabeth asked. "I will be back before visiting hours. Are you steady enough to greet Mother if she chooses to surprise all by appearing early?" Sophia gazed at her, sadness still visible on her face.

"I am endeavoring to alter my feelings. If I put the

sight of Captain Mark Estermire dancing merrily with that saucy Susan Tillburry in my mind, then anger will hold me steady. How about you? Think you are serene enough to meet the public? What if you meet the duke on your outing this morning? How will you handle the face-to-face confrontation?" She pushed an escaped curl back from her face.

"I have a plan. Never will I admit to ignorance of his real identity. I will pretend it was all a game, a light-hearted adventure of no real consequence. I will insist it was a hoydenish lark brought on by my tender years. What say you? Will it serve?" She pulled on butter-colored kid riding gloves as she stood and made ready to leave the room.

"Perhaps, if you can maintain your countenance," Sophia answered. Elisabeth contemplated her sister with interest, evaluating her critically. Sophia had her own way of coping with disappointment. She might appear fragile, but her sister was made of sterner stuff. Elisabeth nodded with pride in her sibling. Now if only she could exhibit the same inner strength.

"I will leave you and keep my appointment with Matthew. Deny yourself to visitors if you please. I shall return before you know it." She leaned over to kiss her sister on the cheek and left by the side door where her groom was waiting with her mount. Mr. Diver-Jones was there as well walking his horse slowly up and down the street. He raised his head and called out a greeting.

"A strikingly beautiful red bird arrives to keep me company. Will you whistle a merry tune? Do we fly away this morning? I s-say, Miss Elisabeth, you are a s-sight for my weary eyes. That is a particularly clever design for a riding habit, but what's with the unusual hat?" He tossed her into the sidesaddle and allowed the groom to assist him into his own.

Elisabeth had replaced her red riding costume from two years ago. Her old one never recovered from its dip into the murky waters of the lily pond. She preferred the military style, cherry red for her riding habit, but she had changed the design of the matching hat to one with a bigger brim. "You are naughty to speak of my hat, good friend. Have you not noticed what the sun has done to my face?" Lately, she had declared war on her tiny freckles and tried to shield her face whenever she could.

Her mount frisked a bit and held her attention until they were started down the street on the way to the park. Halfway there, they were joined by Lyndon Peron and, at the gate, James Wilkerson. Inside the park they greeted a new friend, Miss Eloise Larkin, riding with her groom trailing. The other four chattered together in a noisy cluster until forced to split up in twos by the narrowing of the bridle path. Elisabeth rode ahead with Matthew, Eloise with Lyndon with James riding behind. Soon a newcomer edged Matthew out and, with a salute and a smile, her friend dropped back to ride with James.

Riding beside her now was handsome Viscount Teasdale, Arthur Bridges, who had lately been paying her excessive attention. He would be put in his place if her mother caught wind of it. Elisabeth was aware his reputation was shaky, and she had heard some call him outright a rake. His was an old title and his father's estates were vast. Nevertheless, hopeful parents had crossed him off their list of possibilities after watching him flirt outrageously but then give freezing set-downs to more than one assertive debutante. He rode usually with a fast crowd, friends with the Regent, most whom were rumored to be high-stakes gamblers. Elisabeth enjoyed his witty repartee and was in no hurry to dismiss him. She used her crop to touch the tip of her red-brimmed hat to him in greeting. He saluted her with his own, tapping his high top hat.

"Miss Barrows, you left the ball early last night. I was crossing the room to beg for a waltz when I spotted you disappearing out the door with your family. Imagine my disappointment." He grinned what Elisabeth could only surmise was his unique custom for seduction or flirtation. It was powerful—he was a fine example of a handsome rake, but she was immune. She offered a half-smile in return and changed the subject. One thing that disgusting duke had taught her, and she would not forget, was to never let a pleasant smile be mistaken for honesty.

"La, Lord Teasdale, I made certain you enjoyed a plethora of dance partners. One missing could not possibly disturb your evening. Shall we canter?" She nudged her horse which sprang ahead. The viscount was directly by her side, handling his mount with an easy, almost negligent, expertise, albeit somewhat aggressive. Elisabeth gave him a sincere smile of approval in acknowledgement of his skill.

"You are a handful for your mother, I suspect," he said, glancing at her from the corner of his eye, as his horse reached to take a nip out of Elisabeth's. He soon brought it under control, but it danced with dainty steps as if it wanted nothing more than to run wildly in the wind. It was a beautifully formed piece of prime horseflesh. Elisabeth admired the animal while she had neutral feelings for its owner.

"My mother!" she exclaimed. "You are acquainted with my parent?" she asked all wide-eyed innocence. "Lord Teasdale, I knew you surpassed me in years, but never did I think you were a contemporary of my mother." She tried not to smile, but knew she failed.

"I see that dimple, Miss Pert, and you know perfectly well, I am not of your mother's age, although she is a wonderful example of her set. I was about to ask what day you set aside for callers? I pray I might be one of their number?" He held her eye almost challenging her, a habit which she intensely disliked. *Arrogant man.* It was just such behavior that she abhorred, but she took the time to consider his request.

Elisabeth thought of the stress both she and Sophia were under and almost said no, but then she reflected having callers come to admire them might be just the distraction both needed. "We receive callers on Tuesday. Our hours are one of the clock until four. It would be pleasant if you were counted among that gathering."

He nodded, said his goodbyes, and trotted away to greet a cluster of older gentlemen gathered at the corner of the park. Elisabeth wondered briefly if she had disturbed a hive of bees, but became distracted when she recognized a large, black stallion pacing steadily toward her party. Her mount moved with restless energy, and she realized she had tightened the reins. She could feel her face starting to warm. *Please, God. Don't let me blush.* Richard's seat on that brute of a horse was impeccable, just as she remembered. Flashes of him holding her snugly to his chest, she in wet riding habit, flitted through her mind as he approached.

Quickly, she struggled into her adoptive role as gay sophisticate.

"Here is Lord Roderick, a childhood acquaintance of mine," she called out gaily. "Do you join us, Your Grace?" Elisabeth could not read his face. Always before when they had met he expressed a friendly greeting with a broad smile for her. He guided his mount into a tight circle and took the empty place beside her.

"Well met, Miss Elisabeth. How fare you since last we met?" He turned to fix her with a green-eyed solemn expression. She stifled an urge to scream at him for his perfidy, for breaking her heart, for behaving a cad to a young girl, for not loving her as she had loved him.

"Have you been gone a long time? Oh, la! I had not realized. Your duties kept you away, did they? It must be a great thing to be a duke." She tossed the words over her shoulder to Lyndon and laughed merrily.

"You have changed your hair," he said quietly. "I like it very much, but perhaps I was as fond of your braids as well." His boot brushed against hers as their mounts rubbed closely together.

She trilled a laugh as silly as she could make it. "Braids! You do me no service to remember my childhood ensemble. We all do nonsensical things when we are young. I have been out for two years now, Your Grace. Can you imagine how quickly one grows up in that time?" She laughed, turning it into a titter, once more refusing to look directly at him. It might work, she thought desperately, if only her heart would stop its loud thumping in her ears. Surely he did not expect her to be the same foolish chit as when he left.

"It does seem a long time since I rescued you from

your leafy bower, Miss Elisabeth. Have you forgotten me? I see you are keeping smart company these days. Is the viscount a particular friend of yours?" He stared at her steadily, but his stallion moved too restlessly to allow much intimacy.

She nudged her mount forward and as expected, he kept up with her easily. Before she could answer, Jamie rode forward and greeted the duke with an enthusiastic shout. The talk turned to war. She dropped back and found Matthew, suggesting they end their ride early. He raised his eyebrows at her, but acquiesced without argument. She called a general adieu to the group, reminding them she would see them the next day, gave a casual wave to Roderick and turned her mount away.

Her middle section seemed to always take a hit when Richard was around. Sheer willpower kept her upright as they rode back through the park and toward the gates. An intense feeling of relief surprised her. She had not realized the great tension until it left. Now that the initial confrontation was over, perhaps she could manage to maintain her composure whenever he appeared.

Matthew Diver-Jones, eyeing her with raised eyebrows commented, "Flying a bit high for my blood, Miss Elisabeth. Friend of yours? Heard Roderick was back from the wars, but not a familiar of mine. You neighbors?"

"Oh, just a casual acquaintance from a long-ago house party. It was my sister who caught his eye, not me. She, however, was not interested." She laughed out loud at the surprised and shocked expression on her friend's face at the idea that any lady would not be interested in becoming a duchess.

## Chapter Ten

It took all the willpower he had to sit and watch her ride away. Damn James Wilkerson's eyes. Nice chap and all that, but Richard had not finished his conversation with that...what was she now? He could not call her a child; she had grown up. He could not call her a hoyden; her manners were correct, even her hair was tamed. He missed those saucy curls fluttering around her piquant face. Good Lord, but his pulse was beating as if he were a green lad meeting a beauty for the first time.

She was not married, he thought, his pulse soaring. He tried to keep his mind on talking crops with James when he wanted to ride away and be private with his thoughts. All the while he had been away, he tried to forget her. There were many beautiful women in the world. Several of them had crossed his path in the last two years, but none had rid him of the sound of a husky voice whispering his name in the dimness of his own garden. Even now the memory of her lips under his had him releasing a heartfelt sigh.

Elisabeth, little Lizzie, prompted emotions he thought long left behind in his salad days. How had he managed to leave her? A man does not refuse a call from his royal, and he had not. He and Mark had ridden out the very next day and only returned a week ago. Mark had decided to keep his appointment and act as a permanent diplomat for England. He was at present on leave and awaiting his next assignment.

Mark had confessed he intended to woo and marry Elisabeth's sister, Sophia, if she were still available. They had talked long into the night on the trip home. Richard was shocked to learn that he and Mark had left both sisters so abruptly. What boorish behavior was this from two who called themselves gentlemen?

"I made a serious mistake, my friend," Mark had confided. "I thought it was concern for her, but it was not. My pride has kept me from making the match I most sincerely desired. If only she has not taken another, I will not make that same error again." He had been disappointed when the sisters left the ball the night before. "I wanted to demonstrate how much I have healed," he said to Richard after the women deserted the ballroom. "I wonder why I keep ruining my chances," he lamented. "Surely she was not unsettled by my not addressing her immediately?"

Richard did not return the confidence. He knew in his heart his love for Elisabeth was not proper. She was a child...no, not a child anymore, but he was so much older. He could not ask a young girl to tie herself to a man old enough to be her father. For two years he had argued with his heart and thought he had finally conquered it, as they sloughed through the countryside on their assignment. His solace during those bleak days was that she would find a match more appropriate and likely have at least one heir for the lucky scoundrel, damn his eyes, before they returned.

"My God, but she is lovely." He groaned aloud and startled a man and his wife strolling on the roadside as he passed by. She had taken his breath away as he glimpsed her from the doorway of the ballroom. She was all ice blue with diamonds. Would he ever forget his first sight? His Lizzie, but not his Lizzie: a grown-up Elisabeth in her milieu interacting happily with her young set. Exactly where she should be, he acknowledged, his heart taking a beating. Neither she nor her sister had made marriages. Now that snake Teasdale was moving in on her innocence. He could not permit that to happen.

So, she had learned his real identity, had she? He chuckled at her attempt to fool him into thinking she already knew. Perhaps it wasn't the most gentlemanly prank he had ever pulled, but he was, after all, in his own home. She had been such an innocent. Their relationship began accidentally when, hidden, he heard her voice asking for a kiss. From that moment on, he longed to silence that husky, musical voice with a kiss she would not soon forget. Those kisses were seared into his own mind, amazingly difficult to disengage.

Kissed her and left her, and thought he was doing the correct thing. Tell it to his heart, which had ached for two long years. He had made sure he would tutor this young girl so she would never ask for a kissing lesson again. Instead, she had been the teacher and he the pupil. Unaffected, innocent, and full of life, she had taught him to love, taught him to care deeply for another person so much he denied himself that which he most ardently desired. Would he ever again hear her whisper with affection that he was her Noble Rescuer? More like he was a Dastardly Cad.

She might never treat him to that trusting blink from those glorious blue eyes again, but he vowed that no-good Teasdale would not be the recipient instead.

Why had she not chosen one of those young men who seemed to cling to her side? It was amazing to think that both her sister and Elisabeth were still unclaimed. It could not be from a lack of courage of the young men in the *bon ton*. Two debutantes, gorgeous and well-endowed on the marriage mart for two years must surely mean the ladies were difficult to please.

Might she love him? He dismissed the thought immediately. How could she trust him let alone love him? Trust lost could never be regained. He felt a deep regret when he remembered how he was about to reveal himself to her. But then he kissed her instead and forgot everything else. He could regret the decision to keep silent, but he could never regret the kisses.

Chapter Eleven

At-home hours in the Barrows' town house were held on Tuesdays from one o'clock until four. The popularity of this family was apparent in the group gathered there deep in noisy social interaction. Widowed Helen Barrows, head of a circle of men and women with interest in the arts, occupied one end of the drawing room where her friends looked with indulgent eyes upon the noisy children playing cards at the other. The gaggle of young people ranged in age from seventeen to late twenties, normally more sophisticated and aware of their newly granted status as adults, regardless of how their parents and their friends treated them.

The new parlor game had them enthralled and involved much crowing and congratulations when one team topped the previous play on words, with groans and recriminations when it did not.

"Ah!" shouted Lyndon Peron. "You cheated, Matt, you know you did," he yelled when said cheater had them all groaning with a pun, instead of the malapropism the game called for. Matthew laughed so hard he only shook his head in answer. Sophia actually giggled at the antics of the two of them. Elisabeth, a member of the other team, noticed her sister relaxed and amused and was relieved.

The young men stretched out long legs, mindful of

their shining boots with various decorations—the latest high fashion they declared. Fluttering tassels seemed the favorite addition, and Elisabeth wondered how the horses regarded this silly affectation to footwear. One long and muddy cross-country ride would put it quickly to rest. How she would love that ride! She turned her thoughts away and observed her guests.

Gentlemen must bend from the waist since high collars restricted their movements. One young man called Chubs, Elisabeth uncertain of his actual birth name, had reached and stripped his collar open, his very red face convulsed in laughter. His merriment was echoed by two younger ladies not out yet, siblings of their older sisters.

"You have taken the round, Mr. Diver-Jones. It's our turn!" Eloise Larkin protested. Matthew gave her a mock bow in submission.

"He is ever a selfish brute. Nanny was fond of blue ruin. No doubt gave him a sip or two instead of milk," Lyndon Peron said and aimed a mock bow toward his cousin.

"Let's make another team, Lily," Eloise said adjusting the skirt of her fine sprigged muslin. She and her friend Lily were chiding Matthew who received this gentle onslaught with a wide grin and protestations of innocence. Elisabeth excused herself to call for tea service.

"Yes, Mother?" she asked, noting a signal from her parent.

"You are calling for tea, Lizzie?" she asked with a slight smile on her face. Her daughter wondered if that expression had anything to do with the handsome older gentleman sitting by her side. A viscount, she thought, who had known her mother in their salad days. Did this reaction from her mother have any significance? If so, she sincerely hoped her parent's romance progressed along more successful lines than those of her daughters.

She turned when she detected a commotion at the door. The footman ushered in a tall, handsome gentleman with a deeply tanned face. It took a second before Elisabeth recognized Captain Mark Estermire. He was dressed in a blue superfine coat, worn loose on his shoulders with trouser legs tucked into brown leather boots, scuffed a bit. His collar was not the fashionable height but was more relaxed and anchored with a jeweled pin. She took a deep breath and gave a short prayer for the Maker to send courage to her sister.

Sophia stood and even now walked sedately across the room. With a small but polite smile of greeting, she held out her hand to the solemn-faced gentleman. Elisabeth released her breath. Her sister was a champion with a steady hand. It could have been anyone entering their drawing room for their at-home day. How did Sophia manage to remain so serene?

"Here is Captain Estermire, Elisabeth, arrived just in time to take tea with us. Do you not wonder at how sunbaked he is? Have you been to distant lands fighting some dreadful war, Captain?" She gestured him to a seat a distance away from the still noisy, interactive crowd of young people arranged in a group at the end of the drawing room. None of them glanced up at the newly-arrived visitor, so entranced in their game they were.

"You are too busy for my visit, Miss Barrows, but may I engage you for a walk tomorrow? A ride in the park?" Estermire asked with his eyes fixated upon

Sophia's face.

"Do sit down and take tea with us, Captain. I'm afraid I am engaged for most of the week, but certainly you are a welcome visitor today. Do excuse me for a moment." She glided gracefully across the room and whispered to her mother, who promptly stood and accompanied her to greet the captain.

"Yes, I do remember you, Captain. You are a good friend of Roderick, are you not? You have been away? Can you tell us about your adventure?" She steered him gently toward the older group of visitors, while Sophia returned to stand by Elisabeth.

"Thank goodness tea is about to be served," she said. She took a deep breath and clasped her hands tightly together.

"Oh, I say. S-s-sustenance is here!" Matthew Diver-Jones sang out gaily. "Good thing too, as I was about to expire from s-s-starvation." All were quickly arranged on the facing couches in readiness for food. Together, the sisters turned to supervise the serving of the small cakes and platters of biscuits even now being eagerly sought by their younger guests.

A correct thirty minutes later, a cup of tea and a biscuit consumed, the captain took his leave. His face was grim but he said not another word to Sophia, nor did he beg for privacy to speak to her. Elisabeth was puzzled. Had he come to resume his courtship? If so, she was proud of her sister, who declined to be tossed into a flutter over a love so badly treated.

As their guests trailed out by twos and fours, a late guest came through the open door and was announced to the room. Viscount Teasdale, tall and handsome with his wicked grin, held out his hand to Elisabeth even as he greeted her mother with a cavalier bow. Elisabeth drew in her breath.

"You have only now missed tea, Lord Teasdale. How sad." She stood near the doorway not inviting him to a seat. "How may we serve you today?" She gave him a polite smile.

"Beg pardon, Miss Elisabeth, I was unavoidably detained. May I have the pleasure of your company for a ride tomorrow? I understand you have a keen affection for the sport. Tomorrow at eight? I will meet you outside." He gave her a wide smile, turned and left. Elisabeth stood perplexed.

"You did not invite Teasdale to stay, Elisabeth?" her mother asked, a small wrinkle of concern on her pretty face.

"I do not intend to encourage visitors so late in the day, Mother. Viscount or no. He asks to accompany me riding in the morning, but didn't stay around long enough to find out our set has planned an excursion to the country for a picnic. I suppose he will make part of the party." She shrugged her shoulders as if not worried about this titled visitor.

"He has a reputation, Daughter. He rides in a fast crowd, not one I would wish a daughter of mine to join. If the party is a large one, I doubt there can be any harm. Your sister joins you?" she asked.

"Sophia, Jamie, and several more known to you. Eloise's mother and her older brother accompany us. You will not worry, will you?" She gave her parent a quick hug and kiss on the cheek.

Her mother was never one to fret over her daughters, as long as they were properly chaperoned, except to chide gently now and then about the waste of tossed aside suitors. She didn't press her daughters to marry, but sometimes she scolded a bit.

"In my day, we were not given…" she said as she trailed away toward the stairs.

Sophia held out an arm to her sister and they climbed the stairs to their shared room. Elisabeth studied Sophia for signs of stress but could only admire her calm countenance. She could only hope her own face displayed a courage she did not feel. She placed a hand over the flutters in her stomach. How could she be a firm support to her sister when her own emotions were in such turmoil?

## Chapter Twelve

"Oh, yes, she was there. So was half the town. I was decidedly *de trop*," Captain Estermire said bitterly.

"You no doubt engaged her for another day, did you not?" his friend Richard asked, seeking information for his own benefit. He had not yet thought how to approach Elisabeth with his own serious intentions. Were his intentions serious? He was beset with doubt. He could not change his age, nor Elisabeth grow older. Why did his heart continue to insist he solve the problem?

"She explained she was too busy to see me for the next week. I wondered she actually remembered my name." He hit his muscular thigh with his riding crop. "I am so exasperated, mostly at myself. How could I have been so blind? She is the most beautiful lady I have ever dreamed of."

"You were worried that you would never heal properly," Roderick returned mildly. "It seems to me a natural concern, and one I am happy proved wrong." Your leg is perfectly recovered now." He surveyed the furnished apartments he had taken on his return, since his own town house had been let for another month. He and Mark had decided to share accommodations for the time being.

"Did you hear from the government office about your appointment? I know you aren't planning anything permanent." He was distracted thinking about Viscount Teasdale and that ride in the park with his—no, not his—Lizzie.

"Any day now I'll be informed, I suppose," Estermire said absently, his mind clearly not on the topic either. He continued his rant.

"In my sappy mind, it seemed only yesterday that we parted. Her face was forever in my thoughts and dreams. How could two years go by so quickly? She has obviously moved away from the feelings she expressed. Damnation! She told me my leg was of no consequence to her. Why did I not listen?" He flung himself into a wing chair beside a small fire burning half-heartedly in the grate.

"You are not to be defeated so soon, are you, Captain?" Roderick asked. "What this situation wants is an organized campaign." He chuckled when Estermire turned his head and glared. *Good. Anger was better than this.*

"What do you say to a late supper at White's tonight? We shall discuss an organized attack on an enemy." He laughed aloud when the captain shook his head.

"You have lost your mind, Roderick, my friend. This is a gently bred lady, not a stinking Frenchie convoy." He leaned forward with his hands clasped in front of him, his handsome face earnest.

"Ah, but courtships can be similar to war tactics," Roderick said. "What we need is reconnaissance. Our absence from the country for so long leaves us seriously depleted of the information we need to progress. What we need is a rattle."

"A…what are you talking about? You mean

someone who spills information whether you want to hear it or not?" He was trying to suppress a smile, but was failing.

"Of course. Is that not how we worked our spying? There is always someone eager to become important by the sharing of every piece of information he can glean."

"I see what you mean, but who?" The captain stood with an eager expression. "How can we find a rattle when we need one?"

"White's for supper," Roderick answered firmly. He would work for his friend and see what his efforts availed for himself.

"I'll go as your guest?" Estermire asked. Roderick nodded and clapped his friend on the shoulder.

Shortly afterward they entered the elegant but smoky room filled with men with cigars hanging from their mouths, either quietly reading or gathered over a table. Mark drifted over to watch a game in progress, while Roderick settled in a chair near a group of men playing cards and discussing a race.

"Teasdale will win without a hair on his head out of place," one said. A man universally called Fat Jelly disagreed and the two proceeded to argue loudly. Jelly seemed in danger of an immediate apoplexy, his stout face bulging and growing scarlet.

"Been out of town," Roderick said. "Where is this race being held and when? Need all the news." He leaned back in his chair and waited. The argument ceased and the two men turned eagerly toward him, both vying for the biggest gossip-mongering prize.

"They say Prinny's carriage was pelted with rocks when he rolled down the streets of Town," one wag offered. "Spent the Treasury broke on that monstrosity he built in Brighton. I heard he had a pool built down the center of that long dining table, then he—you will never believe this—put goldfish in it. They were swimming all during the time they dined, some of them belly up dead, if that doesn't cure an appetite. They say taxes will go up because of it."

Another screamed with laughter, then whispered, "He wears corsets and creaks when he walks."

Roderick allowed the conversation to range freely. He was by far too experienced a spy to ask directly for the information he sought.

"Rumor has it he's gone off completely, thinks he was leading the charges in the battles. He might be the Regent, but I never heard of him riding to war. Can hardly sit a horse—pity the poor animal—so fat has he grown. Takes four grooms to get him into the saddle." The gossip flowed, and Roderick despaired of hearing any of the information he needed, but then the subject switched to the current crop of debs.

"The Barrows ladies are called the 'Unattainables,'" Fat Jelly summarized. With his ears filled with *on dits* enough to last him a year, Roderick stood and looked around for Estermire. He spotted him finally sitting in on a card game in a corner. He caught Mark's attention and signaled that they tend their supper.

During their meal, he shared what details he had gathered. "Sophia has refused at least two very eligible suitors. She is well-regarded by the ton, even by her deb rivals. Parents advise their daughters to emulate the conduct of Miss Barrows. You've settled on quite a prize, Estermire." He chuckled when his friend held his head in his hands.

"Don't despair. Think, man. Why is she turning down all those available potential husbands?" He laughed aloud when his friend's head came up, eyes blazing with what he supposed was hope?

"Are you serious? Could it be? But she was so…well, not cold, but not what I remembered."

"Mark, Mark. How would you expect her to respond after two years and not a word from you? You probably broke her heart, and she is not going to trust it to you any time soon. Can't blame her. If you want this young lady, you will need to court her again."

"Don't mind that if I thought she could ever feel affection for me again." He looked up as a man approached their table.

"You back in town, are you, Roderick?" Viscount Teasdale said, smiling widely at the two men. "Pity I didn't engage to race you on the morrow. What kept you away so long?"

"Teasdale. Still up to your tricks, are you?" Roderick said. "Been away on the king's business…well, the Regent's, that is. How is Prinny? Heard he needed help mounting his ride."

They chatted desultorily for a minute, with Teasdale acknowledging Mark with a friendly nod. Roderick had known the viscount since school. He was a couple of grades younger, but the man had a reputation for shady dealings even then. Elisabeth would probably be putty in the hands of a rogue like the viscount. The duke thought his heart would never stop reacting to the very thought of that sweet hoyden—hoyden no more.

"Saw your mount in the park the other day. Nice ride. Is that the one you're racing tomorrow?" He was fishing for information about Teasdale's relationship with Elisabeth. How to get at the truth without revealing his own interest?

"Not made the decision. I have two new ones bought at Tattersall's auction just a month ago. You missed them, Roderick." He laughed and clapped the duke on the shoulder. "I know you and horseflesh." The duke nodded at the hit.

"Thought you'd have set up your nursery by now, Teasdale. You're holding out longer than I am, say what?" He made himself chuckle and appreciated that Mark was holding his peace.

"Might be in the market for a change, now you mention it. Found myself a lively filly and mean to tame her before long. Have fun breaking her to bridle," Teasdale said. He pulled up a chair and joined them at the table.

"Ha! New mistress, right?" Estermire interjected and started when the viscount laughed loud and long.

"Since when does a doxy need taming?" he asked. "This is a lady, and I mean to make her my wife. Time I set up my nursery, got myself an heir." He straightened, a deep ruby winking in a jeweled pin holding his neck cloth in place.

Richard Edmond Hawlester, the present Duke of Roderick, clenched his hands underneath the table. *Over my dead body!* Elisabeth Barrows might never trust him again, but he was still her Noble Rescuer, and he would never let this cretin harm or have his little love.

Chapter Thirteen

Early the next day, the picnic goers gathered outside the Barrows' town house creating a commotion in the street. Young men vied for position as they started the procession, trailing horses and riders, three carriages filled with those who preferred not to ride, and a special coach filled with food and servants. It was a large group of lively, jostling young people and their chaperones.

"Will you ride up front with me, Miss Barrows?" Lyndon Peron said as he tried to control his skittish bay. It was a beautiful animal, but Elisabeth thought it too fresh for such an excursion.

"Don't pay any attention to Diver-Jones. With that nag he's riding, it will be tomorrow before he gets to our destination." Elisabeth laughed.

"I'll catch up with you when we are past the town traffic. I want to assure everyone manages to get safely underway," she said and turned her head in surprise when Viscount Teasdale rode into view. His sardonic grin evident, he waved his crop and nudged his mount forward.

"Well met, Miss Elisabeth. I was unaware you were involved in a parade."

"You left before I could explain, Lord Teasdale. This picnic was planned some weeks ago. We are off to the estate of the late Baron Sanders. Riverside Manor it's called." She gentled her horse as she watched the servants' coach rattle across the cobblestones. "There, that's the last one. We may be off…if you intend to join us, my lord." She nudged her mount, holding the reins tightly as the mare surged forward to catch up.

Without hesitation, Teasdale guided his mount to keep perfect pace with Elisabeth. "Riverside is not far, only a few miles outside town," the viscount said. "We shall be there before long. How is it you are able to procure an invitation? The Dowager Sanders is not usually accommodating." He turned to speak to Elisabeth and narrowly missed a vegetable cart coming the other way. The tradesman yelled something that caused the viscount to shout with laughter.

"What did he say?" Elisabeth asked. "Something about where to keep turnips?" She hadn't understood much of the words the man screamed.

"Best you remain in ignorance," Teasdale returned. "He has quite a colorful grasp of the English language." He reached forward to pat his mount on the neck fondly. They entered a street with newer homes, larger and more gracious, set back from the road. The traffic was dwindling to an occasional carriage or single horseman. It was a fine day with the promise of full sunshine.

Lyndon Peron rode back, raising his eyebrows and narrowing his eyes when he spotted Teasdale riding tandem with Elisabeth. "Thought you were joining us at the front, Miss Elisabeth," he said. "Been expecting you." He bowed to the viscount who gave him a cursory bend of his head back.

"Sorry, Mr. Peron. I thought it wise to keep an eye on the stragglers. I will see you later near our destination grounds," she said with a friendly smile. He gave a half bow from the waist acknowledging her words, wheeled his mount around, waved goodbye, and left them.

"You have a fond set of friends, do you? It must make life comfortable."

"I imagine friends are a valuable asset to anyone. Are you not fortunate in those you choose to surround you?" Elisabeth tipped her head to gaze at him. She knew what a fast crowd the viscount preferred. Even if she didn't see them together often in the park, the gossip wags buzzed with their exploits. Once, she had spotted a cartoon in a shop window, a drawing of rather vulgar behavior involving the Regent and his friends. She thought one resembled Teasdale.

"Oh, as to that. I'm not certain all those I see regularly could qualify as friends. Colleagues, perhaps. Merely long acquaintances. A man is fortunate if he can boast of even one close friend. Does your mother accompany you today?" he asked, adroitly changing the subject.

"No, we have another parent as chaperone. I believe she is some relative of the Dowager Sanders, which is to answer your earlier question. We were granted permission to picnic on her grounds through the parents of Eloise Larkin. I believe they are riding in the first carriage. I should ride ahead and visit with them. I'll speak to you later, my lord."

She trotted away leaving him no choice but to stay behind. She refused to look over her shoulder to see how he handled her dismissal. Truth, she was uncomfortable in his company, although she could find no logical reason for it. His behavior was everything a gentleman's should be. *There is no accounting for a person's preferences, is there?*

What did the viscount want? Surely he was not entering the list to court her, was he? How unfortunate this would happen just when she had to cope with the return of the dastardly duke. She suppressed a fleeting surge of feelings for the man called Richard. Teasdale was no lightweight to be turned aside lightly, although she found him handy as a foil for Richard Hawlester. *Careful as you go, Elisabeth. Impulsiveness is not your friend. Surely you have learned your lesson by now.*

She spoke to Mrs. Larkin and found Sophia in the seat beside her. Her sister was chatting happily with Eloise's older brother, a ruggedly good-looking man home from the war. He made a formidable extra chaperone for his younger sister, Elisabeth thought with a grin. After a few pleasant words, she passed on to join the more ambitious set at the front of the procession. Lyndon called out to her, and she joined him sliding into a space created by her friends, with whom she had no need to build a guard against her behavior or her words. She relaxed and let the tension flow away.

The next hour brought them to the grounds of a lovely manor house set in a slight rise overlooking the river. Grooms who had ridden ahead took charge of the horses, hobbling and setting them to graze in the lush grasses near the riverbank. Elisabeth looked down on the exquisite gardens displayed to one side of the old mansion. The faint, but distinct fragrance of roses teased her nose as a gentle breeze puffed by. On the other side near the back door, Elisabeth identified an herb garden, located convenient to the cook she guessed. It was arranged in an intricate design, curiously resembling a bird in flight.

She shifted in the saddle when the carriage containing Mrs. Larkin and Sophia drew near. The ladies descended and stretched. They stood admiring the views, but Mrs. Larkin was eager to initiate the plans.

"We are invited to set our picnic over there," the chaperone said and pointed to a small grove. "There are tables and even some benches for us to take our leisure. My Aunt Sanders has graciously planned for us to enjoy our stay."

"How lovely," Sophia exclaimed and strolled toward the shady wood. Several guests joined her. The young people milled about, some flinging themselves to sun in the soft grasses. Groups formed and shifted as friends visited and others became acquainted. Elisabeth had not bothered to count, but she guessed that Mrs. Larkin had encouraged more than twenty to join in this excursion. Elisabeth was pleased with the congenial group.

The servant's coach arrived, and soon the tables donned white table cloths and baskets of food set up for their picnic. Jugs of lemonade with available cups occupied one small table and became instantly popular. Thirsty from the ride, the guests circled and helped themselves to the cooling drink. Platters of chicken followed by loaves of bread were displayed, and baskets of fresh fruit tempted young appetites. The servants placed jars of pickled beets and eggs out for those adventurous enough to taste them. More food followed, most of it of the dessert variety. Small pies, biscuits, and cakes soon decorated the last empty picnic table.

Already, the eager men were circling the food tables helping themselves to plates and piling them high. The servants set out blankets and quilts for their comfort, and the young ladies staked their claims, resting like bouquets of flowers on the pallets made comfortable by the lush grasses. Those with riding habits were more careless toward their attire, while those who had chosen muslin day gowns made a fuss as they settled. The young men claimed their favorites and shared the food.

Teasdale invited Mrs. Larkin, the chaperone, to join him and turned his charming smile to Elisabeth. She made a moue and begged pardon, but she had already promised another. Teasdale maintained his sangfroid, but she noticed a tightening around his eyes. She felt a slight guilty pang but remembered he had joined them uninvited. She collapsed on a blanket beside Sophia and Eloise, who were soon joined by several of their close friends.

"What a muffin face you are, Lyndon. How did your parents ever manage to feed you?" Matthew Diver-Jones and his cousin were soon enjoined in a jostling match to grab all the available biscuits. They stuffed their mouths past full and soon had the women in full-blown laughter. Formal manners forgotten, the two clowned and teased. Eventually with their appetites sated, many sauntered off in twos and threes. Some shut their eyes and napped.

Elisabeth left the group and walked quietly in the shade of the trees. She wanted the solitude to think over her meeting with the man who had kissed her and made her a dupe by withholding his identity. She could not stop the pictures forming in her mind of him wrapping his arms tightly around her, his lips roving over hers, his tongue teasing her mouth. Even now, her knees grew weak remembering. With the memory came despair as she recalled he was only playing a game with her naiveté.

"You are enjoying a visit with nature, are you, Miss Elisabeth?" She whirled around to see Viscount Teasdale who stood directly behind her. She had not heard his approach, although she acknowledged she should have expected him. Immediately, she altered direction and strolled toward the river and sunshine.

"Why, yes, Lord Teasdale. Is it one of your favorite pastimes as well?" He kept pace with her, touching her hand once or twice as they strolled.

"Miss Eli-Elisabeth, would you do me the honor of a private minute of your time?" Startled, she paused. They were within sight of the river. Down below she could see a barge anchored at the small dock.

"How may I be of service to you, my lord?" she asked warily. He was as handsome as could stare, but his presence had all her warning signals nudging her to be away from his presence. He stepped closer and took her hand. She looked up into brown eyes that seemed to twinkle with some amusement he held privately.

"I thought perhaps I could kiss you, Elisabeth. You are a very beautiful lady, are you not?" he said as his lips found hers.

Elisabeth froze as he kissed her with persistence. His manner was forceful and very different from a first kiss she remembered. Even so, she tried to respond, as she felt his hand behind her head forcing her closer. It was no use; her heart was not with her. Finally, the most eligible suitor released her and stepped back with a teasing smile.

"Your first kiss, Elisabeth? I feel honored to be your first, sweetling. I intend to pay suit. I will speak to your parent soon." He tilted her chin up and grinned.

She nodded that she understood but squeaked in alarm when he rushed past her.

Teasdale tore down the riverbank like a madman, waving his arms and shouting. A man leading a horse onto the barge stopped and turned around. The horse whinnied and seemed to recognize Teasdale as its owner. Elisabeth was astonished at the tableau being played out and walked quickly toward Mrs. Larkin, their chaperone. Others attracted by the noise came toward them.

"What is going on, do you know?" she asked, as the older lady stood watching the puzzling action on the dock below with her hands clasped before her. She faced Elisabeth with raised eyebrows and a worried expression.

"Why, I'm certain I could not explain. There was a groom—I guess he was a groom—who came to me and said that horse was to be taken down to the barge. How could I know it belonged to the Viscount Teasdale? Is he a thief, do you think? How very dreadful!" She held her handkerchief to her nose, and Elisabeth could detect the odor of lavender.

Still puzzled at the strange interaction of the viscount and the thief masquerading as a groom, she gazed past her chaperone. What she spied made her think perhaps lightning had struck. At least, that was how the sight caused her to feel. The Duping Duke was strolling toward them with the Dowager Sanders' hand tucked familiarly in his arm. The usually taciturn lady was smiling up at her escort; the sound of her bubbling laughter came floating up to them.

A total sense of unreality overcame Elisabeth. How could all this be happening when she had been so very careful to obey society's rules? When would her heart lose the tender feelings it still possessed for that wayward nobleman, and how in blazes could one kiss be so very different from another?

"Why, it's Aunt Lily with Roderick, and she is laughing!" Mrs. Larkin exclaimed. She seemed astonished that her elderly aunt would be on genial terms with the duke. "Never recovered from the loss of Uncle William," she whispered to Elisabeth as the couple approached. "Always grumpy, though she has a heart of gold. Now here is Roderick, and I make certain I don't know how we are to entertain him. The refreshments are all gone. Who would believe those young men could consume so much food?" She wrung her hands and tried to smile, although her agitation was evident.

"Niece, look who has decided to come for a visit. He's been out of the country on the Regent's business for two long years, he tells me." Mrs. Larkin bobbed him a curtsey and Elisabeth followed suit trying not to meet his eyes. Her heart raced, and she clenched her fists in an attempt to gain control of her runaway emotions.

James Wilkerson hurried forward to greet the duke, who promptly clapped him on the back. The two of them moved a step away to discuss a newly purchased piece of horseflesh James felt had promise.

"Had your picnic, did you?" the dowager asked gruffly. She surveyed the lounging and napping gathering of young people. "Not got the gumption we had when we were that age," she muttered underneath her breath. Her gaze found Elisabeth, and she inquired about her mother.

"She's fine, ma'am. She is perhaps pleased to be excused from following my sister and me around town today." She managed a smile and a casual reply.

"Where is the older sister?" the dowager asked, glancing at a gathering of young ladies conversing with accompanying giggles. Sophia was with a group near the wood. Elisabeth beckoned to her.

"Are you closely acquainted with our parent, ma'am?" Elisabeth asked, certain she had guessed correctly.

"Certainly, knew your whole family. Haven't been a recluse all my life, have I?"

Sophia came smiling to join them and bobbed her bow. She moved away with Dowager Sanders and Mrs. Larkin leaving Elisabeth standing alone. How was she not surprised when Richard slid into place by her side? Where Jamie had disappeared to, she couldn't guess. Had she lingered there purposely? How much humiliation could she gather for herself?

"You are surprised to find me here before you, are you not, Elisabeth?" He held out his arm and she was obliged to give him her hand. He tucked it securely into the crook of his arm and covered it warmly with his own.

"I'm sure I gave your whereabouts not a single thought, Your Grace." She busied herself tucking up her riding habit with exaggerated care, lest the long skirt catch on small shrubs.

"You were once pleased to call me Richard. Can

you not bring yourself to do so now?" She felt his breath tease the curls on her forehead. His nearness was disturbingly familiar.

"How could I miss the Duke of Roderick when I did never meet him, Your Grace?"

"Ah, but you had a good friend named Richard, did you not? Did you miss him ever?" He squeezed her hand and she glanced up. He gazed straight down into her eyes and locked the stare.

She felt the familiar clench of her stomach. *Drat the man!* Could he not remind her of her humiliation?

"I knew a man named Richard I once called my Noble Rescuer." She managed a curt reply and felt her balance returning. "To my dismay, I learned he was only a Deceptive Duke, hardly noble for all that."

"Do you think you could forgive me? You were very young and so very beautiful. I could not resist the enchantment of pretending I was someone else, however briefly. I did not mean for it to last so long or…you were irresistible, my dear, but I most ardently assure you. I did not mean you harm."

Elisabeth thought of the nights she cried herself to sleep. Was the man ignorant of the impact of his devastating behavior toward a young girl?

"Indeed, I reasoned my call to duty by the government providential," he continued. "You were free to concentrate on your début and join a group your own age. Did you soon forget me?"

"Almost before I left your estate, Richard. Surely you knew I too played the game. I was too easily bored as a houseguest at the residence of the old duke." She waved to Sophia, who left the dowager and came to join them. "I am grown up now, Your Grace. I do not play silly games anymore. Real life is much more rewarding." She released his arm and walked away with her sister, leaving the Duke of Roderick standing alone in the meadow.

He turned when the Viscount Teasdale climbed the bank, pulling his horse behind him. "Teasdale. You here? What brings you out so far from town?"

"Damn groom tried to steal my horse. I told him a thing or two, I assure you." He puffed from the climb. "Claimed he must have gotten the message all wrong, damn his thieving eyes."

Elisabeth looked curiously back at the sight of the two noblemen on the bank of the river, both devastatingly handsome, powerful men. She had allowed both to kiss her. The contrast between these two provided no conclusive information. She would not contemplate the theory that Richard was the better kisser. He was probably the most experienced, and that didn't bear thinking of.

What would her mother say to an offer from Viscount Teasdale? No matter. She had no intention of accepting him, but would she ever fall in love again? How could she even guess whether love was what she felt? Perhaps it was only a part of the false atmosphere created by a Deceptive Duke playing a game with a young maiden. All too ready to return to London, she hurried to find her horse, as the rest of the party sought theirs or their seats in the carriages now being brought round. The country was far too full of surprises to suit her taste.

Chapter Fourteen

"He insists he wants to make you his wife, Lizzie. Are you not interested in becoming an important hostess? There are not many opportunities for a young lady like this one. Dare you turn it down?" While Elisabeth had been out on her regular morning ride, Helen Barrows had received a visit from Viscount Teasdale with the promised proposal. Her mother had invited her to her boudoir for a discussion of the offer.

"Mother, I am not very well acquainted with the man, but when I have been in his presence, I have felt uncomfortable. I have no logical reason for it, but I can no longer deny the truth. He came on the picnic excursion with us, and his strident nature puts me off for some reason. He is used to taking charge of those around him, perhaps." She looked out the window and thought absently she would walk to the lending library for new books. It was a fine, sunny day.

"He has an important title and a pleasing countenance, but you are never one to be led, Daughter. I understand and will respect your decision, but you are to inform me if you change your mind." Her mother chuckled quietly, leaned over and caressed her youngest on the cheek. "Well, he asked only to be allowed the opportunity to court you. I will tell him you are not interested, but I doubt he will take no for an answer immediately. You may be plagued with his visits for a while yet. May you tolerate it?" She stood and pulled a tasseled cord for her maid to join her.

"I will remain polite, if that's what you're asking. He can visit on our at-home day like all the rest. I will not accept exclusive rides in the park with him, but he is free to join my set when we are out, I suppose. I do hope he accepts my rejection soon. What a nuisance it will be if he does not." She stood and kissed her parent on the cheek.

"I will ask Sophia if she will accompany me to the lending library. If not, I will have Sally accompany me. Should you have an errand for me to run, dear Mother? It is lovely out and I long to be enjoying the bright day."

"No, child. I'm shopping with Mrs. Larkin presently. I have in mind to buy a new hat. I am dismayed at how shabby my blue one has gotten. It seems I purchased it yesterday. I saw one in the window of that new shop that had the cleverest blue feathers…" She drifted to her wardrobe to stare pensively at her clothing. Elisabeth understood she had been dismissed and left quietly.

****

After her youngest daughter left the room, Helen turned to her writing desk. Soon her pen flew across the page. After a time, she sprinkled fine sand on the letter to dry the ink, sealed, and addressed it. She rang for her maid, and when the woman arrived, instructed her to post the letter immediately. Helen hoped no interested party noticed that it was addressed to Her Grace, the Duchess of Roderick. She sat at her dresser staring at her reflection in the cheval mirror and wondered how long it would be before she received a reply. Helen suspected it might be time for the two of them to conference.

Chapter Fifteen

Sophia declared a visit to the lending library was just the thing she needed to lift her spirits. The sisters walked out of the town house to delightful sunshine. Elisabeth's wide-brimmed straw hat decorated with artificial red cherries protected her fair skin and discouraged freckles. Sophia carried a parasol, ruffled and fringed with pink lace, since her close bonnet furnished little protection. A slight breeze greeted them with no hint of rain, and they arrived at the lending library within twenty minutes of leaving the house.

Elisabeth was flipping the pages of a stylish magazine for young ladies while Sophia sought more serious reading. They browsed throughout the rooms in no hurry to make their selections. Elisabeth pulled a book from one of the shelves and was startled by a face peering through at her. To her dismay, Lord Teasdale popped into view around the corner with his wide, knowing grin. He crowded her in the narrow corridor, placing his hand on the wall, encircling and closing off her exit. Immediately she felt her temper flare, but managed to stifle hasty words. It would not do to make a spectacle.

"You are looking for reading material, are you, Lord Teasdale?" she commented as casually as she could and nodded a slight acknowledgement as she pushed forward forcing him to back away.

"You are a pleasure for my eyes today, Miss Elisabeth. What luck to find you here." He followed her as she sought her sister's presence.

"What plans have you this fine morning?" she asked, holding her magazine in front of her. "I vow you must be a leisurely man with time to linger in a library." She had searched all the rooms with no sign of her sister. Where was Sophia? Teasdale pressed behind her occasionally touching her elbow as if guiding her along. She longed to slap his hand away, but restrained herself.

"Oh," she said softly as she finally spotted her sister, standing red-faced, looking up into the grim expression on the handsome countenance of Captain Mark Estermire. Should she give them privacy, even though she knew how angry Sophia had been at the man who had broken her heart? Perhaps she still loved the captain. Whatever the result, they would need the time to settle their differences. Only this removed her best hope of detaching Teasdale.

"Oh, la, Lord Teasdale, do you think I might find more suggestions to make up new gowns over here?" she said and trilled a laugh. He followed her away from the intense conversation of the young couple, his hand now firmly attached to her elbow. Elisabeth glanced back and observed her sister. She was gazing at the captain with a slight smile on her pretty face. It seemed hopeful after all. How now to rid herself of this nuisance?

"You have plans to ride in the morning, Miss Elisabeth?" he asked, leering down at her.

"Of course, Lord Teasdale. I frequently ride with my friends in the park." She edged away and picked up another magazine. He followed close behind her.

"I make it my business to escort you tomorrow," he said aggressively reaching for her hand. She sidestepped him and turned to the lending counter.

"Teasdale, well met. That your equipment outside? Dismayed to inform you your groom has wandered away and so have your cattle." The duke stood negligently by a table of books, idly picking up one or another. Elisabeth drew in a sharp breath, but Teasdale was already hastening out the door. His abrupt exit was pleasing to her, but the presence of Richard was not. She turned and rounded a corner with bookshelves blocking her sight.

"Elisabeth?" He poked his handsome head around the corner and peered at her with hesitant smile lighting up his face. His eyes crinkled with laugh lines. She knew that look. He was amused at the situation, and, in her anger, she burned to box his ears.

"My friend Mark is occupied in a serious conversation with your sister. May I keep you company? I am reluctant to interrupt them. I will keep my distance, unlike that boor Teasdale. I can see by that glint in your eye you would dearly love to box my ears."

"This is a lending library. I assume you are a member. You may occupy any space you desire. How comes it you are here? A duke could have the entire library shipped directly to his house." She heard her sarcasm, and he winced indicating he heard it as well. "And by the by," she added, "why don't you?" She ducked past him and reached a table covered with more magazines.

"Elisabeth, I acknowledge how badly I have

behaved, and I profusely apologize if I have hurt you in any way. Do you think you could ever forgive me and allow us to be friends again?" He stood quietly by her side, making no attempt to touch her.

"You are perhaps looking for new friends, Your Grace? A man with such a high title must always enjoy popularity. He has no need to consort with lowly personages like me. Unless, of course, you desire to play silly games again. In that case, my answer would be definitely no. I am a dupe for you only once. You must find another victim for your juvenile amusements." She had heard his apology, and it seemed only to increase her anger.

"Elisabeth," he pleaded, "what can I do to entice you to forgive me? I long for your good will. We were fast friends once, were we not?" He reached out his hand, but she turned her back on him.

"Were we? Ah, Richard the Duke. I was a fast friend to you. I fail to understand how you include yourself in that statement. You were my Noble Rescuer. In my mind, I thought that meant you were a good friend who wished me well—a sad mistake. I was very young and had not been much out in company as yet. My naiveté amused you, did it not?"

"My dear, if you only knew how I longed to…I meant to tell you all that night when you came down to the garden, but…I lost my head. You were sweet and beautiful, and all I longed to do was kiss you. If I had been honest that night, never would you have allowed me to hold you." He reached both hands out to her, but she walked away.

"Stop, Richard. Sorry, Lord Roderick, Your Grace. Richard was an imaginary friend, a good friend that I lo…liked, but he never existed except in my silly, young head. Go away. Can you not see it is painful for me to remember my humiliation? Even as a green girl, I understood a duke would not notice such as me. You were amused with your little deceit, and I a plum ripe for the plucking." At last Roderick dropped his arms and turned away.

She stayed with her head down staring at the floor until she heard her sister's voice calling her. She wiped a small tear from her cheek, forced a smile, and greeted Sophia, whose face was so radiant it made the sun seem dim. Good, thought Elisabeth, at least one of us may find happiness.

"And so you are reconciled, are you, Sister? I'm happy for you." She reached out and hugged Sophia, holding her own emotions on a tight leash.

"Pray, do not think I am as easy as all that to forgive. Mark understands now how badly he upset and hurt me. I have been candid with him about how much he…well, that he wounded me. We have agreed to become friends again, but he will not be freely granted a place in my heart. In time, if I think he is a steady man with sane thinking…well, we will see." But she grinned with delight over their meeting. Elisabeth was proud of her sister.

"He is not in the army anymore, did you know? His wound makes him ineligible, even though he has overcome most of his infirmities." She tucked her hand in Elisabeth's arm and they left the library.

"Is he to settle in England, then? I know very little of Captain Estermire's situation or his family. I presume they are all that they should be?" She turned with questioning eyes to Sophia who smiled.

"Yes! Quite respectable. Mark is a fourth son and must make his own way in the world. He is fast friends with Roderick—I'm sorry to bring up his name—and would be given a position with him if necessary."

"He will not work for the Dastardly Duke, then?" She grinned when Sophia whooped with laughter at her name-calling.

"No, he has applied and been accepted to become an ambassador for our country. He is awaiting a new diplomatic appointment now, although he is on leave from his long stint overseas."

"Oh? How do you feel about that? If you and he were married, you would be forced to live in some foreign county. Do you long to serve as a diplomatic hostess? I know Mama would be upset over your absence as would I."

"I know, and part of me is sad about that. But I must confess to you, dearest Sister, another part of me is very excited to think of travel. I have always longed to, but never did I think the opportunity would present. You are surprised?" They passed a bakery and sniffed the pleasing fragrances of fresh-baked bread.

"Somewhat. Wanderlust doesn't seem to suit your personality, or have you have been hiding things from me," Elisabeth accused. "What else do you have in that head of perfection?" They paused while Sophia adjusted her parasol in the brief gust of wind while Elisabeth clutched her hat.

Sophia shook her head. "Perfection is not a word to apply to me, and we are discussing the subject of marriage too soon. I have simply given him permission to visit with an opportunity to regain my friendship. Perhaps he will fail me once more. Let us talk instead of your own unexpected visitors. There were two of them, I saw."

"Ha. Neither was welcome, I can tell you. First came the Beast who cannot keep track of his horses and then the Duping Duke begging pardon, as if I ever would. Pity me," she pleaded, when Sophia covered her grin with her hand.

"I do, I promise you, I do, but you will keep me laughing with your name-calling."

"I assure you that barely covers my anger. I longed so to box his impudent ears. What do you suppose would happen to a lowly person as me if I physically harmed a duke? Just one sharp smack," she said as she slapped her hands together fiercely.

"Oh, Elisabeth, I do hope you will soon rid yourself of your disappointment. He must be regretting his behavior if he keeps appearing and apologizing like that. Do you not think?" They lingered beside the gate to a square enclosed with an iron picket fence.

"Would you like to sit in the square for a while?" Sophia asked. They entered by a gate and found a bench. It was quiet and peaceful in the pretty setting. The scenery served as a balm to Elizabeth's excited nerves. She sat thinking for a moment and then confessed to her sister her worries.

"I'm not certain His Most High Deceiving Duke is my biggest problem right now. Teasdale is more pressing, I think. I cannot give him my answer until he actually asks the question. I thought I would need to box his ears this morning, he was so persistent."

"I am sorry I did not see him with you initially. Mark and I were talking."

"I know. I led him away to give you more privacy.

You will forgive me?"

Sophia reached over and squeezed her hand. "We are a pair, are we not? What do you think Mother would say to all this agitation?" They smiled at each other. Elisabeth thought there was a sheepish look on her sister's face and imagined one on hers as well.

"No doubt astonished if we explained this all started two years ago when the Dutiful Duke planned to announce his engagement to everyone—and then left."

"He was called away by the government," Elisabeth said. "I keep forgetting that, but he could have said something that night before he left."

"And never announced his engagement to anyone," Sophia added. "I wonder if you had anything to do with that, Sister. I'm guessing that you did."

Elisabeth said nothing but sat gazing at the pretty park. Had their secret trysts anything to do with him not announcing his engagement? Always she had thought his hurried departure was the cause. But then she did not know Richard was the Dreadful Duke, even as she remembered Richard left the same day…oh, it was too confusing. Again, against her will, came the feel of his arms wrapped around her with his lips descending toward hers. She squirmed on the bench and thrust her thoughts away.

"Let us go home now. I think we are beginning to obsess on the topic of these men, and for me, I can tell you, they are more aggravating than important." She stood up and pulled Sophia to her feet. The sisters, with their arms wrapped around each other, left the pretty park across the street and entered their mother's town house.

"Where have you girls been so long?" their parent

greeted them as they entered. "I made sure you were not buying out the book shop. Is life so boring you have turned to reading—surely you do not aspire to become bluestockings instead of spending time with your friends?" She smiled at them and offered her fragrant cheek to be kissed.

## Chapter Sixteen

"I beg you will join me. M' mother has arrived in town to help sponsor a young relative making her come-out. Could have sworn she'd intended to confine her assistance to writing a few letters, but there she is opening up the town house. She insists I make a visit early to Almack's. It seems I have a second or third—it's difficult to remember them all—cousin who has lost her spots and is making a showing tonight. I must lead her out I am informed. One dance only I promised her, so knee britches it is. It's difficult to believe after all this time Almack's dictates this antiquated attire. Only in London." Richard moaned.

"Once I show my face, she promises we may leave for White's. There's a new gambling hall just opened if you'd rather drop in there. I hear their late suppers are excellent." He stood tying his neck cloth in a way simpler than most. He disliked not moving his head freely. He reached for an emerald pin to anchor it. Adding his signature ring, he turned to face Mark, who was lounging nearby in a red velvet chair with his legs thrust out. His friend bent over to rub his knee, shaking his head.

"Not certain I'm fit for dancing tonight, Roderick. Walked on my leg quite a bit today, and it's aching tonight." He stood and ambled closer to the small fire burning in the grate. "I despair of my leg ever regaining its original health. I think it recovered and then, like tonight, it reminds me of the insulting injury. Perhaps I still make a poor specimen to ask a lady to share life with me," he said, reaching up to lean one arm on the mantle.

"Well, rejoice, my friend. You are much closer to your goal of gaining a wife than I am. I thought Miss Elisabeth would punch my nose today. She has a fiery temper, that one." He tilted his head but shook with amusement. "I cannot help but admire her tenacity in refusing to forgive me." He held out his arms for his valet to assist him into his coat.

"I did not play the poser with Miss Barrows. Richard, it was unforgivable how you treated her sister. What came over you to play that game?"

"It was badly done, I admit. My excuse is that you have no idea how tiresome it is to be admired for your title alone. I had no plan of pretending to be another; it just evolved that way. I was in turmoil to choose between all those giggling debutants at the time I rescued Elisabeth from the dip in the lily pond. I had actually almost decided on her sister, but you had that taken care of." They smirked at each other.

"The problem came about when I did not immediately confess my real identity. Who would ever believe she could be a houseguest for two days and not realize the identity of her host?" He stood still for his valet to brush the shoulders of his coat and toss his hair in the careless style of the day. Did they call it the Brutus? He had obviously been out of the country too long. He would need to pay better attention to the current styles.

"I find that difficult to understand as well, but

Sophia assures me her sister learned the truth only recently. She has not had two years to allow her ire to cool. Unfortunate for you, I believe." He shifted his stance and rested his weight on his more solid leg.

"You have healed the breach with your interest, have you? I do not mean to pry," Roderick asked.

"Sophia has agreed to allow me to visit. That's as far as I have managed to gain, but do not misunderstand me. I am very pleased to have come that far. Do you plan to pursue your interest with Miss Elisabeth? Or are you merely making amends for your unfortunate behavior?"

"I can confess to you at this point that I am a lost cause. No matter how many times I tell myself I am too old to court that beautiful young lady, my heart refuses to listen." He turned to dismiss his man.

"Do you worry your private matters will become a topic of gossip?" Mark glanced at the closed door. "You speak freely in front of your servant."

"My valet? Do not worry. He guards my privacy more thoroughly than I do." He paced the room and returned to the subject close to his heart.

"She may never be friendly again, and I know I deserve that, but listen to this. Who do you think has decided to pursue her for his bride, declaring he is ready to set up his nursery?"

"I am guessing it's Teasdale. I saw how you manipulated his groom so his horses wandered." He laughed and clapped his hands. "No one could be more upset than Teasdale. He spends all his time either challenging to race or racing. Did you hire that groom after he fired him?"

"I hired him before Teasdale fired him." He raised

his eyebrows with a look of disdain. "I have vowed he will not have her. I've heard uncomfortable gossip about his treatment of women. Elisabeth is able to take care of herself, but as his wife, she would be a victim of his brutality. That is not going to happen," he declared firmly.

"Listen, if you change your mind about going out later, I'll stop by to check. I must leave now or the doors will close. An example of another antiquated rule, but the master excludes everyone from Almack's if they arrive late. I believe they would deny Prinny himself if he were minutes late." Richard clapped his friend on the shoulder and hastily left the apartment to provide the promised escort to his second cousin to a ball which was nicknamed the "marriage mart."

****

Mrs. Helen Barrows shepherded her daughters through the doors of the social club known as Almack's. She had received vouchers for them from Sarah Villiers, Countess of Jersey, and without fuss. Both young ladies already had permission from the patronesses to waltz and thought of themselves as veterans of this important event. Elisabeth preferred to spend the evening reading a new book she had taken out purported to be written by "A Lady," but her mother, usually never one to pressure her daughters, suggested she attend. There was no way around it. She had to give up her plans for a quiet night to read and make herself presentable.

Inside the room, which was lit by a large chandelier, Elisabeth greeted friends, although she was surprised to see the company so thin tonight. She nodded to Miss Eloise Larkin, who stood conversing with others of their set. She and Sophia moved to join them, while their mother met two chaperones of her own age. They settled against the wall in the chairs placed there.

"I s-say, are you in for the trip tomorrow?" Mr. Matthew Diver-Jones asked as they walked up. His enthusiasm for social outings infected them all.

Handsome as could stare, thought Elisabeth, and no one nicer or better mannered. *If he were only older, I could marry him and stop attending this "marriage mart" which I so dislike.* Her feelings toward marriage in general had undergone a change since both Viscount Teasdale and the duke had disturbed her peace.

"What exciting adventure have you discovered for us tomorrow?" she asked, smiling at Matthew. She patted her tight curls and glanced down at her blue pastel gown. She was especially fond of the capped sleeves filled with tiny ruffles. It was her own design and she hoped the low neckline did not activate the disdain of Lady Cowper, one of the patronesses, although her mother pronounced it quite acceptable.

"Did you ever wonder why we subject ourselves to the scrutiny of these ladies, who set themselves up as arbiters of us all?" Elisabeth whispered to Sophia, who shushed her.

"Do not, Elisabeth. I know it is silly and unfair, but it is the way of society. You do not desire to be ostracized, do you?" Sophia whispered back. They plied their fans as they whispered behind them. In the corner the musicians tuned their instruments. Dancing would soon begin.

"Balloon," Matthew was saying as they rejoined the conversation. "You ladies must bring food. We will make certain there are enough carriages for us all. There is no way we can guess what time the balloon will launch s-so we must go early and wait." His grin was as wide as the Thames River. "S-sometimes the owners allow others to s-stand in the basket for a price. I am keen to try that. What a ride that would be if it really went up while I was s-standing there."

"Ha. No doubt you would tip over and land on your head. Clumsy all your life, what?" Mr. Peron chimed in. His friend protested loudly, earning the group a censorious glare from Lady Jersey, known to all as Silence for her non-stop conversation.

"Permit me to beg you for the first dance, Miss Elisabeth?" Matthew bowed to her and held out his hand.

"It would be my very great pleasure, Mr. Diver-Jones." They joined a set forming in the middle of the floor. Sophia danced with a tall, good-looking gentleman who was Eloise Larkin's oldest brother. He had been smitten with her sister since the picnic at the Dowager Sanders' riverside estate. Sophia enjoyed his company, but Elisabeth knew he was only a friend. Captain Mark Estermire was her only love, and it seemed the two would finally make a match of it.

The sisters enjoyed a popularity that had them on the dance floor for every set. Eventually they collapsed on a sofa set up for resting, plying their fans to cool their warm faces. "He begs me for another dance, but never will I accept," Sophia confided. "He knows I cannot grant that favor without inciting gossip."

Elisabeth fluttered her fan in front of her face. "Probably that is exactly what he desires, Sister. One more dance and gossip will have you engaged. Another after that and you must either marry him or be considered hopelessly fast. Never will we be tricked into marriage that way. He is a brash young man, is he not?"

"Yes, but he amuses me. I welcome a respite from thinking of Mark tonight. I am too smart to be caught in the mouse's trap by eager young men. I am almost on the shelf, if it comes to that. Old enough to be a maiden aunt, only we have no nieces or nephews to be cared for." Sophia looked around the room and then touched her sister on the arm in warning.

"I see him," Elisabeth said between clenched teeth. "Will the man allow me no peace?" The Duke of Roderick was escorting his mother, the dowager duchess, and a shy young lady wearing a white gown which did not flatter her very pale complexion. She had the family signature of thick black hair which was pulled up to display her slender neck. Her eyelashes feathered her cheeks accenting her shyness. As furious as she was at Roderick, Elisabeth felt sorry for the debutante who was clearly terrified to be there. Had she no friends?

Roderick led the young lady out for a dance, which she executed by staring at her escort's feet. Nothing could be more fatal, and Elisabeth noticed two of the patronesses with their heads together. Surely they would not revoke the young girl's vouchers when her patroness was the dowager duchess and the Duke of Roderick her escort? Elisabeth cringed for her shyness. They could rescue her if she hadn't wanted to avoid Roderick.

"We need to rescue that poor child," Sophia whispered behind her fan. Elisabeth nodded. So be it.

Surely Richard would conduct himself mannerly and leave them to invite the young girl to be their friend.

Roderick returned his dance partner to his mother and shortly afterward left the room. He glanced over his shoulder and caught Elisabeth's eye, gave a half wave and disappeared out the door. She could not decide if she was pleased or disappointed that he had accepted her rejection.

"Mr. Diver-Jones, do rescue that poor girl from the line of chaperones and bring her over here to meet us," Sophia suggested. "But first, dance with her, will you? We are much too tired to join another set."

Matthew amiably presented himself to the dowager duchess and asked to be presented to the deb. The young lady's face flushed a bright red as she took to the floor with Matthew, who was on his best behavior. Eventually, he teased her until she raised her eyes to his. A small smile appeared on her face as she whirled, dipped, and bowed with Matthew.

"Knows Roderick would call him out for upsetting the girl," Lyndon Peron said wisely. "Man's a dead shot." The group parted and reformed, circling Sophia and Elisabeth, who perched resting on the sofa at the center of their group. As the country dance ended, Matthew returned the girl to the dowager, but after a short conversation, he escorted her over to be presented to the group of young people.

Her name was Miss Jane Hawlester, a distant cousin to the Duke of Roderick. She confided she was the eldest of four sisters and had only arrived in Town recently.

"For I love living in the country, but my parents insisted I come to stay with the dowager. I must find a husband so my mother may bring out my sister, Laura, who is eager to be presented. I offered to exchange places with her for I truly love another, but my mother..." The young lady rattled on, fortunately speaking in a low voice.

Elisabeth was pleased the shy Jane felt comfortable enough to share intimate details, but wondered what to say to warn her how inappropriate it might be if she confided in the wrong person. Gossip could spread like a river of tumbling water, especially when it was connected, even if only slightly mentioned, to a peer of the realm. Would Roderick be upset at all this family history being bandied about? As angry at him as Elisabeth was, she had no desire to see his family embarrassed by a young girl's indiscretions. It reminded her of another naïve young lady who had no town bronze, but never would she be revenged on him like that.

"Need to count the potentials," Mr. Diver-Jones was saying. "S-see how many want to meet at the park. Early, mind you. Don't want to miss the launch." He touched each candidate on the shoulder until he had a list of Balloon launch promises.

"Suggest we meet at the Barrowses' with its wide street. It's a better place to gather up," Mr. Lyndon Peron said. All nodded at the wisdom of this advice.

"S-sometimes you can be a handy fellow, Lyndon. Nice to have you around." He flashed his engaging smile which made it difficult for a person to stay grim.

"So handy, I need to beg the pleasure of a dance with Miss Hawlester here. Pleasure, ma'am?" Lyndon asked. He gave her an elaborate bow and had her giggling as they took the floor together.

"He's a good boy, what s-say?" Mr. Matthew Diver-Jones said, making Sophia and Elisabeth laugh at the antics of the two.

"Sounds like an interesting excursion. Wonder if we have time to warn cook we need a food basket. You know how the boys are prone to eat everything in sight," Sophia said. She stood up to take the floor when a gentleman a little known to her asked for the pleasure.

Elisabeth, too, was solicited to join a set. Soon it was time for refreshments. There was an insipid punch and a stale biscuit.

"Do you suppose this drivel is presented to discourage us from enjoying ourselves?" Miss Eloise Larkin whispered, sipping gingerly from her cup.

"To remind us passions of any form are considered improper, I presume." Elisabeth returned with a smile. Their fans hid their expressions and allowed a hint of privacy.

"Miss Sophia, Mr. Diver-Jones has mentioned a treat tomorrow morning. Can you tell me if it is a proper place to visit? I must ask permission from my relative. Will there be chaperones?" Jane Hawlester asked prettily.

"I am not certain what arrangements he has made, but I suspect at least one careful parent will be joining us. I assure you this group is not improper, but ask permission if it worries you." Sophia smiled kindly at her.

The very young debutante was already relaxing and smiling with the attention of their set. Pale and washed out in her white dress, nevertheless, young Jane was attractive in her quiet way. She had a tendency to babble in her soft voice, but as she became more acquainted with everyone, she calmed down. Her laugh rang out more than once. It was quite a difference from the strained little face looking down as she took to the dance floor with Roderick.

Elisabeth wondered what news of this event Jane Hawlester would take back to the duke and then questioned why she would care. *Because he matters to you.* Now that she was somewhat over the initial shock and horror of learning she had been romanced by her host, who had been pretending to be someone else, she started to reevaluate the affair.

At some point, she ought to try to have a rational conversation with him to learn why he had tricked her so badly. Truly, it was astonishing she had not learned his identity sooner. His mama and not he had greeted them on their arrival, and then she had heard someone refer to "the old duke." From there she assigned a different person to the title. She had no interest in the old man, understanding they were invited because of her sister.

Also, she was embarrassed to admit, she had kept her relationship private from everyone. In other words, she thought with a chuckle, I collaborated with Richard. At the time, it seemed to add excitement to what was otherwise a dull visit. It had been fun to share a secret. Oh, she had enjoyed the horses very much. She still thought of the wonderful rides she had on that beautiful white-faced mare.

The problem, the crux of the matter, was that she had trusted him implicitly. He had known how young and innocent she was, no doubt being well acquainted with her parent and sister. He took advantage of her naiveté with no intentions to anything but play.

Perhaps that was the part she could not forgive. It was all a game to him when she was falling deeply in love. It hurt when he left so abruptly, but it was a horrible pain when she learned she had been tricked as well.

Sadness began to overcome her, replacing the anger. Determined not to allow that Despicable Duke to ruin her night, she draped her shawl around her shoulders. Tomorrow would be an amusing day if she managed to sleep tonight. Dreamless, she prayed.

Wrapped in her own thoughts, she belatedly noticed how much of the evening had passed with her mother and the Duchess of Roderick in close conversation. What would that good lady think if she knew how outrageously one of her houseguests had behaved with her son?

## Chapter Seventeen

The trip to the closest park was accomplished with much less confusion than when they left for their picnic. It was a subdued collection of young people and chaperones, some with sleepy faces, which traveled in both carriages and on horseback. Elisabeth rode mounted on her favorite rented hack, but Sophia chose to share a carriage with Miss Larkin and her mother. She packed a food basket carefully into the back.

Mr. Matthew Diver-Jones encouraged them all as they trailed through the busy early morning cobble-stoned streets of town. Merchants glanced up as they rode by, disturbed in the task of arranging their wares. Young boys hired to sweep the streets paused and cheered the carriages and horses on. The distance wasn't far, and they soon set up camp near a tall tree on a slight rise. They pulled the carriages in a semi-circle around the tree and hobbled all the horses over to one side.

They could see the balloon engineers in a clearing below, moving slowly with colorful silks bunched at their feet. Ropes leading to a woven basket sat in the middle of the confusion. Elisabeth with the others stared at such a strange contraption.

"Do you really think that silk will hold them up?" she wondered aloud.

"How many people do you think could ride in

there?" Sophia asked, peering down below. She popped her parasol over her head as the sun peeked from behind a cloud. Today, she chose a deep blue with tiny ruffles to match her walking gown. She leaned forward to watch.

Elisabeth wore her red habit, a new wide brimmed hat perched on her curls with a red ribbon tied underneath her chin. She stood holding the reins of her horse until Matthew Diver-Jones came forward with several young teenage boys hired to mind the horses. She released her mount and walked forward with Mr. Lyndon Peron.

"Stay back. We need you to stay back." The men were shouting at several young boys crowding close to the balloon. One burly gentleman chased them with a stick held over his head. They fled, but like a flock of birds, crept back as soon as the man's back was turned.

"It is a fascinating exercise, is it not, Mr. Diver-Jones?" Elisabeth asked, holding tight to his arm, but her escort was too enthralled to give her the attention she deserved. Elisabeth was not disturbed about being ignored but was amused at his intense interest. They returned to the large tree where young ladies with several servants were spreading quilts and unpacking food.

"Not much happening right now," Elisabeth said as she joined her sister and Eloise Larkin. "Goodness, what a feast! Cook certainly outdid herself. Always she loves a challenge." She looked up as a new carriage appeared, driven by Roderick with Jane Hawlester tucked neatly by his side. Elisabeth shrugged. She should have expected this development and refused to allow her ire to return. Time she dealt with this man in a logical manner.

"Miss Barrows, Miss Elisabeth!" Jane called, excited to meet them. She ran and threw herself down on the quilt and reached out her hands to Sophia. Her straw hat tipped over her eyes, and she giggled. Obviously, Elisabeth thought wryly, the girl had learned to relax.

Roderick did not join them immediately, delayed by tending his horses. He flipped coins to the teenaged boys and then strolled toward his relative sitting on their quilt. James Wilkerson waylaid him and the two of them walked away together. Elisabeth released the breath she was holding, annoyed at herself for allowing the man to create such tension.

They heard a shout and stood up to check the action. Matthew Diver-Jones was beckoning, his face red with excitement. He ran toward them waving his hands. "They are inflating the balloon. Come on! You want to s-see this."

They could already see without moving down the hill. The bright panels of the balloon were slowly inflating, a mystery to them how it was happening. It was large and very striking, each panel a different color. There was a noise sounding exactly as Elisabeth imagined a dragon sprouting a flame of fire might.

"Oh, this is so exciting. I can barely breathe," Jane said, standing with her hands clasped before her.

"It is an amazing feat, is it not?" Sophia added. "I would be terrified to go up in that basket, would not you?"

Elisabeth stood silent, her mind occupied with thoughts of the duke, who was standing a little way beyond them. His back was turned to her, so she allowed her diligence against her attraction to lapse. She stared at the black hair curling on the back of his neck, remembering when she had buried her hands there while he kissed her. Butterflies started their fluttering in her stomach as she remembered how delicious his kisses felt. Her face grew warm and she turned away, hoping no one noticed her blushing.

"Come on, Lizzie!" Jamie shouted running back to grab her by the hand. They walked rapidly toward the commotion, looking up at the slowly inflating balloon.

"It's an amazing sight," she said, craning her neck skyward. The balloon puffed its dragon sound, and they could see it rise above the treetops. Two men moved around inside the basket as it rose; one of them leaned over and waved to the gathered crowd. Before they expected it, the large colorful object disappeared behind the treetops and seemed to shrink as it moved swiftly away.

"Did you enjoy the sight, Lizzie?" James Wilkerson asked, as they walked slowly back toward the quilts spread on the ground in the shade of the oak tree.

"Yes, and do you long to fly, too, Jamie?" She leaned her head briefly against his shoulder. Her childhood friend had matured in the last few years, and sometimes she felt he was moving away from her.

Their long-time relationship was a comfortable one. How nice to be with a male member of society and not need to always be on guard. A person who knew you when you were still in the nursery could never be impressed with pretensions. She grinned at the thought of attempting to assume airs around Jamie.

"It is an intriguing thought," he admitted, "but I

fear I am destined to keep my feet solidly planted on terra firma. My father counts on me, Lizzie. Wouldn't want to disappoint him, what?" He laughed and squeezed her hand. He flicked her cheek gently, then walked away to join a couple of his friends standing near the horses.

Elisabeth smiled at his brotherly treatment of her. Had she ever begged and nagged him to teach her to kiss? She laughed aloud at the thought. Of course, after the Duplicitous Duke kissed her, she understood what Jamie had been trying to explain to the impatient, young Lizzie. What a difference two years out in society made! She felt completely changed from the silly child she had been, but she had to admit a home truth: kissing still puzzled her.

Still reminiscing, she walked up the hill, looking down at her feet but glanced up to see Roderick staring directly at her. She flashed him a smile before she had a chance to think. His face lit up as if the sun had taken up residence in his eyes. She looked quickly away and sought her sister, who was emptying the food basket and handing out pieces of bread to eager hands.

Jane Hawlester had settled like a soft blossom on the quilt by Sophia. How could they not include the duke? They couldn't, of course. Elisabeth realized manners dictated she invite him to share their basket.

"I did not know we needed to bring food," Jane was apologizing to the sisters. "Do you have enough to share?" She was ducking her head again, presumably in embarrassment.

Sophia glanced over at Elisabeth with raised eyebrows. She nodded her permission. There was no help for it, and why make a big fuss? It was time she gave up her anger. She didn't need to welcome him back into her life, but why make everyone uncomfortable? It was, after all, a long time ago.

"Jane, ask your cousin if he will join us on our blanket for refreshments," Sophia said. Jane immediately jumped up and approached the duke, who again was chatting with James Wilkerson. Both men turned around and ambled toward them.

"I made certain your invitation included me as well," James said. He collapsed at Elisabeth's feet holding out his hand for bread from her sister.

"When did you ever wait for an invitation, Jamie," Elisabeth retorted. "Always eating all the biscuits."

"How about that time we left to explore the ruins on the hill? I let you have all but one of the sweets we brought along." He propped his head on his hand as he chewed. Jane stared at him fascinated. Elisabeth laughed at his blatant falsehood.

"You had just had a huge tea, and you took a bite out of every single sweet before you gave it to me, you scoundrel." Jamie grinned and did not defend himself.

Roderick took a napkin and a bite of the cheese and bread Sophia handed to him. He thanked her quietly, refraining from joining James and Elisabeth's bantering. Jane, apparently fascinated by James and his casual attitude, continued to stare at the handsome young man.

"Do you live close by the Barrowses' home, sir?" Jane asked timidly. She nibbled on her bread but continued to gaze at James with big pansy eyes. They started a conversation which excluded the others. Shortly afterward Sophia wandered away and joined Eloise. Elisabeth lifted her eyes and met those of the duke.

"Well, Your Grace, here we are and must converse or be thought ridiculous," she said. She reached into the basket and handed him a peach, which he promptly began to peel. He reached forward and offered a piece to her. The juice was succulent and sweet, but dribbled down her chin as usual. She searched in the basket for a napkin when he offered a big, white square to her of his own.

"If you had rather not, I will accept your wishes, Elisabeth. I never want to be the cause of your discomfort." He offered her another bite, but she shook her head no. A girl could stand only so much intimacy and remain distant. He leaned forward slightly, bracing his weight on one hand with the other on his bent knee.

"Miss Elisabeth," Lyndon called. "You must come and be the judge. That disturbed person, Matthew Diver-Jones, has wagered me over this caterpillar, and how long it will take to make it up the bark of that tree. You know how he mistakes what he sees. I must have you as witness." Elisabeth grinned and prepared to leave her quilt. The duke stood and reached his hand to assist her.

"Ah, Elisabeth. How I wish…will you ride with me tomorrow? I must take Jane up for a turn in the park, but will you ride with me afterward?" he asked. He had not released her hand, and Elisabeth was finding it impossible to pull away.

Finally, she looked up at him. "To what purpose, Your Grace? You and I may not argue for the sake of our friends, but why would you want my company?" She jerked her hand away and turned to find the tree with an interesting caterpillar.

"Elisabeth, may Jane and I join your set for an excursion in the park? Would you object to that? I know you ride there almost every morning. Would you mind? I would very much enjoy the company and must needs bring Jane with me." She turned at the mention of Jane.

"Perhaps," she said. "It is an analogous selection of young people. Would it be beneath you to be seen with so many commoners? I dare say you are unfamiliar with most." He moved closer to her as they conversed.

"I would be grateful to have assistance entertaining Jane. She is shy and needs the support of her peers. You and your sister were very gracious to receive her into your set last evening. I thank you. My mother was pleased. She is appreciative of your parent and your sister." Elisabeth forewent answering, as they made their way together toward the tree where Matthew and Lyndon were creating a commotion.

A stack of money was growing on a large stone as the young men gathered to place their bets. They were staring at the trunk of a small sapling, shouting encouragement to some small worm's progress up the tree. As they approached, a tiny robin red breast swooped in, nipped the caterpillar in its beak, and flew away. There was a stunned silence. A moment later bedlam broke out.

The Duke of Roderick bent over in gusty laughter while the younger men screamed pleas for the little bird to come back with their prize. Roderick with tears still streaming from his eyes held out his arm to Elisabeth. She accepted gratefully, as she felt weak from laughing so hard at Matthew and Lyndon's faces.

It was perhaps the best part of the day; certainly it

was the end. They gathered up their belongings, found their carriages and mounts, and left the park. There were calls back and forth regarding the ride in the park the next day. Elisabeth sat silent, aware that Sophia kept glancing at her with a worried expression.

She held her peace until they had gained their shared bedroom and were putting away their shawls, parasols, and hats.

"Do you hold me in anger, Sister? I excuse my behavior today in leaving you with the duke because you thought it best to give Mark and me privacy at the library. Was I wrong? Should I have stayed?"

"No, you were perfectly free to pursue your own interest. I had already decided it was time I put my anger aside. I do not expect to enjoy a friendship with the duke, but it is nonsense to hold a grudge over something that happened so long ago. He asks to join our rides in the morning, seeking to gather support for his cousin. He mentioned his mother was pleased that we offered Jane our friendship." She reached down to unlace her half boots and noticed they would need cleaning. The park had hosted patches of mud here and there.

"But, Lizzie," her sister pursued, "are you not still struggling with your feelings for him? I know I am not over the captain. Although we have managed to reconcile to a friendship, I have not overcome my tender emotions for him."

"I confess to you, Sister. I do have strong tendencies to prefer Roderick to others. As unwelcome as they are, it appears, even with all the rational reasons to do so, I cannot forget the partiality I felt toward him. Especially when I thought he returned my sentiments."

"I will never pester you with questions, but imagine my curiosity as to the exact nature of your time with him. How many times were you together? Why was no one else aware of your friendship? It is all so mysterious to me." Sophia held out her hands with a slight smile.

"Sometimes I think it was all a dream. Mostly it was chance that created the opportunity for Richard, for he was that name to me, to remain anonymous. My young naiveté could be blamed for the rest, I suppose. Also, I admit it was very exciting to share a secret. You will laugh when I tell you I mistook the duke for that fat squire. Because Mama had confined me to my room, I missed dinner and not been introduced to either of them. I heard someone mention the old duke, and I made a supposition." She sat at her dresser and removed her red hat.

"You had no idea when you met that he was your host? How incredible!"

"I paid not the slightest attention to the politics of the duke's choice to wife. If I thought of it at all, I presumed you were the one he would choose. I knew his mother was friends with ours, but I suppose I was too silly to notice she was too young to have been that old man's mother. I remember wondering at the time how you would like being spouse to a fat, old man." They both broke into giggles.

"It is even more unbelievable to find out later that we both had secrets. Since you were meeting the captain, why do you think my activities so surprising? And did you really desire to be Her Grace? What a lot of responsibility that would be."

"I was thinking what to say if I were the one

chosen. You must admit, now that you are aware of his identity, the gentleman has a pleasing demeanor." She laughed when Elisabeth ducked her head and smiled. "Yes, I see you do agree."

"It was shortly after we arrived that I became aware of the captain. We started to talk and everything progressed from there. He was deeply troubled over his wounds. I tried to boost his spirits, and it seemed for a while I had. He began to get about more. We finally confessed our fondness for each other, but he declared it impossible to go further. They left soon after that. As you are aware, I was devastated."

"As was I, even not knowing the total of his perfidy at the time. I considered myself in love with Richard the Stranger. I called him my Noble Rescuer in jest after he helped me when I trapped myself in the tree." She giggled when Sophia gave her a stare of incredulous shock. "Ah, I would relate to you all the mischief I have gotten into in the past, but I need a nap, as do you. We are to attend the Smyth's ball tonight, are we not?"

"Yes, do you wear that gown trimmed with blond lace? I will wear my white with the sapphire necklace mother loaned me. It has a matching pin for my hair."

"Yes, the blond lace it is. Now to sleep, my sister. Or we will be fagged half to death before supper is served." Elisabeth tucked herself up in her bed and rested, but she did not sleep. She was still as much in love with Richard as she ever was before, and she had no idea what to do about it.

Chapter Eighteen

"He is attentive to his cousin. That says positive things regarding his character. You must admit his good qualities and not always dwell on the bad. It might make your recovery easier, Sister." Sophia was whispering behind her fan to Elisabeth again as they sat out a dance they had arrived too late to join. "He is graceful on the dance floor."

Elisabeth eyed the duke as he cut a swath through the gathered cream of the crop at Almack's. She fluttered her fan in frustration.

"I am more than aware of his charm, Sophia, and obviously susceptible to it. That is why I need always to remind myself of his faults." They watched the couple as the music swelled into a newly acceptable dance called the waltz.

The patronesses granted permission to the debutantes to participate in the dance, but only on an individual basis. Both Sophia and Elisabeth had been given the nod in their first year out. Not all young ladies had been so lucky, but some breezed through the extensive examination by the patronesses.

Jane Hawlester was a prettily behaved ninny, an opinion universally accepted, but she was popular. With the Duke of Roderick escorting her, the dowager duchess sitting chaperone, and her manners meeting the acceptable standards, her only duty for this her first social season was to enjoy herself and perhaps choose an acceptable suitor. Elisabeth predicted she would be engaged before the season ended. The sisters, having been privileged with her confidence, understood her to say she was in no hurry to leave the social scene. The love she left behind seemed forgotten.

It was a common problem. Parents kept their daughters home or in some ladies' finishing school until it was time to present them to the ton. Then the young girls were dressed, drilled to behave, and thrust onto the social scene. It had the makings of a disaster and, all too often, it was.

"Thank goodness our mother introduced us to the neighborhood young people as we were growing up. It's sad to see those green girls flounder year after year," Sophia said. They were watching a prime example make a cake of herself with some young man wearing collars so high he could not turn his head.

"That's the second dance she has taken to the floor with him." They shook their heads wisely. It was a fatal mistake unless he had approached her parents and made an offer. They could see two of the patronesses with their heads together. Monday morning would have them evaluating whether to remove the vouchers of unacceptable debutantes.

"Jane will not make a misstep. The duke and his mother are watching her very closely. He, at least, is well aware how quickly naïve young ladies could get into mischief even with a careful parent." Sophia patted her on the arm with an understanding smile.

Elisabeth remembered too well her own sly behavior and the secrets she had kept from her mother. At the time, she knew she was breaking the rules but was too intrigued to modify her behavior. It struck her all at once that she was lucky the duke was called away. He called it providential, and she began to understand his viewpoint. Absence was the only behavior modifier operating at the time between either of them.

She shivered. She had been compliant and easily manipulated. How could anyone consider her a proper lady if they knew she had been so willing to break all of society's rules? It was a lesson she vowed never to forget. Endeavoring to keep her promise, she placed such strict structure on all her behaviors until even her parent weakly protested she had gone too far.

The waltz came to an end, and Roderick returned his kinswoman to his mother sitting chaperone on the sidelines. He glanced at the Barrows sisters posing idly on the sofa, nodded his head in a semi-bow, but kept walking toward the card room. Elisabeth felt a physical jolt and was instantly disappointed in herself. How could she feel regret when he behaved exactly as she wished? How would she react when he finally picked his duchess? She was thankfully diverted by the noisy return of her young friends.

"The sisters agreeable," Eloise chanted when she joined them. "I shall call you that forever," she said, giggling and waving her fan vigorously.

"Oh, ho!" James Wilkerson exclaimed. "Elisabeth don't show it now, but there was a day when..." He ducked when she pointed her fan directly at him and frowned. "It is no matter. We all have our secrets from when we were children. Lizzie is all grown up now," he admitted. "Still a bruising rider, our girl is." There were murmurs of agreement by all to this sentiment.

"Papa threw me up before I could walk," Elisabeth

said with a chuckle. "I protest it is not my fault if I would rather live in the saddle than out."

She was startled when Viscount Teasdale pushed through her circle of friends, loomed in front of her and demanded she stand up with him. Elisabeth was instantly conflicted. If she turned him down, she could not accept another invitation to dance. Manners dictated she do the pretty and take to the floor even as she wished him far away. There was no help for it. Drat the man, she thought, seething inside.

She was about to rise when Roderick swooped in and almost snatched her hand out of the grasp of the viscount. He bowed before her. "My dance," the duke said firmly. Elisabeth stood, gave him a curtsy, and walked away from underneath the frowning nose of Teasdale.

It was a country dance with very little chance for conversation. Elisabeth managed a faint thank you as they passed in the figures, shoulders touching now and then.

"Your card game was not of interest to you, Your Grace?" she asked, privately wondering where he had come from. She could swear he had been sitting in the card room before Teasdale appeared.

"Lady Luck has been denied me this night. Are you and your sister attending the musicale tomorrow?" he asked. Elisabeth understood he was making polite conversation, and when next they met she answered in kind.

"Yes. Do you bring Jane to enjoy the performances?" She dared glance up and met his eyes. It was a mistake. She missed a step, and he gripped her hand to keep her from colliding with another in the movements of the dance. Feeling weak in the knees, she rejoiced when the music ended her ordeal. He escorted her from the floor, returning her to the couch where her friends still clustered.

"Still the rescuer, Your Grace?" she murmured. "I do thank you for your intervention. I do not welcome the lord's attention, but he seems not to understand my preferences." He gazed at her with a solemn face, but said nothing.

They parted at the sofa, where Lyndon Peron claimed her hand for the next dance. When Viscount Teasdale returned, she said with all honesty she had no more free dances. Soon, her mother signaled she was ready to leave, having no interest in the poor food served at supper.

In the carriage on the way home, her mother commented on her partners in the dance. "Lizzie, you are sailing in high company with a duke and a viscount both claiming your hand at the same time. I thought for a second we would be witness to a challenge. Will you have a duel fought over you, Daughter?" Elisabeth covered her face with her hands.

"I tease you, but a word of caution as well. It will not do for any gentlemen to be seen competing to beg a dance with you. I understand it is not your fault, but you must do your best to discourage that sort of contest."

Elisabeth remained silent, but nodded to indicate she understood. Truth, she was clenching her teeth to keep tears from forming. The strain of unwanted attention from the viscount and the distant but attentive favors from the duke were beginning to wear on her composure. Confusion was her unhappy lot. Sophia reached over and squeezed her hand in sympathy. At least someone knew how conflicted she had become.

Chapter Nineteen

"How goes your campaign, Captain?" Roderick asked Mark Estermire as they walked through the drizzle toward White's. They hoped to play a hand or two of cards before retiring for the evening.

"Ah, Richard, she is the most beautiful, even-tempered girl I have ever set my grateful eyes upon. She invites me to join their at-home day. It is more than I could ever expect. I believe she forgives me a little. As soon as I think it possible, I will ask her to be my wife. I do not want to take the chance at losing her a second time."

"There is a musicale at Rex's place tomorrow night. Should you go with me?" he asked with a grin. Mark understood instantly and agreed to meet. They entered the doors of the club with nothing on their minds but cards.

Before they could get beyond the first corridor, Teasdale waylaid the duke, placing an arm on his shoulder. Roderick stood still, looking at the man as if he had lost his sanity. Teasdale dropped his hand, but his tone was aggressive.

"Just a word with you, Roderick. You forgot what I said to you about Miss Elisabeth Barrows, I presume. Set to make her my wife. Don't mean for there to be interference. I declared for her first." He stood with legs spread, fists clenched at his side with a pugnacious frown, as if he were in the ring.

Roderick just stared at him with a faint smile. He would not bandy Elisabeth's name about in a men's club. Did the idiot have no manners? No wonder she refused him, he thought, but then he winced, wondering if his manners had been any improvement.

"Thought you might like to test your grays against my bays," he said. "Heard you won your wager against the last opponent." Teasdale dropped his frown immediately.

"You want to name a day for the race," he responded eagerly. "Wagers recorded in the book tonight?" He clapped the duke on the arm, all conversation concerning ladies apparently forgotten.

"I intend to play cards tonight. Name a date and we will record the wagers the night before." They walked into the card room with Teasdale eagerly discussing possible racecourses.

Richard Hawlester, conscious of his position, wondered whether he could discuss the viscount with Elisabeth's parent at some future date. He could only distract Teasdale for so long. The title was long and respectable, but the present viscount did it no honor. He knew of dishonest dealings the man had conducted. There were *on dits* he cheated at cards, although he had not been directly challenged. He was horse mad and spent vast sums on the best and fastest trotters. Then he would manipulate unsuspecting novices to a race, bid up the wagers, and ruin more than one green lad. His reputation among the demi-monde was unsavory, to say the least.

Unfortunately, it was his treatment of women that had the duke seriously worried. What if the Widow

Barrows approved of the viscount's quest for Elisabeth's hand in marriage? What parent in good conscience could refuse such an offer? It would be difficult to explain why she should not.

Briefly, he speculated whether the viscount could be cash poor. He would inherit a vast amount of land, but could he possibly have bankrupted it in his pursuit of the best horses in the land? There were rumors the viscount's father, the earl, was on his last legs.

He was not certain what Elisabeth would bring to the marriage table, but he knew it was substantial. Her father had not been a titled man, but a member of an old and well-respected family whose ancient name preceded that of several who claimed titles. He had been wealthy beyond belief and left his widow well supplied. His mother would never have invited possible candidates to replace her who were not well shod. She was careful that way.

On the way home that night—he had elected to walk since the steady rain had stopped—he allowed himself to speculate if he could possibly convince Elisabeth to be his duchess. No longer could he deny his strong attraction to her, although it pained him to see her so subdued from the impetuous young lady he remembered. Had that happened because of him? God, he hoped not. How stupid of him not to evaluate the effect of his behavior on such a sweet, young girl as his Lizzie had been. He had fallen in love with the lovely Elisabeth, and his strong emotions unsettled him. Never had any female affected him as did she.

All he had wanted was a little fun, a tease of a young lady who wanted to become experienced at kissing. He chuckled a bit at the memory of a very young, adorable Elisabeth. How could he have been beyond the pale vain and stupid? She might never return his love after the callous treatment he gave her, but he was a lost man and had to try.

It wanted only a determination on his part. He would become her Richard again. She had loved him as her Noble Rescuer. His pulse had quickened tonight when she dropped the Noble and just referred to him as "a rescuer." Nothing could have been more poignant than to hear he was noble to her no more. He vowed he would never make such a mistake again. Even if she never forgave him, he would be cognizant and cautious of others' vulnerability to his position.

As deep in thought as he was, he did not fail to hear a faint scuffle behind him. He turned just in time to see two ruffians rapidly approaching. In the dimness of the lighted street lamp ahead, he could see one carried a cudgel. There was no doubt in his mind the man meant him no good. Thank goodness he carried a walking stick. Almost, he had decided earlier tonight he would leave it at home. He flicked a switch and a sword popped out. He took up a fencing stance and tipped the first one to reach him with a prick. He didn't intend to kill the chap, but he meant not to be harmed himself. The man screamed and dropped the cudgel to the ground. The other man paused.

"You want to try your luck with me, do you?" The duke hissed the words in warning. He paced with sliding hops toward the man who stood hesitantly for a second more, then turned and ran. Roderick faced the first man who stood moaning and holding his arm. He held the sword toward him and demanded to know who hired him.

"I be a'bleeding. Be in the grave fo' day. 'Ave pity, milord." He sank to the ground, holding his arm and rocking back and forth. The duke thought with satisfaction the prick must be pretty painful. Served the scoundrel right. He wouldn't die of the wound, but hopefully he would remember not to attack honest people anymore.

"Who paid you?" he demanded once more menacing the man with his sword.

"Hit were a toff is all I know. 'E stopped his carriage and asked us to follow you.

"He was driving his own horses?" the duke asked, pulling the man up by his sound arm. He pulled out his handkerchief.

"Hit were big gray beasts, a'snorting and pawing the ground. Gave us coins. We wuz mighty pecked, guv'nor. 'Ungry to death. Beg pardon. Weren't meaning your lordship no harm. 'E said hurt y'a mite is all."

Roderick tied his handkerchief around the man's arm and sent him on his way. Now why was Teasdale trying to have him hurt? He needed the race to end in his favor that badly? He would need to watch his back. Perhaps Mark would be his close friend for the next few days.

Roderick was even more determined Teasdale would not get his hands on Miss Elisabeth Barrows now that he knew what the man could be capable of. He was quite willing to harm another. He would look into the viscount's finances as soon as he'd had a chat with Elisabeth's mother. That good lady needed to be strongly warned.

Discouraged, he gained the front door of his town

house and shed his damp clothing. What could he do to convince the Widow Barrows of the danger Teasdale could present to her youngest daughter? Ask her permission to court her daughter? His pulse took a jump as the idea took fertile root in his conflicted brain as a possible solution. Could he talk Elisabeth into accepting his proposal in order to discourage Teasdale? The Duke of Roderick paused with his hand on the banister of his stairs, wondering if Miss Elisabeth Barrows would box his ears then or later.

Chapter Twenty

"You should have seen how he abused those proud grays. One of them was limping, but he whipped him anyway. He raced them up that long hill—they were blown long before they got halfway. How that man wins races, I vow I don't know." Lyndon Peron was sitting on the floor with his long legs stretched out before him. He leaned his head against the arm of the sofa which Eloise Larkin shared with Elisabeth. The room was filled with groups of chatting young people who favored the Barrows home on their visiting day. They were sprawled across the room, several of the young men on the floor.

"Well, he didn't win that race, did he?" Matthew Diver-Jones said slapping one fist into another. "S-soon as he came around the corner with his poor horses, wind gone completely, the duke just pulled around him and trotted down the hill to the finish line, pretty as you please. It was pitiful to s-see. Those s-sad horses of Teasdale's must have been in pain. I say, he shouldn't be allowed near good horseflesh."

"Lord, you see how crazy the viscount acted? He shouted and shook his fist and complained Roderick had cheated him. Thought the man would challenge the duke to a duel." Lyndon reached up and tweaked Eloise's book. She glared at him and went back to reading the new novel Elisabeth had just loaned her.

143

"He might like to, but everyone knows Roderick would have carved him into pieces," Matthew Diver-Jones returned. "Man's an expert with a s-sword; s-spot on with a pistol, better driver as well. Thought maybe his bays would beat the grays and they did. Won a bundle, I can tell you. But the real reason was his driving s-skill. Viscount just don't have it, s-say what?" He was smiling widely, as he had been since he came in the door. Winning a wager obviously put him in an excellent mood.

"Wouldn't have believed it if I hadn't seen Teasdale whip those beautiful animals up that long hill. Who does that?" Lyndon asked twitching his face in disgust. "Must have thought he was winning when the duke held his animals back. They started up that hill and fell quite a ways behind. Kept them from harming themselves, though. Keep that in mind if I ever need to race."

Elisabeth looked up as Captain Mark Estermire was ushered into the room. Sophia stood up to greet him and settled with her guest on a window seat across the parlor. Elisabeth allowed herself a satisfied smile as she observed the two in earnest discussion and diverted Lyndon when he started to bring attention to the new arrival. Her mother looked over at her eldest and then at Elisabeth who nodded. Sophia had finally confessed to their parent regarding the liaison which had begun two years before.

As she watched her sister, she felt a wave of envy. Sophia was close to having her life settled, even if she held the captain at arm's length for a while. A sister knew—Sophia had found her true love. It was just a matter of time before Mark Estermire proposed, and her sister would marry the captain, becoming a diplomat's helpmate, traveling the world.

Elisabeth would be left alone, an aging aunt doting on her sister's children. It was difficult not to feel self-pity. Sophia and Mark did not need to deal with broken trust. Mark had made his decision to leave based on what he thought was a permanent infirmity. It was an unfortunate mistake but not a betrayal.

Elisabeth thought she could have forgiven Richard for leaving her, but how could she ever trust him? Sometimes she longed for the man she had thought he was. Her Richard, the imaginary one, would never have behaved like that. He was her Noble Rescuer. He had loved her, looked after her, and taught her lessons about kissing that she could never forget. She had finally understood what Jamie had been trying to tell her that embarrassing day in the library.

A kiss is not just a kiss unless it has some meaning behind it, at least for her. Only she could not figure out what the fake Richard had in mind. Perhaps kissing was something gentlemen could do without meaning. She had not enjoyed it when Viscount Teasdale kissed her. Oh, it was still most confusing.

Someone new came into the salon and, startled, Elisabeth thought for a moment she had conjured the man up. As Roderick entered the room, his presence was almost palatable and powerful. She sat staring at him, tall figure slender and shoulders wide. His blue superfine coat was worn over a figured vest with a white froth of a neck cloth cascading down the front. His collars were high but not ridiculously so. He handed his high top hat and cane to the butler leaving his coal black hair mussed in the popular style. His rugged face was still deeply tanned leading Elisabeth to wonder what his two-year absence in service to the country entailed. Hours out of doors was the obvious answer. He looked over to her side of the room and bowed, but quickly turned away to find her parent. Jane had not accompanied him.

Elisabeth thought she would lose her breakfast so upset did her stomach become. What did he mean by a visit to her mother? What could he mean? Surely he did not come to ask to court her. Never would she permit him to do that, and so she would tell her mother. A horrible thought occurred to her. How could she explain why she would have nothing to do with a duke, for heaven's sake, to a mother who had been lied to? Oh, she would never forgive him for placing her in this impossible situation.

"Oh, I say. Look who's here," Lyndon said. "It's the winner of the race himself." He stood, but hesitated when he saw the duke in earnest conversation with the Widow Barrows. He wrinkled up his forehead, paused, and then glanced back at Elisabeth with raised eyebrows.

"Came without Miss Hawlester, did he?" Lyndon queried quietly. "Know anything about that, Miss Elisabeth?" She shook her head, not trusting herself to speak.

"Best keep my mouth shut, what hey?" Lyndon grinned and sat back down. His behavior captured the attention of his friend.

"What's going on?" Diver-Jones asked staring around the room as if his friend were holding some secret from him.

Elisabeth thought to control the pair before they

started a fuss. They were good young men, and she liked them well enough, but they would create a commotion. In fact, they positively reveled in creating chaos.

"Likely, Roderick came over to give my mother a message from the dowager duchess. Nothing to concern us. Perhaps Miss Jane is not feeling well. I'm certain my mother will let us know if we need to visit her." Lyndon gave her a wise glance, but held his peace.

Elisabeth thought her head would explode with the agitation she felt. Why would that man not take his leave? A duke must always attract attention, but must he do it at her home? A glimmer of what his life must be like shimmered briefly in her mind. Was this kind of notice why he preferred to meet in private? He had created a private bower in his garden, or had some distant duke who disliked being the object of attention? Almost, she began to understand his actions as she saw everyone in the room craning their heads toward the titled visitor.

She remembered seeing him in the dim light of the moon, smiling down at her saying he needed to tell her something important. But he never had. Only that he was leaving the next day. For two years, the memory of those kisses had haunted her mind, the kisses and the fact that he left the very next day. Was he truly intending to confess to her his real identity?

"Is it time for tea?" She stood and made ready to signal the butler. She'd try anything to divert attention from Roderick, who was still in serious conversation with her mother. In the window seat, Sophia was smiling and holding hands with Mark Estermire. The two of them had obviously settled their differences, just as she suspected they would.

Richard looked up and caught her eye. He smiled and nodded just as her mother stood and walked with him to the door.

"Come and say goodbye to His Grace, Elisabeth. He professes not to have time to take tea with us." Elisabeth walked forward mesmerized by his intent stare. As she drew near, he held out his hand to her. She felt the warm squeeze of his fingers and fought the butterflies in her mid-section. Could she be forgiven for wanting to throw herself into his arms? How vulgar had she become?

"Your Grace," she managed, and dipped in a small curtsy. "We wish you would join us for small refreshment." He wouldn't cause her to mangle her manners. He would not, she vowed silently. She could not break the gaze, could not tear her eyes from his. Her mother touched her on the shoulder and gratefully, Elisabeth faced her as the butler appeared with Roderick's hat and cane. In a heartbeat, the duke turned and was out the door.

"We entertain important visitors today, do we not?" her mother commented mildly as she returned to her corner of the room. Had her legs turned to wood? Elisabeth walked stiffly back to the hall doorway catching the butler's eye. Shortly afterward tea appeared and, after what seemed like an hour but was only a few minutes, their guests left.

Sophia, her mother, and Elisabeth retreated to their private, small parlor located in the back of the town house. A window there looked out into their tiny garden. They often settled there to relax *en famille*, but Elisabeth clenched her hands, waiting to hear what had been said by the duke to her mother.

"Daughter, our family must be flattered by a surprising intelligence from the Duke of Roderick. He has offered his name to shelter Elisabeth from the unwanted advances of the Viscount of Teasdale. He tells me the viscount has such a reputation that no young woman would be blessed to agree to wed him. I have answered how grateful we are to the honor, but do not feel at this time his generosity is warranted. He assures me the permanence of such an engagement would rest solely upon your acceptance of it. I am surprised by this attention, but perhaps you have something to add, my Lizzie?"

"I do not think such an offer is at all necessary, Mother. In fact, I do not desire either man's offer, if truth be known. Let us relax and enjoy our time together," Elisabeth said, but their butler appeared once more with disturbing news.

"The Viscount Teasdale begs entrance to speak with you, Miss Elisabeth. I informed him you were not available to visitors at this hour, but he is insisting you will see him. What shall I say, ma'am?" Elisabeth stood and made ready to leave the room.

"You do not need to meet him if you had rather not. I can give him the news that his attentions are not welcome, Lizzie. It's your decision."

"Best I get it over with, Mother. Once he understands I'm not interested, he will leave me in peace." She walked forward with determination to deal with the unpleasantness as soon as possible, returning to the front parlor. There, Teasdale stood staring out the window with an impatient expression on his handsome face. As she reentered the room, he faced her and gave a wide smile, holding out his hands eagerly.

Elisabeth acknowledged his pleasing countenance, his very important eligibility as a spouse, his political connections, but she could not like him. This would be her third proposal, and she had turned them all away. Elisabeth knew her mother must grow weary of squiring two eligible daughters with no results. Even so, she could not marry the viscount. She could not even convince herself he was worthy of friendship.

"You are late to our at-home hours, Lord Teasdale. Perhaps another day you could come earlier to visit with our friends." She stood a bit apart, and he frowned and dropped his hands.

"Beg pardon, Miss Elisabeth, but I had something important to impart to you. May we sit down and have a discussion." He gestured impatiently toward the sofa.

His manner was still forward and his expression aggressive. It was the very thing about him that Elisabeth disliked.

"Lord Teasdale, you can have no business with me that could not wait until my family is receiving visitors. Let us part until another more convenient day." She spoke firmly but with a slight smile, hoping to keep the situation on friendly terms. He reached for her hand, but she managed to step quickly back. He frowned then flashed a wide grin.

"You will change your attitude when I tell you what a treat you have coming. Miss Elisabeth, I have come to bestow on you a great honor."

"Oh, pray do not, Lord Teasdale. I am not the person to receive or deserve honor." Elisabeth hoped against hope the disgust she felt for this arrogant and puffed up peer did not show upon her face. She struggled to maintain as bland a demeanor as she could.

"You cannot be surprised that I have come today. I have previously contacted your parent and received permission to speak to you. She was gratified by my quest, I can promise you."

"The surprise might belong to you, my lord. My mother is quite the lenient parent. It may shock you to understand she expects her children to make their own life's decisions." This home truth did not seem to faze him one iota. His smile grew even wider than before. Obviously, he expected nothing but a fawning agreeable answer to the question he even now had not asked. How she wanted to slap his arrogant face, but she must compose an acceptable answer if he ever did come up to scratch.

"Miss Elisabeth, Elisabeth, I may call you now. I desire the ceremony to be held as quickly as possible. I am even now late in tending business at my estate. You must hurry to purchase your bride clothes and be ready to leave town within a fortnight. My lawyer will be over to discuss the dowry you are to present to me. Substantial, is it?"

"Lord Teasdale, I can have no idea what you are saying. Is it that you expect me to become your bride?" *What a ninnyhammer this man is,* she thought with disgust.

His face turned red and he glared at her. "Have I not been saying? Are there slow members of your family? I intend us to be married next week. I mean to purchase a special license, and I see no impediment to it. Already spoke to your parent. Father gone, right ho?" He turned from her to pace around the parlor.

"Lord Teasdale?" She endeavored to return him to

reality. "Could you stop walking around and listen carefully to what I have to say to you?" He stopped and glared impatiently at her.

"Well, out with it, my girl. No time to waste. Must get on the road. Be back for you in a few days." He stood, restlessly rubbing his hands together.

"I am afraid you have given me such honor I cannot possibly answer you in the positive. I must decline your so gracious request to be your wife." She could not help a wince as he stared at her as if she had lost her mind.

"Of course, you will be my wife. No impediment is there? Spoke to your mother. Agreeable woman. Substantial dowry. Attractive girl. Thought it through and decided we would suit. Need an heir. Time to set up my nursery. You be ready in ten days, you hear?" He started for the door, and Elisabeth thought it necessary to reach out for his hand. He must understand she would not marry him.

"No, Lord Teasdale. I will not marry you. Alas, I love another." Elisabeth had no idea where that confession had been hiding. Hopefully, she would not need to name the man. If the viscount's face had been red before, it was purple now.

"Ridiculous woman. What do you prattle about now? Spoke to your parent. We are to be married in ten days. Stop this nonsense. I have business to attend. Did I not come to you to make the arrangements?" She stepped back as the menace on his face grew. She was not afraid of this man, but he seemed to be losing his temper.

"Understand. You want romance, do you? Kissed you once. Should be enough, but come here and we will do the job right." He grabbed her arm and pulled her roughly onto his chest. His mouth descended hard, causing her teeth to cut into her lip. She pushed against him with all her might, but he had one arm pinned to her side. She tried to scream but he had covered her mouth with his. The pain was excruciating, and she thought she tasted blood in her mouth. Finally, she jerked free.

"Be fun to have the schooling of you, young filly," he said grinning. "Have you broke to the bridle before you know it. Enjoy it, mark my words. They always do. See you in ten days. Do not keep me waiting." With that, he opened the front door and left.

Elisabeth wiped her mouth with her hand and, as she expected, it came away smeared with blood. Her lip was already beginning to swell. Her fury was unbelievable. How could this man, this arrogant idiot, come into her home and demand she marry him?

"Elisabeth? Dear, are you still in conversation with Lord Teasdale?" Her mother came into the room followed by Sophia. "You were so quiet in here, we dared not interrupt. Dear God! Elisabeth, what happened to your mouth?"

Chapter Twenty-One

"I can't believe you're heir to the Duke of Roderick. Ronald, you must be fourth removed cousin on his mother's side. Is that even legal?" Teasdale tooled his grays down the road with his companion riding in the carriage beside him. The fast pace of his curricle left swirls of dust in the road behind him.

He glanced at Ronald Harrison, a small man with untamable red hair. He was first-born son of a squire, but some said he was actually the baseborn son of a local redheaded baron who had paid for his schooling. He and Teasdale had been in the same year at school.

"Checked with m'lawyer. It's legal all right. Family ran to females what can't take over the reins. He probably thinks he's safe because of that one what lives in America. Heard he died. Arrogant cousin probably isn't even aware of the threat to him." He laughed a nasty laugh and punched Teasdale on the shoulder.

"Watch what you are about, Harrison. Just because we were in school together don't give you the privilege of breaching protocol. I am the Viscount Teasdale and you are…what are you? Oh yes…nothing." He laughed long and loud. His companion snarled but turned away to watch a vegetable peddler pull over to the side of the road. With his cap pulled down, the man gazed at them with dull eyes as the carriage whizzed by, covering his cart with a thin coating of dust.

"The plan is to rid the world of your predecessor and my competition. Filly thinks she has me fooled. Put her sights on Roderick, did she? I'll set that to rights soon enough. I will not be trifled with." He grimaced and flung his whip high over the gray's heads with a sharp crack. The team surged forward, sweat pouring from their shoulders.

"How did you know he was courting her? I haven't heard gossip about that. The man doesn't usually make a move that isn't reported as an *on dit* in those single sheet papers. What do they sell for now? A penny?"

Teasdale glared at his companion. "How would I know? Y'think I spend my time reading them? Almost everything in them's pure falsehoods anyway. Maybe some truth, but mostly just exaggeration. I set a man on her house, and I know every move she makes. Caught him hanging around her three times now. She said her heart was given to another. Has to be him. He's going to wish he had stayed wherever he went to for the last two years before I'm finished with him."

"Think he's about to set up his nursery? Get his own heirs? It won't happen. I'll kill 'em off before they can take over, I promise you," Harrison said with a sneer.

Teasdale turned to stare at his colleague, Ronald Harrison. "'Twas you shot his uncle, was it? Ye gads, didn't think you had the nerve to do it. Shot him in the back, did you? Doesn't take much courage to get that done. Why didn't you tell me about it at the time? Few years back now, wasn't it?" Harrison said nothing, but grinned.

"How come you didn't kill Roderick instead? What good is it to kill his uncle? You are mad." He chuckled with derision and cracked his whip over the team's heads again. He liked the sound it made, the jerky reaction of his team, the power he felt as they surged in direct response to his whip. He'd paid a king's ransom for them, and then they'd lost him the race. If they weren't worth as much as they were, he'd shoot them. Lost too much on that race. If he couldn't pull a bit from the sire, he'd need to rusticate, and that didn't fit his plans. Why didn't the old cawker die like he was supposed to?

Lost in his own thoughts, he was surprised when Harrison responded to his last question. Even more, he realized his former roommate was admitting to murder. An involuntary shudder ran across his shoulders. Fellow was mad, completely mad.

"Didn't want to draw too much attention to speculation on the new heir. Anyone could read the book of peers and find out. I made this plan a long time ago, and I can wait it out. Don't want to wind up in gaol. This way nobody will suspect me. Patience is a virtue, you know." He laughed in a high-pitched giggle and snorted.

"Ha. They'd need to be very interested to go as far as you, Harrison, but don't worry. I'll be glad to help you get rid of Roderick. He's now made himself a pest. I don't tolerate those who interfere with my interest."

"Lost your race to him, I hear. Heard you called him a cheat. Lucky he didn't call you out. Thought you were going to have him beaten up before the contest started." Harrison smirked. "I was hoping you'd do the job for me."

"I had a thing or two to say to those two scoundrels...I paid them good gold, too. Got it back and gave them a new job." He scowled and grew quiet.

"Might not be as easy as you think to rid yourself of the man. He's known to take care of himself wherever you think to meet him. Heard he's pretty good at the fancy, but better with swords. Not looking for a duel, are you?" He twisted around to stare at Teasdale, his mouth hanging open, wet lips dribbling.

"I'll decide what to do this week. They tell me my father is on his deathbed. Might be earl before the day is out. Ha! Then that silly chit will be glad she is to give me heirs." He purposefully kept his eyes on the road in front of him. Harrison was not a handsome fellow.

"I assume you need her dowry. Heard you lost a bundle on that race. I was surprised you decided to keep these grays after he humiliated you." He ducked as the viscount swung at him but snickered his odd laugh, holding his hand in front of his face.

"He cheated. I don't know how he did it, but I know his bays should not have beaten these grays. Cost me a fortune. Sell them if I don't come about soon.

"We need to plan how to handle this meddling duke," Teasdale continued. "I plan to stop in at the Fat Ducks Inn tonight. We'll have a word or two." They laughed together as Teasdale cracked his whip.

****

Later, they sat drinking a pitcher of the dark brew famous at the inn.

"Shooting's too obvious. Too risky for me. What say you do the shooting since you've already got one murder behind you?" Teasdale was uneasy. He found Harrison useful, but he had no fondness for him. Truth to tell, if he didn't claim an old friendship, he would be leery. Man had something queer about him. Teasdale was almost shocked by the admission Harrison had shot Roderick's uncle in the back. Rumor was the man had been killed by road pirates, robbed and shot. Now he learned it was Ronald Harrison all the time. He stared at the redhead and bent forward to disguise a shudder. If he wasn't in such a bind…

"Don't care much about shooting him. Always planned to do him in at some point. Where you want it done? Might take me a while to set it up, mind you." Harrison paused to drink deep from his mug.

The room was filled with locals enjoying their beer and visiting in loud voices. The noise provided a sense of privacy to their conversation, even as they hunched over the table to speak in close confidence.

"Listen," Teasdale said between gritted teeth. "I'm not telling you what to do, but I need that dowry. Whenever you want. But soon, I think. Already told that chit to be ready in ten days. Two gone already. Don't think it will cause much of a stir in her household. They weren't engaged or anything. Think he might just have gotten interested in the last week or so. Been out of the country for a while."

"If he's looking to get himself an heir, he's a dead man. I can promise you that for truth." Harrison laughed loud and long, stopping conversation around him as the honest country folks turned to stare.

Teasdale cringed at the attention and wondered again why he bothered with this poor excuse of a man. *Something definitely wrong with Harrison's mind.* He didn't care much knocking folks out of his way, but Harrison seemed to enjoy it, and he knew that wasn't right.

Chapter Twenty-Two

"Wish me happy, Roderick?" Captain Mark Estermire and his friend, the Duke of Roderick, walked in the twilight toward White's where they intended to have their supper and perhaps, if the crowd was congenial, a few cards.

"Said she'd take you crippled leg and all, did she?" Richard asked with a grin. "No accounting for taste. Congratulations, you gudgeon. Long time coming, I say." He clapped his friend on the shoulder and laughed at Mark's chagrin. "When is the happy event to take place? You are waiting for an appointment any day now, aren't you? Does she go with you?"

"Haven't had a chance to discuss it. Stop by tomorrow. Need to be soon. Have to leave when they send me orders. She doesn't mind the travel. Did I tell you? Always wanted to see the world and is looking forward to going with me. Doesn't care where it is. Is that a miracle or what?" He beamed.

"Mark, you really have the devil's own luck. She is perfect for you, beautiful, of course, but intelligent and well-read, poised and well-mannered. Almost asked her myself until you stepped in and caught her attention. Best friend you turned out to be." Mark laughed out loud while Richard grinned good-naturedly.

"You're not fooling me. You had an eye on the lively younger one. Saw you paying attention to her when you rescued her from the duck pond. Thought at the time you were a little too fond of green apples." They walked underneath a street lantern which shone with dim light. The fog had crept up from the river and mixed with smoke from the ubiquitous belching coal fires. They could see no more than a step or two ahead of them.

"Tried to fight it. You don't need to remind me I'm too old for her. Thought when I left that was the end of it, but she came right along with me. I could never get her out of my head or my heart, for that matter. I am embarrassed to say I would now get on my knees and beg her to wed me tomorrow. Don't think she ever will, though. She trusted me, and I failed her. She's the kind of person who doesn't forget that quickly, I can tell you."

"Sophia mentioned how disappointed her sister is with your behavior. Nothing I could say except I know how sorry I am." As they gained the light of another lamp, two men emerged from the dim light of the fog. Roderick tightened his hand on his walking stick.

"Trouble, think you?" he whispered from the side of his mouth, never taking his eyes from the shuffling sound of the two as they neared. "I have the one on the right."

"Right-oh. Left for me," Mark answered as the men appeared before them, their caps pulled down over their eyes.

"Ho, there! You two here for more punishment, are you?" Roderick called out. He recognized the two for the ruffians from the other night. How stupid could they get?

"No, all wrong, guv'nor. Look'n for you. Toff still

after you, but we'uns got nothing to do with 'im." The one with the wounded arm came closer with his hands in the air. "Just thought we could make a deal, guv'nor."

"Deal? Just what kind of deal are you proposing? What have you got to make a deal with?" Roderick paused, his sense of humor tickled.

"Man with the gray horses, guv'nor. 'E threatened to do us cause we didn't 'urt you like 'e said. Might be 'e got a worm in his head. Made us promise to try again and took 'is money back. Mayhap you could pay us to tell you what da bloke is up to? Eh?" He stepped closer to the street light and smiled with snaggled teeth.

"Name is Jake and dis 'ere be Joe. We need work. 'Ungry as wolves, we are. What say, guv'nor? Us work for you?"

"Sounds like a deal you can't pass up, Roderick. Turn the tables on him with his own paid thugs. I like it." Mark laughed.

"How do I know you won't go to the viscount and try the same thing?" Roderick asked. He watched the two squirm and thought he had it right. They intended to play both ends to the middle. "If I catch you trying that, I'll call the runners in on you," he warned.

They vowed they would work only for the duke. Roderick flipped them both a gold coin which they promptly bit.

"You come straight way to me if he tries it again." Roderick concluded. The two shuffled off into the dimness of the night. Who knew what might come of that?

"Teasdale is playing rough, is he? I wish I could say I'm surprised, but I'm not. His reputation seems to be well deserved," Mark said, disgusted.

"He's pretty stirred up since he lost that race. Money problems, I expect," the duke said. "Should have seen him, Mark. He almost destroyed those beautiful animals, forcing them to run flat out up that steep hill. I couldn't help cringing to watch it happening. Nothing to do. Can't stop a man from abusing his own property. He lost quite a bundle on that race, and then screamed at me that I cheated."

"Witnesses?" Mark asked.

"Oh, certainly. There were many spectators to the entire racecourse. He made a fool out of himself yelling foul like that. Could never prove anything at all except what an incompetent whip he is. Probably disappointed I wasn't with a broken arm or leg since he hired those two thugs to rough me up the night before." They entered the club with supper on their minds and were promptly seated.

"I spoke to Mrs. Barrows. Told her I'd offer for Elisabeth if the viscount gave her any trouble. Elisabeth can decide if she wants to continue the engagement or break it off after Teasdale loses interest."

"What did she say to that?" Mark asked. "You surprise me, Roderick."

"I fear for her safety. I can have her under my protection this way. She'll probably box my ears for my presumption, but it helped to convince her mother how serious this is. Teasdale is set on making her his wife, and I can't distract him forever. I did some plain speaking as to the man's character, and Mrs. Barrows was quick to understand my meaning."

"Does she know how you feel about her daughter? I think from what you related to me she had no idea you two were…interested in one another at one time."

"I managed to tiptoe around that as best I could. I hesitate to explain with honesty how matters stood between Elisabeth and me, before and now. Embarrassed as I am over my own behavior, I cannot stand by and allow that scoundrel to run roughshod over Elisabeth."

"I understand. You know, Richard, I'm about to become a member of that family. I might have a word or two to say to Teasdale if he keeps pressing the issue." He thumped one fist into another.

"What say? You are correct. How fortunate it is you have managed a firm connection with Sophia. I still think I need to keep an eye on Elisabeth myself, but how pleased I am to have you in place to help." They turned to pay attention to their supper, ceasing all conversation for the nonce.

## Chapter Twenty-Three

Helen Barrows sat in her boudoir in her undress with her forehead wrinkling in thought as her maid attended her hair. Even if the alliance she hoped for did not come to pass, she would never allow her daughters to be bullied into an alliance they did not choose. As shocked as she had been at the violence inflicted when she had helped put a cold compress on Elisabeth's lip, she acknowledged that forced marriages were not uncommon. A man in the viscount's position could take liberties that would make such a marriage a necessity. Public opinion would, no doubt, support his claim if Elisabeth refused his offer. Options were few.

With her husband gone, there were no male members of the family who could be appealed to protect them. They might flee, leaving no word where they could be found, but there were few places they could shelter where word would not reach the viscount. If the man was determined, he would eventually run them to ground.

To protect one daughter might endanger the happiness of the other. Sophia had announced her decision to wed her captain. No one was more aware of the threat of embarrassment to a diplomat's career than Helen, who had lived her life in the harsh light of the *beau monde*. Estermire might lose any chance he had of advancement if the Barrows family were subjected to scandal. He could be dismissed before ever an appointment came for him. How could she choose one daughter's happiness over the other? She could not. She turned with a half-smile to thank her maid as finishing touches were added to her coiffeur.

"That will be all, Sally. You've done an exceptional job today. Will you let Miss Elisabeth know I need to see her as soon as she is dressed?"

She had relatives on the continent, but with the fatal consequences of the turmoil that raged, it just would not be feasible to remove her family there. There was a solution if only she could think clearly. The Duke of Roderick had offered her family protection through an engagement to Elisabeth. It puzzled her why this had come about. He owed them nothing that she could discern, and Elisabeth refused to discuss it. It was time she had a frank dialogue with her youngest daughter.

Helen was not unaware something had transpired between Elisabeth and the duke. Her friend, the duchess implied as much, but Helen could not believe it. Whatever happened obviously had its roots in that house party some time ago, since the man had been out of the country for two years.

She was certain the duke had been on the verge of proposing to Sophia when he was abruptly called away. How Elisabeth was involved was a complete mystery to her. She prided herself on a light touch with her girls. Never had she thought to be an oppressive parent, but she would have the truth now and not just the parts her old friend, the duchess of Roderick, had learned. It was very important she have all the facts in this situation. They must make a plan soon.

"Come in, Elisabeth. Oh, it's you, Sophia. I

thought Sally was bringing your sister to me. Oh, how lovely you are this morning. Is that a new style for your hair?" She gave Sophia a fond squeeze and gestured for her to sit.

"Mother, may I have this time to discuss something with you? Elisabeth is still making herself ready for the day. Our maid always tends to me as the elder as you know. It will be some minutes before my sister is released to come to you."

"Of course, you may. What is troubling you? Wedding nerves? I must have that mother-daughter discussion with you soon, must I not?" She smiled and patted her daughter on the cheek. "Never fear, sweetness. If you love this man, nothing that happens when you are private with your husband will be distasteful to you. I loved your father with all my heart and found his arms around me a most glorious experience. I'm certain that you will, too." She laughed and reached to hug Sophia.

"Yes, I see you blush, but I am your mother and these things must be given our full attention before your wedding night." She was surprised when Sophia stood up and paced to the window.

"Why, what is troubling you, dear child? You aren't that frightened of the captain's endearments, are you? Sometimes these young men can be too eager in their attempts to demonstrate their love. Never you mind. It will all straighten itself out in time."

"You do not understand!" In her agitation, Sophia threw out her hands and tears of anguish rolled down her cheeks.

Helen was experiencing the beginnings of true alarm. What could be threatening this family now?

What new disaster loomed over their heads? *Oh, why had you to die, Robert. I need you more than ever now.*

"No, of course I do not know when the two of you refuse to share your secrets with me. Sit down now and let me understand." She was aware of annoyance in her voice, but after all, a mother could only take the stress so far.

"I am in conflict, Mama, between loyalty to my sister and a wish to make her life better by confessing to you." She sat down on the chaise lounge beside her mother and put her arms around her. She rested her head on her mother's shoulder as Helen patted her.

Irritation at the reticence of her children to confess what troubles might be afflicting them warred with concern for their well-being.

"Sophia, dear child. How can I help you in ignorance? Let me know the facts and we will sort them out together." She pushed her gently away and reached for a handkerchief to wipe her daughter's eyes. "It's about Elisabeth and Roderick, I am guessing. Something has happened between them, or he would not be acting as he is now, I'm sure."

"Oh, I begged her to tell you, Mother. She is too embarrassed to let you know how she told so many falsehoods when we were guests of the duke. She was a totally different person then, you understand. That was before she made a vow to never break society's rules. You remember how she changed so after our visit there?" Helen nodded.

There had been a complete change in her rebellious daughter, but she had not connected it with the visit to the Roderick estate.

"And then are you going to continue to withhold

the secrets, or will you finally allow me the facts that will give me the information I need to straighten these problems out? I understand your desire to keep your sister's confidences. It is an admirable trait, but you must see the importance of allowing me to possess all the facts before I make important decisions for this family."

"Yes, I know I must. I ardently dislike the necessity, but with the latest offenses by that wicked viscount, my loyalties must be to my sister's well-being." She searched in her reticule for her vinaigrette, and Helen thought she must shake her eldest soon if she did not come to the point.

"You see...Elisabeth and the duke..." She was interrupted by the entrance of her sister.

"No, Sophia. You are being forced into betraying my confidence by my stubbornness, and I cannot permit that to happen. I will confess my failings to my mother." She glanced pleadingly at each of them, as she stood twisting a handkerchief between her fingers, a sorrowful expression on her face.

Helen thought heaven had blessed her with two gorgeous daughters, but now she could see how beauty attracted evil as well as good. Elisabeth was as comely as her sister but in a more piquant way. Unfortunately, her liveliness usually attracted more attention.

She had lost count of how many young men had pleaded to be allowed to address the popular Miss Elisabeth. Most she turned away and sometimes never even mentioned it to her daughter. Whatever had happened at the Roderick estate must have been traumatic. Both her daughters had shown no interest in their proposals. Now it seemed she would finally know the reasons why.

"I was a hoyden, Mother. I disobeyed all the rules and ran practically wild when we visited the estate of the Duke of Roderick. It took me a long time to realize why you taught me to pay attention to the taboos of society. I thought it was to keep me from having fun. Now I know rules are for protection."

"Yes, dear. Well, to tell the truth, I sometimes wonder...but never mind. That is not the topic today. Let me know what happened, if you please." She sat trying for patience and a neutral expression. It would not do to show censure at a time like this.

"Yes, of course." Elisabeth took a deep breath. "I had an affair with the Duke of Roderick. It ended when he was called away by the government." Helen gasped.

"You bedded with the duke?" Helen exclaimed. "When...how...what a scoundrel! No wonder..." She broke off, her calm shattered.

"No, no, Mother. I did not...it was not...perhaps, an affair is not the proper word. I did not—I was never in bed with him." Elisabeth's face turned a fiery red, but she uttered a short laugh.

Helen relaxed a bit. Surely, her innocent daughter had exaggerated the situation.

"Start from the beginning and tell me exactly what happened. Do not leave out a single thing. Now begin," she directly sternly. She was concerned enough at this point to leave behind the finesses she had earlier vowed to use.

"I had an unnatural curiosity about kissing," Elisabeth began, refusing to make eye contact with her mother. "I believe now that started the whole thing. Well, that and I was racing this beautiful mare with

169

Jamie, and when a rabbit ran in front, I fell into the lily pond." Helen took a deep breath, held it, and then released it with a sigh.

"I wondered what happened to that lovely red riding habit of yours," she said calmly. "Go on."

"Jamie helped me out, but the duke...Mother, I had no idea he was Roderick. I thought the duke was that fat old squire. Until recently, when Sophia told me it was Richard. He told me to call him Richard and...I digress." She, too, took a deep breath and let it slowly out.

"He took me back to the manor. After you...when I was confined to my room for several days, I escaped when you were not around and walked to the wood. I climbed a tree and got my foot stuck. Richard came along and helped me pull it out. I called him my Noble Rescuer." Elisabeth was speaking faster and faster now as if she wanted to get the ordeal over with. "We talked sitting in the grass. He was a perfect gentleman, Mother, you must not think he wasn't, but I had these weird feelings. I tried to discuss it with Sophia, but I was too ashamed." She paused and stared ahead as if remembering.

"You had feelings for the duke, Elisabeth? This is why you have behaved as you have?" Helen asked with a sinking heart. What had that careless man done to her innocent daughter?

"It's much worse than that." She met her mother's eyes. "I still have feelings for the duke."

"That's what I was going to tell you, Mama," Sophia added. "My sister is in love with the Duke of Roderick. It is such a very sad situation."

Helen thought she was going mad. She looked

from one to the other. "Let me get this straight. You are in love with Roderick. He has come to me offering to become engaged to you to protect you from Teasdale, to be broken off later if you do not like it. But he will not break the engagement himself, and he has been paying you attention of late. Am I clear on this so far?" Both daughters nodded.

"You are calling this a sad situation, Sophia. Would you explain how you have come to this conclusion?"

"But don't you see?" Sophia said. "She can never trust him again! How could you be wed to a man you can never trust?"

Helen stifled a laugh. Her innocent daughters were perfectly serious. She could name many marriages not established on trust. Mostly they were made on alliances, estates, dowries, titles, and any number of not so transparent motives, including the kind of force Lord Teasdale might use. She had been fortunate in her own husband, but they had not been in love before the ceremony. Love had grown over the years, and now she thought of him with regret, wishing she had those early days back.

"Tell me exactly what he did to lose your trust, Lizzie. What did he promise you that he did not deliver? Had he proposed marriage to you?" She saw that he had not by the shocked expression blossoming on Elisabeth's face.

"No! Let me explain. I understand it is difficult to believe, but I did not know who he was. I thought of him only as Richard, my rescuer. Do you remember the picnic? He beckoned to me when I was out walking with my friends and took me to a secret garden room where we had a private luncheon. I thought he was a friend of the duke's. You must understand. I was falling in love with him even then." Her face flamed once more, but she soldiered bravely along.

Her mother thought she did understand, and the anxiety she had been feeling started to fall away. There was a solution to this problem after all. She made an effort to keep the smile from her own expression.

"The worse is yet to come, Mother. Brace yourself. I received a note inviting me to meet him in the garden in the evening. He said at the beginning he had something to tell me, but he never did. Instead, he kissed me. He kissed me a lot...and I liked it. I...anyway. He stopped and then told me he was leaving the very next morning. That's it."

"That is everything? You are certain?" Helen was almost convinced their troubles were over. She began a mental exercise writing a note to the dowager duchess explaining their plans to unite their children might work out after all.

"Well, only that some days ago he apologized after he came home. Sophia helped me to learn his real identity when we saw him at the ball that night. I was furious as you may have imagined. How dare he play games with me?" She stood and paced the floor.

"What was his excuse, if he gave you one?" her mother asked. Surely this information would spike the guns of that arrogant viscount.

"That to answer his government's call was providential. He thought me far too young for him." She stifled a sob and was hugged in sympathy by her sister.

"He certainly set you up for a disappointment, but

had either of you discussed your affections?" Elisabeth shook her head as she sat wringing her hands.

"Elisabeth, will you tell your mother if that was your first kiss?" she asked amused. Elisabeth nodded. It was just as Helen expected: A young naïve girl on the brink of her come out had over-reacted to the sophisticated advances of an older gentleman.

"And have you received more kisses since?" she asked. Elisabeth's face seemed in perpetual shifting color. She nodded with a shamefaced grimace.

"Only once more besides yesterday's horror, and it was not at all pleasant. Teasdale forced one on me when we were on our picnic. He caught me walking alone near the river. That's when he mentioned speaking to you."

"But you were not upset when Roderick kissed you, right?" Helen persisted. Elisabeth shook her head. "In fact, you welcomed it?" Elisabeth nodded.

"This is an interesting topic, my daughters. Elisabeth, you will accept the generous offer from Roderick." She held up her hand as both daughters began to protest.

"Enough! For once you will do as I bid." Both girls looked as shocked as she had ever seen, but Helen ignored them and continued. "I cannot think what kind of scandal we face if we do not. Teasdale is out of town, I understand, but due back soon. We must be settled in our plans before he returns. I will contact Roderick and let him know what has happened." She closed her eyes to the dismay on Elisabeth's face. This time she would make a few decisions.

Helen dismissed her daughters and sat to write to her old friend, the Duchess of Roderick. It would be interesting to see what her good friend had to say about this turn of events. She was now in possession of two pertinent facts: one, her daughter loved the Duke of Roderick. Two, he loved her daughter in return. How else to explain his offer? Being engaged to Roderick and later jilting him would protect Elisabeth from Teasdale, but it would also brand her a jilt in the eyes of society. Helen had wondered whether the man was thinking straight—now she knew why he was not. It seemed Helen could ensure her daughter's happiness, if she was careful.

Chapter Twenty-Four

"I assure you, Elisabeth, nothing could be further from my mind. You are in danger and I want only to come to your rescue." Richard held her closely in his arms as if she would disappear if he did not. The tabbies would be squeaking for a week. The music swelled as he swung her round and round in the waltz. When Elisabeth whispered urgently for him to loosen her, he insisted engaged couples were permitted a greater degree of digression.

"You are deliberately trying to create gossip," she insisted.

"I'm telling you, I merely want to express my happiness to have you in my arms once more." He grinned down at her.

Elisabeth missed a step. Her anger at the situation, her humiliation almost overcame her good manners. Elisabeth could hardly believe her mother had promptly sent the notice to the papers. Oh, she understood why her mother insisted she accept his proposal, but she railed at her fate just the same. She wanted to scream at him, stomp on his feet, box his ears, and kiss him.

The engagement would be announced alongside that of her sister to Captain Mark Estermire. Details were already sent to the papers. They would spend a week more in town and then retire to the duke's estate with a house party. Her mother and his mother had planned the itinerary carefully. There would be no chance for the gossips to wonder how it had all came about. Roderick had informed his mother the connection was of long standing, and she accepted it with surprising grace. After all she had been the one to pick the family two years ago. If she thought her son had engaged the wrong sister, she kept the thought to herself.

Everyone was happy with the arrangement but Elisabeth. The conflict within her threatened to explode her head. It was an impossible situation to be engaged, without ever a "yes" uttered, to be deeply in love with someone that you mistrusted. How did this all happen? She held herself tightly in check, tension riding her shoulders constantly, lest she expose her feelings to the one person she longed to share them with. How much misery could a person contain without completely melting away?

"That is quite a fetching gown you're wearing, by the way." Roderick held tightly to her hand as he guided her toward their mothers, standing alongside Sophia and Mark. They were at the coming-out ball of the Cutterdoles' daughter Cleo.

"Smile, Daughter. Do not disgrace your breeding," her mother whispered to her as they arrived to join the group.

Elisabeth plastered a smile on her face, hoping it did not more closely resemble a grimace.

"Not bad, Lizzie," Roderick said, leaning over her with his hand lightly touching her back. "Just hang on for a minute or two more and the deed will be done."

"Do not call me Lizzie," she said between clenched teeth behind her fan. "Elisabeth or nothing. Just say *you*, the naïve girl from my past that you enjoyed duping, and I will answer you."

"Certainly, Elisabeth. I long to call you wife; be it something that interests you?"

"I told my mother you kissed me, you know," she said spitefully and felt gratified when he winced.

"I cannot in all honesty claim I'm sorry for that. But I am embarrassed your mother had to know I rushed my fences too soon." He squeezed her hand. "It was a delightful interlude, my dear. I know you mistrust me for my deceit, but would we have had as much fun if I were the duke?" he whispered close to her ear, his breath stirring her curls softly.

"No, for Richard was a much nicer person than you," she replied tartly.

They stepped forward as the announcement was made and Roderick held up her hand smiling down at her. There was a smattering of applause and perhaps a groan or two, as mothers in the room signaled their regrets; and then Sophia and Mark were announced. The music started again with couples taking to the floor and it was over. If Cleo Clutterdole was appalled to have her ball usurped by the surprising news, she didn't show it. In fact, her parents seemed to be gratified their ball was the chosen one.

The Duke of Roderick had become officially engaged to Miss Elisabeth Barrows whether she liked it or not. It was a dilemma not to be envied. Elisabeth was deeply in love with her fiancé, who had rescued her again—he pitied her. Although she would never allow him to guess, she credited him with the title Noble Rescuer again. After her encounter with Teasdale, she had been truly fearful the beast would manage to

177

manipulate her into a marriage she detested. She had been on the town long enough to understand how it could be done. The viscount's title, soon to be an earl, was a powerful one, but not more so than Roderick's.

The night ended finally, and she bid Roderick's mother goodnight. She was a placid lady easy to gain friends. Elisabeth did not look forward to the disappointment on Her Grace's face when she would need to end the engagement. That unpleasant duty was months away, and she decided not to think about it now. She was to accompany Roderick, Sophia, and Mark tomorrow to see the Elgin marbles. Her mother declared it socially acceptable for young, engaged ladies to visit that museum. Exhausted and with a heavy heart, she tossed and turned in her bed long before she fell asleep.

Chapter Twenty-Five

Next morning, Richard and Mark arrived in good time in his barouche, an attractive four-wheel carriage, wheels picked out in red and yellow and sporting a fold-up hood, and a smart driver dressed in the duke's livery. Richard had purchased the vehicle only two days before, and he was pleased to hand the lovely sisters up for the ride to the museum. The two couples sat facing each other and Richard enjoyed watching the happiness play across Sophia's face. She and the captain were well matched. He was attentive and obviously loved her very much. Sophia returned his affection and was all smiles underneath her pretty parasol, which she sometimes twirled to give the two of them privacy.

Elisabeth had chosen a broad brimmed hat instead of a parasol. Roderick chuckled when he observed this obstacle to dalliance. It prevented him from coming within an arm's length of his newly declared fiancée. Also, he hoped that shade did not erase the delightful freckles which strayed across Elisabeth's tiny nose. He was particularly fond of them, especially the one shaped like a minute heart that sat near her dimpled cheek. One of his goals was to be allowed to touch her right there.

They soon arrived at the museum and entered the building with a small crowd of other visitors. Richard looked down at Elisabeth but could not see her face underneath the hat. How these young misses would handle anatomically correct male statues, he could not guess. Their mother wanted them further educated in the realities of the male species, he supposed, since it was she who proposed the excursion. He soon forgot about their ingénue status and lost himself in the splendid art from so many years past.

He could not imagine how Lord Elgin had thought it a good idea to cut the friezes from the outside walls of the Parthenon. His claim that he was rescuing art from destruction did not hold up, when one could see how difficult it had been to remove them and the damage it caused. He was studying one particularly breathtaking example of horses in battle, when he felt Elisabeth move beside him.

"How do you like the art, Elisabeth?" he asked, stepping back to see her face. She turned her face up to him with glowing eyes, her hands clasped beneath her chin, a tiny reticule dangling from one wrist.

"It is the most wonderful thing I have ever seen!" she exclaimed. "Have you ever seen such beautiful horses?" He should not have been surprised at her comment. He remembered he thought she might judge a man by the health of his horses. He turned his head to keep her from noticing the smile on his face. He was pleased that the frieze—maybe Lord Elgin had been right, after all—had made her forget her anger with him, if only for a while. It had been a cold ride through town for such a warm day.

"The man who carved this marble had to know and love the animals. He made them come to life even in this cold stone. See how you can practically see that one breathe?" She leaned over to almost touch the statue and trace its back with her gloved finger.

He allowed himself the pleasure of feasting his eyes on Elisabeth as she concentrated on the artwork. Her half dress was cut low at the neck but sported a tucker in a cerulean blue with an added small train. There were two matching feathers in her hat, and she carried a shawl draped across her elbows. His mind drifted with pleasant memories, imagining a red blur that was Elisabeth and her favorite mount as she took a low hedge at a dangerous speed.

They moved on down the line where a lone male statue rested. All four stood gazing silently at the form. Richard cleared his throat and uttered in a squeezed voice.

"Although most of the statues are anatomically correct, you must remember that many of the statues are damaged. Parts—important parts—have been broken off. Arms, legs, and even noses," he managed to get out. Mark made a snorting noise, but refrained from commentary. Roderick rested his hand in the middle of Elisabeth's back and steered her firmly onward. She said not a word, but he could guess the expression on her face. She was not ignorant of the anatomy of horses, and he knew she was not without intelligence. True to his suspicions, she tilted the hat and gave him a completely roguish grin before hiding behind the wide brim again.

Roderick was about to take her to task when a party of young men surrounded them.

"S-stole the march on us, did you?" Matthew Diver-Jones said to Roderick. "Congratulations, old man. S-she's a handful, but a terror in the saddle. Take care s-she don't run you over." He moved over to give

Sophia his best wishes and greeted the captain while Lyndon Peron wrung his hand.

"Wondered where you had gotten off to. Haven't s-seen you in the park lately. Is this engagement thing keeping you from riding?" Matthew asked Elisabeth. He stepped aside for James Wilkerson who swooped upon Elisabeth.

"Couldn't have picked a better man for you, Lizzie. Congratulations, Roderick. She's lively, but suspect you'll be able to handle her. Just give her a good mount and stand back. She won't bother you much if she's got a good seat in the saddle."

"Well met, you three. Are you up for some country living for a week or so? We are moving down to my estate next week. Inviting a few people. Be best pleased if you would join us," Roderick said, while he was being slapped on the shoulder and having his hand wrung.

"What ho! S-sounds like a great invite. You going, are you, Elisabeth?" Matthew asked. She nodded acquiescence, unable to form an adequate reply. Her social status was severely changed, and she was rapidly becoming aware of it. How would all this play out when she ended the engagement? The young men gathered in a clutch and joined them, making remarks as they examined the artifacts. They soon had Elisabeth laughing.

"I say, look at that warring steed," Lyndon said, pointing to one of the horses with a warrior perched on his back. "Think they bred bigger horses in those days? Don't know how he keeps his seat without a saddle."

"Not to mention his pants," Matthew added sotto voice, but they all heard.

Their noisy laughter caught the attention of other visitors, and Richard thought it time they left the Elgin marbles to rest. He was fond of Elisabeth's friends, but they could make him feel the difference in his and his fiancée's age. Once he, too, was a noisy young man full up to the rig, betting on the pace of a caterpillar. Nevertheless, could he but manage to reel his fish in, he would make this woman his wife. Once, he had hesitated. No more.

He assisted Elisabeth while Mark helped Sophia into the barouche for the return trip home. A thought hit him and he whirled, almost putting his eye out, to ask Elisabeth a question. "Would you like a ride in the park while we are out?" he asked. Her face told him the answer, and he spoke to his driver, who found a place and changed the direction of the carriage.

They nodded to several acquaintances as they wound their way through the crowded park. The driver stopped several times while other carriages blocked the path as they visited with their friends. Elisabeth waved gaily to Susan Tillburry, who blew kisses back to her. She was riding with a handsome gentleman in uniform who Elisabeth thought might be her brother.

Elisabeth next spotted Eloise Larkin in a curricle with a man she didn't know. She leaned over to whisper something to Sophia about the man but paused when she saw the startled expression on her sister's face. She turned to look behind her and stared directly into the furious face of Viscount Teasdale, riding on an enormous gray horse with a white blaze. He stared at her with clenched teeth and leaned forward in a menacing manner. An involuntarily gasp escaped Elisabeth's lips, and she turned quickly around and reached to squeeze Roderick's hand in warning. He glanced down at her reaching out, grasped and held firmly to her hand.

"Teasdale, is it? Just keep smiling and ignore him. If he gives us trouble, know that I will handle it. Relax, sweet Lizzie. I've got you now. You're safe," he said in a low voice as Teasdale rode abreast of the barouche.

"Engaged to marry, are you Miss Elisabeth? Funny, I had the impression I had asked you for your hand before I left town. Planning to marry both of us, are you?" he said with a sneer.

"Sorry, Teasdale. Elisabeth and I have a previously arranged understanding. I believe she mentioned it?" Richard was guessing but saw that he had scored a hit. "Wish me happy?" Richard signaled for his driver to move on. The barouche lurched forward, leaving the viscount sitting on his steed in the middle of the path scowling after them.

"There, that should settle Teasdale. The worst is over, Elisabeth," Roderick said.

Chapter Twenty-Six

"You must not allow that dreadful man to curtail your activities. If he thinks he can menace and force you to hide from him, he will cause just the scandal we are endeavoring to avoid," Helen Barrows said with some heat. She had been visibly nervous since she entered the parlor that night and found Elisabeth bleeding from a cut lip.

"Roderick is to pick us up soon, Mother. We are off to Astley's. I confess I am excited to be finally going. I have wished often you had taken us as children to see the wonderful horses I've heard so much about. Did you know they have a riding school during the day for beginners? Is that not a clever idea to use the facilities both day and night?" She was dressed warmly for it had rained during the day and now fog and drizzle threatened. She looked around for her shawl.

"It's best to go with escorts. Your gentlemen will be especially cautious with that irritating man hanging about. Why doesn't he admit defeat and find another young lady to bother?" Helen said crossly. She sat with her needlework in her lap, but was gazing at her youngest daughter. Elisabeth crossed the room and hugged her mother.

"Please do not allow that wicked man to cut up your peace, Mother. I may be upset with Richard on a personal basis, but I trust him implicitly to protect me.

Mark is a former soldier. Surely you're not worried about Sophia's safety? See? We are in capable hands for tonight's festivity." She found her bonnet and shawl and sat in a chair to await the appearance of her sister.

"I saw him ride by at least twice in the last two days," Helen said, disgust in her voice. "He's driving those high-stepping grays that are so restive, pedestrians run to clear the streets. He has no business here that I know of. He only wants to taunt and make us nervous. What a complete cad!" She looked up as Sophia entered the room, a smile blossoming on her face to see her eldest daughter.

"You are in good looks tonight, Sophia. I vow that dress could take you right to the opera if you wore the sparkling jewels, although I approve of you dressing it down for this trip to watch horses prance around. Which shawl shall you choose?" She stood up to rearrange a fold in Sophia's dress.

As her mother and sister talked enthusiastically of bridal clothes, Elisabeth allowed her mind to wander where it would. Memories of an exciting ride on a lovely russet-colored mare with a white blaze put a smile on her face. She wondered if Roderick still had the horse that she had loved so on her visit two years ago. *What if...what if I really married the duke? I could have that mare for my very own.*

Would she really marry a man for the horses he owned? She covered her mouth to hide the giggles. Some light-hearted mood struck her suddenly with champagne-like spurts of laughter. She quieted down when her mother glanced, and Sophia raised her eyebrows. Truth be told, Elisabeth was tired of being angry. Something about keeping company with

Roderick brought out the rebellious side to her nature as well.

Perhaps it was the anticipation of the evening that had her in a good mood. She did love horses, always had, and hopefully always would. She'd heard so many exciting tales of the performance she was to see tonight and had looked for an opportunity to attend. Elisabeth glanced down at an advertisement she had been studying. It declared the horses would perform a country dance, eight all at once. Her pulse quickened. How marvelous that would be, she thought, and wondered who had the training of these animals. Were they some special breed that was easily led into unfamiliar pathways? Surely not a commonly bred animal formerly used as a hack.

A knock on the door heralded the arrival of their escorts. Their butler, in all formality, announced first His Grace, the Duke of Roderick and the Captain Mark Estermire. Mark came precipitously into the room and reached for Sophia's hands. She, just as eager, held hers forward, and they spent a minute gazing into each other's eyes.

Richard gave the couple an amused glance before he turned to Elisabeth and held out his arm. She tucked her hand into it with a grave expression. Never would she allow him to suspect how effervescent her mood had become. Would he try to exploit her good will? With her on his arm, he presented to her mother who nodded her approval.

"I will rest easy tonight with the two of you guarding my beloved daughters. Roderick, you especially, must be diligent, but, of course, you will. I do not mean to sound anxious, but I must report to you that Teasdale has passed by this house at least twice in the last two days. I do not deny this has me uneasy, which I am certain he means to do. Please enjoy your entertainment, but do not allow this wicked man to disrupt it." She gave each daughter a kiss on the cheek and stepped back with a nod.

When the four were seated in the carriage, Roderick expressed his regret. "I am sorry your parent must be bothered by this man. He seems incapable of understanding defeat."

"I am completely astonished he should pursue this course of action," Elisabeth exclaimed. "Why does he not quickly ask another to wife? His title must insure someone would take him for husband." She placed one hand over the other in her lap. Roderick would be quick to hold her hand if she were not careful.

"Perhaps he feels you are the only lady to fit the bill," Roderick answered, amusement in his voice. "That can happen sometimes," he added airily.

Elisabeth was not fooled by his pretending and gave him a sharp glance. Her eveningwear boasted no bonnet, but she could spear him with disapproving glares if she chose. Unfortunately, her elevated mood discouraged sharp glances, and she fought against leaning against his broad shoulder. His proximity seemed to encourage intimacy, a familiar condition from which she suffered when she was near this man. She tilted her chin with determination. She would not allow him to guess. How lowering it would be if he were to find out how susceptible she was still to his charms!

Astley's amphitheatre located at the Westminster Bridge sported a covered entry for arriving patrons. The drizzle of rain had stopped, but the air was damp with swirling fog. Elisabeth and Sophia quickly used their shawls to cover their heads in the moist night air. Gaining entrance was a feat, as the crowd of people gaily talking and visiting made moving inside difficult.

Staring all around at the inside of the huge amphitheatre, Elisabeth gasped at the scope of it. A center ring for the performers covered most of the floor while seats rose three levels on two sides. The third offered one tier of seats, but Richard steered them to the second level. From there they could look down on the entire performance with an unfettered view. Suspended from the ceiling, an enormous chandelier made from glass and lamps provided light for the entire building. The noise from the chatting patrons was deafening but they quieted down at the sound of the orchestra tuning their instruments. The very air seemed to crackle with suppressed excitement in anticipation of the performance.

"Are you looking forward to the antics of the horses?" Roderick asked leaning down and almost touching her cheek. Did the aggravating man sniff her hair?

"I confess I am awed by the size of this building. Even so, how can eight horses perform without bumping into each other? I'm eager to watch. I sincerely hope the animals do not get hurt," she said, whispering behind her fan. The crowd quieted completely as the performances began.

For the next little while, Elisabeth covered her mouth to stop her gasps again and again. She stared in amazement at the precise movements of the well-trained horses. When the animals engaged in a country dance, she crowed her pleasure at the spectacle. At a break in the entertainment, Roderick leaned over to whisper in her ear once more. He brushed against her hair with his face; she was certain of it, but it seemed trivial to mention it when she could hardly contain her excitement.

The noisy crowd immediately drowned out any attempt at conversation. She tried to say how beautiful the costumed women riders were, but he kept shaking his head he could not understand.

She moved closer to him, nearly touching his shoulder and said loudly, "Are the ladies who ride the horses not beautiful?" He laughed out loud, and she suspected he had pretended not to hear. She rapped him with her fan, causing him to chuckle again. She turned her head to hide her smiles. He would not catch her out again.

This crowd was not always studious in their manners. Several rows below, a female dressed in a flashy gown was being soundly kissed by her escort. From her laughter, Elisabeth assumed the lady did not mind this familiarity. Roderick turned and caught her staring and raised an eyebrow. Elisabeth laughed at his antics.

Soon the performers were back on the stage, and the clowns were pleasing the patrons, who responded with roars of approval. All too soon it was over. If she thought of standing and riding bareback a cantering horse, Elisabeth was reticent to share it, but the dazzling visions danced in her head still. No doubt she would ride those beautiful steeds in her dreams. Perhaps not in such revealing costumes!

She waited with Sophia and Mark as Roderick

found their driver. As she lifted her short train safely from the muddy floor, she felt a shove from behind. She fell to her knees and bumped her head with a sharp crack on the tiered step. Mark was by her side immediately with Sophia, making distressed murmurs and holding her hand.

Suddenly Roderick was there, scooping her into his arms and carrying her out to the waiting carriage. The hood was up, and he set her sheltered in the corner until he entered. From there, he took her into his lap and cradled her in his arms. Her head was still all a-swirl, and she fought for calm.

"Tell me you are unhurt, sweetness. Who did this to you?" he murmured while he kissed her cheek and held her hand.

"I think I am not hurt seriously, Richard. Something pushed me and I fell down. I hit my head on something hard. See? I think I have a lump there." She felt her forehead with her hand, which he pulled away to inspect by the dim light of the carriage lamp.

"How is she, Roderick?" Mark asked. Sophia echoed the question, but Elisabeth answered for herself.

"If Roderick would set me back in my seat, I would call myself safe. I have a bump, but I am otherwise unhurt," she said, looking meaningful at Roderick. He reluctantly slid her back beside him and into the leather seat, but kept his arm protectively across her shoulders. Elisabeth was aware of his presence but shaken up enough not to mind him there. Her head throbbed and she suspected she had scrapes on her knees.

"Did someone push you, Elisabeth?" Sophia asked. "I didn't see what made you fall."

"I did see someone there, but he moved so fast by

us, I couldn't tell who it was," Mark answered. "Perhaps it was an accident."

"Certainly, it was an accident!" Elisabeth exclaimed. "It was a rowdy crowd and someone just bumped into me." She had some doubt that statement was true, but why upset everyone?

"I should be whipped for leaving you unprotected. I am so sorry, Elisabeth. I never thought we would have problems at Astley's. Who could possibly know we would be attending tonight?" He curled his hand around her shoulder compelling her to meet his gaze. He was frowning, forehead wrinkled, his eyes locked with hers. She recognized he didn't believe it was an accident either.

"You are not to tell my mother any different. She is worried enough for my safety," she pleaded. He nodded once, but tightened his hand on hers.

"How do you feel now?" Sophia asked. "Should we send for a surgeon?"

"No, of course not. I have a bump on my head. I am not severely wounded. Let us refuse to allow it to destroy what was otherwise an extraordinary evening. Sophia, could you believe how beautifully those horses were turning in the ring? Would not you like to stand up and ride bareback like that? I vow those ladies wore such sparkling costumes."

"They were unusual costumes, what say, Mark?" Roderick said with forced bravado.

"Very striking," Mark answered in kind. "Caught my eye, thought so myself." He chuckled when Sophia glared over at him.

"I am puzzled how those animals could be so very docile to be trained that finely. Who do you suppose is in charge of it?" Elisabeth asked. As much as she wanted to recover some joy for the evening, she really did want to know.

"Astley was a soldier, I believe. It was he who saw the necessity for men to have superior control over their mounts. In the riding school, he takes amateurs and instructs them until they can take part in that country dance, controlling their horses with ease. It is amazing, is it not?" He patted her shoulder.

Roderick joined in the casual conversation until Elisabeth saw with thanks that Sophia had settled back in her seat, once more at rest from worry. She squeezed Richard's hand gratefully, realizing all at once that he had been holding hers all the while. She removed it promptly.

"Please do remember not to make a fuss, Sophia," Elisabeth whispered to her sister as they entered their house. "Mother will see the bump and be upset if we do not convince her of an accident. I beg of you to be careful what you say."

Roderick and Mark said goodnight at the door and left in the carriage.

Chapter Twenty-Seven

"I suspect it was that hanger-on of Teasdale's. Harrison? I've seen him around once or twice lately. Tell you the truth, I can't be absolutely sure it was not an accident. It happened so fast, and there were rowdy people around. I did see the side of his face as he pushed past us." Once back in their quarters they settled in with brandy to discuss the incident.

"Tell me what exactly happened, if you will bear with me and relate it detail by detail." Roderick pulled his coat off and threw it on the bed. He was extremely angry that, under his protection, Elisabeth had been injured. He blamed himself. He cursed loud and long, until exhausted, and then finally he sat down in the winged chair by the fire to listen.

"She was standing right beside us, but I think she bent over to look at something, not sure what. In that position, slightly bent forward, something or someone shoved her from behind. I had only a slight glimpse of that man moving by us, but my attention was on Elisabeth as she went down on her knees. She must have bumped her head on the step." Mark settled in a chair by the small fire Roderick's man had kindled when they arrived. "She was not badly injured, Roderick. You should not blame yourself. Anyone can stumble and fall by accident."

"I should have been there," he insisted stubbornly.

"Her mother trusts me to keep her from harm. Now again I have betrayed a member of that family's trust. What have I to offer Elisabeth now? I cannot even protect her." He shook his head and slammed a fist into the palm of his other hand.

"We have one more social obligation this week, and I can remove them all to my estates. Certainly they will be safe there if no other place. You will accompany us?" Roderick asked, turning to stare at his friend, eyebrows raised in query.

"Certainly, I will join you. You take my Sophia away, think you?" He tilted his head at Roderick with a wry grin. "Not damned likely."

Roderick gave a crack of laughter. "That is one consolation. Where the sisters go, you follow!" He rose to pace the room.

"I may eventually need to confront Teasdale. If I can avoid it, I will, but I will not tolerate him harassing Elisabeth or her family. What can possess the man to fixate on my Elisabeth? Of course, I should understand. I did it myself, but he does not strike me as the type to concern himself with any particular female."

"She has a healthy dowry, Richard. Could that be the cause? I am embarrassed by the largesse I am to receive from Sophia. I had no idea she was so very well portioned." He leaned over to poke up the fire.

"Yes, I knew. My mother investigated her family thoroughly before they were invited two years ago." Roderick chuckled. "My *mater* is crafty that way. I think all the *potentials,* as she called them, were similarly checked. She was determined I would not be caught by some title-chasing chit looking for an easy ride on my pocketbook." He idly picked up his cane and laid it back down. "I had gotten to the point I was determined to pick the best of them and have it over with."

"Yes, my Sophia! What luck I got there first."

"Yes, you cawker. Beat me to the punch, but my eyes were already straying to another by that time. She was so young. I was conflicted. Falling in love with her, but telling myself all the time it would not do. Arrogant imbecile that I was, I never considered she was in love with me as well. How angry she must have been when I suddenly left with no notice I was going. What a cad she must have thought me, and I cannot refute the charge. Imagine my chagrin now that a more complete picture presents to my dull mind."

"You thought time and distance would take care of it? So I thought also. Ironic, isn't it?" Mark added.

"She was about to be presented. How did I know she would turn down every male who asked to court her? I heard all about it. Sophia as well. They have left a string of broken hearts all over Town." He looked over to see Mark smiling and felt his face wreathed in a grin as well.

"Yes, flattering, isn't it? What a boost to our egos, what say?" Roderick said with satisfaction. He paced the floor thinking how to better protect his little love.

"All the more reason we must solve this problem. I will not lose my Elisabeth again—that is, if she ever forgives me for my crude behavior. It is time I do some serious investigation into the life of Arthur Bridges, better known as Viscount Teasdale."

"Knew his younger brother in school. Different kind of man. Loved his books and don't think he ever rode a horse when he could walk or ride in a carriage.

Decent sort," Mark offered.

"Yes, I knew he had a sibling. Too bad he couldn't have been the heir."

"*Pater* on the brink of dying, but then heard he rallied. Bet Teasdale wasn't happy about that." He stood and used the poker to stir the coals in the fireplace.

"How ridiculous this is to be discussing a man neither of us cares for. We need to dispatch this problem with haste. He bores me already," Roderick declared.

"You thinking of hiring a runner?" Mark asked. "Might be a good idea, especially since he hired those goons to harm you. What do you hear from them lately? Anything?"

"No, not a word. I usually ran into them around White's, and I haven't had time to drop in there lately. Think they would be of any use? Didn't impress me as having too much in their heads. That one was definitely a slow top; think the other was just a cork brain." He shook his head absently.

"Couldn't hurt, could it? If you give them ample funds, it would assure their loyalty. They might pick up something. I felt uneasy seeing Ronald Harrison at Astley's tonight. Teasdale is one thing, but that friend…Strange happenings at school when Harrison was around. Dead dogs. Never could pin it on him, but there was enough suspicion to cause most of us to avoid him."

"Is that correct? Don't know as I've ever heard much about him. Think we should have him checked out as well? I can answer my own question. If he was near when Elisabeth fell, I'll have his head on a pike.

Harrison, right? Something about that name rings a bell, but I can't quite remember what."

"You up for cards tonight?" Mark asked. He yawned.

Roderick thought his friend looked more ready for a good night's sleep. He guessed Mark had been on his wounded leg too long, but wouldn't mention it.

"No thanks. I have a book I wanted to read, so I'll say good night."

They parted each to their own chambers. Roderick paced the floor in his room for a bit, but finally succumbed to fatigue as well. He lay in bed staring at the ceiling for what seemed like hours. How could he ever convince the Barrows family his protection was what he promised? Was a duel the only answer?

Teasdale must have it bad to face humiliation by chasing after Elisabeth even after she was affianced to Roderick. Something about this whole business didn't ring solid, but he'd be damned if he could understand what. Sleep was near. He relaxed and allowed it to overcome his worrisome thoughts.

## Chapter Twenty-Eight

Sophia and Elisabeth Barrows entered the black-and-white tiled foyer of the mansion of the Tolberts', Arndt and his wife Doreen. They were chaperoned by their widowed mother, Helen, and the Duke of Roderick with his friend Captain Mark Estermire. The men wore bored expressions, having already professed frankly to the Barrows that a night spent listening to amateur squawking was best avoided. The ladies insisted they had already committed their evening to the Tolberts' musicale and could not abuse their promises with bad manners.

Roderick leaned over and whispered in Elisabeth's ear his approval of her gown. It was one of her latest designs.

"How is it you are managing to look lovelier in each new creation, Lizzie?" he teased. She glared at him at the use of her nickname, which she had forbidden him. Her gown in rose muslin fell in soft folds to a triple lace flounce. The very thin material gave her shoulders the appearance of being almost bare, with the exception of a bead rope twisted around her slender neck. A petite sparkling ruby, borrowed from her mother, hung from the middle of the rope to dangle almost to her décolletage. Her curls were crowned by two small rose-colored feathers twisted around a small ruby pin. Her ears sparkled with matching tiny ruby earbobs. A Norwich shawl draped around her arms, which were covered by white gloves past her elbows. Her slippers were but a scrap of satin barely covering her toes.

Elisabeth took her seat on the second row near a group of her friends who welcomed her gladly.

"Engaged and ignoring us already," teased James Wilkerson. "You are in fine looks tonight, Lizzie." He made room for Sophia on his right. "Where is your fiancé tonight?"

Elisabeth flicked her fan and pointed it over her shoulder. James chuckled when he realized that Roderick had disappeared into a card room set up in the adjourning room.

"Might join him before this is over. Promised my mother I would stay for this deb who is looking for friendly faces tonight. Know her?" he asked casually. He went on to explain the young lady was a daughter of a friend of his mother's from her school days. Elisabeth peeked over Matthew Diver-Jones' shoulder to see a scrap of a young girl sitting on the front row. She waved her fan furiously in front of her bright red face.

"Why they put the debutantes through this nerve-racking exhibit, I do not know," she whispered back. She turned to welcome Jane Hawlester and Eloise Larkin, who settled behind them, chattering and giggling.

"Oh, Miss Elisabeth. That gown is prodigiously wonderful. Which modiste designed it? I must tell my mother to take me there," Miss Larkin said.

Elisabeth gave her the standard answer, keeping her interest in dress design a secret.

The guests chattered with one another until the

noise was exciting the room to capacity. The huge chandelier overhead heated the room, already warmed by the number of human bodies crowded together. Fans were being plied vigorously and often. Fresh air, which would have been welcomed, was kept firmly outside, although it could be debated whether the smoke-laden London atmosphere could be identified as healthy. It would at least be cooling, Elisabeth thought.

The first to entertain was a lovely girl in her first season, plucking the strings of a harp twice her size. It was charming but dull and produced many expressions of *ennui* around the room. Elisabeth was beginning to believe Richard had the right of it. The second performer was the tiny newcomer with the flying fan, a daughter of a friend of Jamie's mother's. Or something like that, thought Elisabeth, sympathizing with the terrified young lady, but when she opened her mouth to sing, all whispering stopped.

It seemed she had a talent. For such a tiny bit of a girl, she had a voice that soared to the roof. She warbled and emoted with such expression as to put Edmund Kean to shame. When the last note ended, applause was thunderous, but there was confusion on the makeshift stage. Elisabeth stood with curiosity and was astonished when her friend pushed by her to reach the front.

James had his arm around the young girl's waist and was assisting her from the room. She was crying and holding up her gown with one hand. Soon they could detect the odor of burnt feathers drifting throughout the room. Elisabeth wondered if she had fainted as well and needed to be revived, or perhaps the lady who swooned was her mortified mother.

"Cast up her accounts, no doubt," Lyndon stated wisely. "Happens sometimes. M' mother says best not to eat before a race. Suspect it's the same here. Too much excitement flips the food." They all turned to stare at Lyndon.

"What?" he asked, eyebrows raised.

"S-something happen to you last night? Charade? Magic? What happened to the real Lyndon Peron?" Matthew Diver-Jones asked staring at his friend with an incredulous expression. Members of the group held their laughter, but snickers broke out intermittently for the next two performances.

Chapter Twenty-Nine

In the card room, Roderick tried diligently to stop a run of bad luck terrorizing a green young man just up from the country. Although the play was not as deep as it could get, still the cards refused to honor the young guest. Perspiration was pouring from his forehead and he held his cards desperately close. The duke wished the poor soul would realize he was in over his head and quit before his losses overwhelmed him. When did the young ever listen? He thought this cub was the offspring and perhaps heir of a country baron who lived near the Scottish border. Just in from the country, no doubt.

Finally, he could stand it no longer and broke up the card game. He clapped the young man on the shoulder and walked him outside where he spotted Matthew Diver-Jones and Lyndon Peron sneaking out of the makeshift theater room.

"What hey," he called over to them, "I see you overcame your deep need for musical talent?" He beckoned to them and introduced Theodore Ragsderit to them with a wink. In spite of the frequent references to being dropped on their heads by their nannies, the cousins were not blockheads. They immediately took hold of the young man's arms and walked out with him.

Roderick nodded with satisfaction. He brushed one hand against another. "That should do it." Those two had been on the town long enough to avoid most pitfalls and would protect the young sprig from the worst.

Richard looked around for Mark, whom he found leaning against the doorway, watching a pretty debutante struggle through a familiar piece were it not for so many mangled notes. He winced at a dissonant chord. He peeked past Mark's shoulder and looked over the still attentive guests.

He spotted the Barrows ladies surrounded still by many of their friends and relaxed his diligence. One more social obligation and they could be away for the country and safe from the viscount and his persistent campaign.

It was still a mystery to him why Teasdale bothered with any one debutante, although he understood the appeal of his love, Elisabeth Barrows. Not to take anything away from her, yet love was not in the nature of what he knew about Teasdale. A horse race, now that was a given. The man would enter into a wager on almost anything. The thought niggled at him, but he dismissed it as being too bizarre to credit.

"I have an appointment in the morning to interview one of the Bow Street runners. Thought I might ask him to investigate the finances of Viscount Teasdale. If Arthur Bridges is desperate for funds, I can understand why he would want to wed Elisabeth Barrows. Not that she doesn't possess ample charms, but never knew Teasdale to care about that."

"It still doesn't add up for him to continue pursuit when her engagement has been formerly announced and posted in the newspaper," Mark said.

"Perhaps the man is stubborn beyond comprehensiveness. He runs with a pretty fast crowd,"

Roderick said. He knew for a fact that several of them drank from morning till they passed out at night. Their adventures were wild and often destructive.

The music ended, and a late supper was offered. Richard wandered back into the room and found Elisabeth and friends arguing over which of tonight's performers had the honor over the other. They welcomed him and suggested he act as judge to pronounce the winner. Since he had not heard anything but the last mangled musical offering, he smilingly refused.

"How did lady luck treat you tonight?" Elisabeth asked tartly. She seemed slightly miffed to be deserted, although reason had it she should have been pleased.

"Oh, so, so. Win some, lose some," he answered, moving with her, his hand at her back as they entered the supper room. He leaned over to inhale her fragrance.

"I met a new friend fresh from the country. Name of Ragsderit. He went off with Diver-Jones and Peron. Think he might enjoy joining our party for the country? I am asking here and there to make up a congenial group. Are there additions you would be pleased to add?" he asked.

She looked up at him with surprise. "You want me to invite guests to your home?" she asked. "What on earth would your mother have to say about someone usurping her authority?" He busied himself with filling her plate with lobster patties.

"She would be delighted to turn over the work to someone congenial. I daresay she will bully your mother into it the minute we arrive." They found a seat near Mark and Sophia.

"Oh, yes. They are friends as I remember," Elisabeth said with a shrug which caused her gown to slide a bit off her shoulders. Roderick observed and stifled a chuckle, as she quickly disguised a tug with a slide of her hand.

"Ah, I see we are not as secure as one might wish," he said slyly to get a rise from her. "What would Lady Sefton say, I wonder?" he added, gazing off into the distance.

"We are not at Almack's, and she would probably ask where I found the design for this dress," Elisabeth retorted.

"One thing I noticed about you, dear Elisabeth. You are never missish. Let me state here and now how much I appreciate that fact," he said, leaning over and whispering in her ear. His breath met curly wisps of her hair, moving them gently. He remembered the fragrance of her mingled with the heady scent of the summer flowers. Would he never stop longing to pull her tightly against his chest and kiss her until she swooned? It was a wonder to him that a grown man could be brought so firmly to his knees by a chit of a girl with blue eyes and curls all over her head. One dimple only.

She looked up and caught his gaze. It was a certainty she read his mind, as her face first flushed, then turned bright red. He admired her courage as she held his stare and gave back as good as he gave. Finally, they both broke the eye lock.

"I was having a wonderful memory, Elisabeth. Are you ever besieged by thoughts of years gone by?" he asked with his mind still afloat on the sea of desire. He spoke quietly so as not to be overheard by others nearby.

"Sometimes," she answered, not pretending ignorance of what he spoke. "But I try to erase such sweet memories. They are overwhelmed by information that rendered them false."

"Ah, love, but they were not false. True feelings were there, just a silly decision to indulge my wishes for privacy in an attempt to go incognito. I loved seeing you dream in Richard's arms. Obviously, you were not there to court a duke, sweet Elisabeth." He took her plate from her and set it on a nearby table, reaching for her hand and leading her into an adjourning room. She followed willingly enough.

"Yes, I loved Richard. I admit my green, country girl indiscretions. I had not been acquainted with very many men when I visited your estate, Roderick.

"What did you love about Richard most?" he asked curiously.

"Ah, you ask, do you? Well, I think it was because he accepted me as I was and did not scold me for my indiscretions. What a total hoyden I was then, always being frowned upon by my parent!

"Now, I think you probably encouraged my wild ways for your own wicked amusements," she added. He could see the one dimple winking in and out of her cheek, but she refused to meet his eyes.

"I confess. It was a delicious sight to watch your happiness and delight. Mine also," he admitted.

"Why did you do it, Roderick? Did you have no feelings for the young girl that I was, to leave me so precipitously? You have no idea how confused I was, how devastated."

"I cannot completely explain away my callousness.

I told myself you would forget about me by week's end, as you claimed you did. Your tender age frightened me. You were a child of the fairies, free from fetters, and I could not lose the title of duke with all the responsibilities that entailed. Does that sound like a fool? Well, I was."

"You held my age against me?" Elisabeth laughed. "I thought I had disgraced myself by breaking all the rules, and you left in disgust of my behavior." She turned to catch his eye. "It was a disastrous end to a lovely week of fantasy, was it not?"

"Oh, you do not, cannot know the half of it. I carried you with me over several countries and under conditions you could never imagine. You were my faithful companion in my daydreams and a delight to remember you at evening."

"But Roderick…it was not you. How could you remember a girl who loved Richard? It is all so confusing to me." She quickly left the room.

Roderick stood frozen. Would she never love the duke that he was and give up the fantasy of her Richard? He shrugged and gave a mental shake to his emotions. One could only try to erase the past. It was a wicked memory for Elisabeth to be abandoned at that age. She was left confused and alone. How could he not have realized the almost criminal results of his choices?

Only twenty now, Elisabeth's behavior was exemplary and exceedingly suited for stepping into the shoes of his mother, if only he could convince her to trust him. Richard longed to ask her in reality to become his duchess. Their time together seemed like a dream to him now. He loved the lady that she was and not the dream from the past.

She had kissed a man named Richard, not a duke. His heart skipped a beat and a pulse throbbed in his neck. What would it be like to have his kisses returned as the Duke of Roderick? Would his Elisabeth kiss him differently or with the same enthusiasm as the novice she had been before? How would she respond if she were tutored by a duke instead of a mere man named Richard? Almost he grinned.

It was a challenge to woo his love, but this time he would convince her as the man with the title. He had a long line of men behind him who had convinced strong women to carry the title of duchess. He would not fail his heritage. He would woo her with all his heart, lay all his worldly goods at her feet, and kiss her until she said yes to his pleas.

He followed Elisabeth from the room and rejoined his party. One thing he knew was on his side: his stables held some of the best horseflesh in the country, and he still owned a mare with a white blaze down her face.

Chapter Thirty

"Have you heard of any plans for an immediate wedding?" Teasdale growled at the man he had hired to spy. So far, his money was wasted. He heard of this foul engagement everywhere he went. That despicable duke had so far successfully intruded into his affairs. Teasdale seemed helpless to stop him, but he had to wrestle Elisabeth Barrows from his clutches. How it had all come about he had no idea. When he rusticated for only a week thinking his father was dying, Roderick moved in and managed to talk the chit into an engagement. Teasdale had to learn of it from the newspapers!

"Probably I need to have him shot," he muttered as he slammed a fist on the table. Meeting this ruffian at a pub in a not-so-desirable part of town had his temper spiking. He had to be careful not to be seen in the bum's company. They may suspect him of haranguing, but he could not be caught for anything more serious.

"No, no, guv'nor. I don't 'old with no killing. 'Ang me from the highest if they find a body. Sure to be blamed for it. No, no. Not me. Be 'appy to be on the look-out for where they go at night, but don't 'old with no murder."

"Devil of a bit, I wasn't talking to you, imbecile. You just keep your nose clean, but follow them wherever they go. Then report back to me what their plans are." He threw a coin on the table and stormed out. Sometimes he wondered how he managed to entangle himself as he had, starting with his father who refused to die.

He didn't know much about his parents. They left him with nannies and then tutors from the earliest time he could remember. He was sent away to school when he was eight years old and holidays were spent in solitary visits to his father's estate. His parents were usually away at some house party or another. When he was around them, they openly preferred his younger brother. He heard his father yell at his mother once that he suspected her of infidelity. Did that mean he was as illegitimate as Ronald Harrison, who was openly supported by a man not legally his parent? No matter. There was nothing his father could do; Arthur Bridges was the heir, false father or no.

Sometimes he looked around the ton for features closely resembling his own, but so far he had not recognized a handsome face that could be his father. What if it was one of the grooms? The horror of it had him breaking out in a sweat. He wasn't well acquainted with his mother. Was she a person of dubious morals? He had little time for women of his own order, nor, for that matter, had he successfully managed to keep a mistress. They complained he was too rough and didn't pay them enough.

He had settled on Elisabeth Barrows as his choice to wife. What had she to complain about? He was a viscount, for God's sake. Did that mean nothing to the simpering idiot? Preferred a duke, did she? Well, in all honesty, he couldn't really fault her for that. Not that her family was hurting for funds, but he imagined titles went a long way with the wives. If only he could afford to let it go! This scrape would put him under permanently. He had to break up that engagement one way or the other.

"Teasdale. Arthur Bridges," he heard, but could not spot anyone in the crowded street.

Finally a redhead popped from around a big, burly farmer pushing a cart loaded with potatoes down the street.

"Oh, it's you, Harrison," he said disinterestedly. "What's with you? Been off tipping the watch again, have you?" He kept walking, meaning to attain the apartment of a crony for a card game.

"No, well, yes, but that's not what I came to tell you. I have news of a particular interest to you. And me, for that matter." He huffed to keep up with the viscount's long stride.

"What now? I already know about the engagement. Nothing I can do to stop it for now. It's in the papers." Some days he just did not like looking at this toady.

"Did you know he is taking a party to his estate next week? They will rusticate in the country indefinitely so I hear. What say that to your plans?" He grimaced when Teasdale whirled on him with a menacing stare.

"They would not leave while the season is still in full swing. What lies are you telling me now?" A sinking feeling in his stomach had him suspecting it was not a lie.

"No lie. Got it from that captain what is a friend of Roderick. Overheard him making arrangements for some high steppers he's hiring for the remove. Seems they've got quite a house party planned. Lots of guests, chaperones, and servants packing, too. He's hired a coach just for the servants. No way you can reach that filly now with her holed up at Roderick's estate." He chortled at his cleverness, but ducked when the viscount took a swing at him.

Teasdale whirled around and headed back to his apartments. Harrison followed, almost running to catch up. The viscount was furious and maddened with frustration. He had to make plans. This could not happen. He had made a fatal mistake to get entangled with Elisabeth Barrows, but he was into it now. Serious plans would be necessary to get his hands on that aggravating chit and away from the Duke of Roderick. How? The estate covered miles and miles of tenant farms owned by the lord. A stranger in that land would be noticed and reported immediately. He had to admit Roderick was brilliant to remove from Town and take his party with him.

He turned to Harrison. "Do you know of a way into that warren? You have a vested interest in this excursion, too. I know you. You would have snooped into the affairs of the duke. Give over, do!" he demanded while Harrison smirked.

## Chapter Thirty-One

Captain Mark Estermire left the stables where he had hired several extra strong horses to pull the equipment needed to remove the Barrows family to the country. It was no small task to remove so many people as they intended. The trip would be accomplished in two easy stages so as not to disrupt the health of the older ladies. He was taking care of the details, leaving Roderick to wrap up any political contacts necessary before he left Town.

The duchess would be traveling in Roderick's barouche, a fast and fancy carriage with a fold-up hood, seating as many as six people, if they were not stout, four if they were. He guessed there would be only four, as Roderick's mother was a bit on the heavy side. Doretha Smyth, the duchess's companion, would be with her as well as her maid and dresser. He'd hired a Berlin, a huge carriage needing four horses to pull it, for baggage and some of the servants. Most of the invited males would ride their own mounts. How they would manage the rest of their necessities, he did not know. He had not been assigned that task, thank goodness.

"I have no idea how many guests have been invited," he said to the owner of the stables. "It's a mystery to me as well." Estermire had been a guest on several of these enormous house parties at Roderick's request, but there had been none since they'd been back in the country. This time however, he would have the pleasure of his fiancée, Sophia, to keep him company. His happiness was almost a tangible thing to him. Never had he predicted her forgiveness and acceptance of his request for her hand in marriage. He had hoped, of course.

A pity that Roderick and Elisabeth could not as easily settle their own affairs. Estermire did understand his future sister-in-law's feelings. It was a betrayal to be lied to and, from what Sophia had relayed, Elisabeth felt humiliated by what she thought of as Roderick's game playing. He did not understand the duke himself, but perhaps it had to do with being chased for his title. Most thought it wonderful to be so titled with all the funds a person could use. They failed to understand the responsibilities that accompanied the title. It must be hell never to be certain whether a person was loved for himself or only for his wealth and title.

The captain shivered and turned around to catch that scoundrel Ronald Harrison peering around the stable door at him.

"Do you have business with me, Harrison?" he asked sternly, understanding that the worm did not.

"Oh, hello, Estermire," he said with a sneer that disguised as a friendly greeting. "Didn't see you there."

"Since you were sneaking around and staring at me, I wonder you didn't," he retorted acerbically. "I know I have no business with you, so farewell." Estermire walked swiftly out of the stables and down the street. He thought the man must be spying on him and wondered if Teasdale had put him up to it. Well, the only thing he would learn was that soon his efforts to harass the Barrows ladies would be at an end.

He entered his apartment to dress. Roderick and he intended to visit Sophia and Elisabeth at their at-home day momentarily. He found the duke at his desk in the library, sleeves rolled up and a stack of papers at his elbow.

"I say, Roderick. Do you still intend to visit the ladies today? It's almost time."

"Damn and blast. I cannot just yet. I promised my solicitor this morning I would attend to some business that must be finished before I leave. Will you tender my apologies for me? I may get over there before too late, but it's doubtful," he said, glaring at the papers.

"Will do. I must dress in haste now. I will be back at four or later. Good luck."

He left wearing his uniform. Although he had sold out, his new clothes were still pending at the tailors. He whistled jauntily as he walked briskly down the street. It was a fine day and he was enjoying the exercise. He tipped his hat at others out for a stroll in the sunshine. Knocking gaily on the Barrows' front door, he was admitted by their butler. He welcomed Estermire with a slight smile, taking his hat and mentioning that the ladies and their guests were in the front parlor. Mark entered eagerly, searching through the guests for his love. And stared directly into the sneering face of Viscount Teasdale ensconced on one of the parlor chairs. He was surrounded by a crowd of young people chatting and visiting noisily.

Confused, he hesitated and took the hands of Sophia as she appeared out of the group and came hurriedly toward him.

"Don't make a fuss," she whispered. "He came to

apologize. My mother allowed him to come in, but Elisabeth excused herself after he said his piece. We do not want to create a scandal, my love. Please?" She took him by the hand and led him to her mother.

"Captain, we have an unexpected visitor, do we not?" Helen said quietly. "Perhaps he will go away now that Elisabeth is not in the room. So far, his manners have been unexceptional." She stood and walked with him to a sofa by the window. "Sit here with Sophia and let us try and ignore him. Soon he will tire of the chatter. When we see the *ennui* on his face, we will know we have succeeded. We want no scandal, Captain," she said firmly.

"When will Roderick get here?" she asked as they settled on the window seat.

"He sends his regrets. His solicitor has him in tow, but he mentioned he might come if he finishes soon. Should I send a servant to fetch him?" he asked.

"I cannot ascertain which would be best. Should Roderick lose his temper, we would be in the boughs. But if his presence warned Teasdale he should leave, then yes. Which do you think? Advise me," she asked with a smile.

"I think we should err on the side of his presence. May I take the liberty of speaking to one of your footmen?" Estermire stood and left the room at a nod from Helen Barrows.

He dispatched the footman to make speed and returned to the room. Sophia, with her usual calm demeanor, had taken up needlework, and her mother had returned to her set, who gathered at one end of the parlor. He glanced over at the crowd of young people where Teasdale had taken a seat and spotted him making conversation with the man known as Chubs. Estermire didn't think he had ever known the young man's real name. He could hear the conversation had drifted into the subject of racing.

"I am trying desperately to calm my own temper," he said softly to Sophia. She nodded her understanding, giving him a flash of her eyes, by which the captain understood his love was struggling with her own strong feelings.

"Whatever could have encouraged him to expect hospitality from this household?" he said, clenching his teeth. He turned his head to see Viscount Teasdale shaking hands with Chubs. He had a sneaking feeling he knew what that was about. The sly viscount was setting up another green youngster to race and destroy. What a despicable human being.

After a few more minutes, Teasdale took his leave. The room settled back into a normal routine and a maid was sent to fetch Elisabeth. The butler was escorting Roderick in just as she made her appearance. He came over to her immediately.

"Elisabeth, reassure me, I beg you. I understand you received a visitor?" She smiled up at him and allowed him to hold her hands.

"I am in great health, Your Grace, and I thank you for your concern. It was a shock, but we survived it."

"What was that imbecile about? He had no reason to be here except to cause you uneasiness." He drew her into the room and settled on a sofa near the window seat holding Sophia and the captain.

"He asked to see my mother, and she made the decision to admit him. He claimed he was here to beg my pardon for his rudeness in the park the other day.

His behavior was unexceptional. We did not desire a commotion to create a scandal, Roderick. I left the room as soon as he tendered his message. Did he just leave?" she asked Sophia, who nodded.

"Teasdale spent the rest of his time trapping that one called Chubs into a race. I saw him shake hands with the young man after they talked of racing. You know his habit, Roderick. He has probably made bets and will cheat him out of his pocket money."

"How sad!" Elisabeth exclaimed. "How can we stop him from taking advantage of someone in our own front parlor?"

Richard threw back his head and laughed loud and long. The other three stared at him bemused, seeing nothing amusing in this episode.

"I beg your pardon," Richard said wiping his eyes. "If Teasdale thinks to fleece that young man, he has another think coming. That boy can drive to an inch. His father breeds racehorses and Chubs grew up testing them out. I buy many of my prime goers from his stud farm."

Light dawned on the faces of the other three and on Helen's who overheard. Amusement grew until they all wiped their eyes in glee that Teasdale had finally stumbled over his own feet. It was a welcome relief from the stress of the afternoon.

"Tomorrow we go to the Atkinson's ball, do we not?" Richard asked after a period of calm was restored.

"Yes," Helen answered. "We are obligated, or else I would suggest we leave on our trip early. You will provide us escort, Roderick?" He nodded.

"Of course, I will." He turned to Elisabeth. "Do you have your red riding habit packed and ready? I know a white-faced mare who is longing to check your pocket for a sugar cube." Elisabeth's face turned from solemn to a picture of happiness at the mention of her favorite mount.

"I did not know if she was still in your stables. Oh, Roderick. Do you say I may ride her once more?"

Roderick chuckled and urged her into a chair, where he regaled her with exploits on the hunting field until her eyes were shining and she clasped her hands in eagerness.

Chapter Thirty-Two

That night at the Barrows household, all three ladies decided on one more visit to Almack's before they left for the country. Helen saw no reason to be absent since Viscount Teasdale had never been allowed vouchers. The captain and Roderick begged to be excused since good friends Matthew Diver-Jones and Lyndon Peron stepped up for escort duties.

Elisabeth mentioned her desire to stay home with one of the new novels making the rounds. Her mother demurred mentioning they must not appear to be in fear of anyone. "As long as we continue to behave normally, gossip will move onto the next exciting scandal." Elisabeth went upstairs to dress.

"I'm wearing my ice blue gown, Sophia. I've been avoiding it since the first night Roderick and Mark appeared at the dance." She pulled on her elbow-length gloves and reached for her white silk shawl.

"We still need something exciting for the ball tomorrow night. What have you saved for that?" Sophia arranged a pale yellow shawl around her shoulders. She wore a pastel green gown trimmed in white lace with a small train. They were ready to depart and had called for the carriage. Matthew and Lyndon were meeting them at the door.

"Not certain. I confess I have given the Atkinson's ball scarce thought. In fact, I seem to have lost my

221

appetite for most social activities. I hate to admit it, and only to you, Sister, but this thing with Teasdale and then the fake engagement with Roderick have begun to stress me. I wish we were already on our way to the country."

"I understand, Lizzie. Really I do, but...are you certain you cannot like Roderick? He seems so taken with you and...he is so big. He makes me feel safe even with Mark around; his air of authority is comforting. I know that part of the reason is his title. It's not every day we consort with a duke, is it?" She laughed a little, and then she put her arms around her sister and gave her a hug.

"I know this is difficult for you. I don't mean to scold or try to convince you to do anything you do not wish to do. I'm sorry, Lizzie."

"I understand it would be easier for everyone if I just accepted Roderick's apology, and everyone would go back to normal. I wonder why I cannot," Elisabeth said, a tear rolling down her cheek.

"You were so hurt that he deceived you, first his rude behavior to leave so abruptly, then to learn of his willful deceptions. I shouldn't wonder if you are still struggling to forgive him. Are you so unhappy with this public engagement? I wonder that Mother could find no other solution to that wicked viscount's persistence."

"I am grateful. I do not wish to seem churlish. Roderick has rescued me again, but this time, at least, it is not from my own folly. I cannot explain it to you exactly, Sophia." She sat down on the chaise lounge and stared out the window into the deepening twilight.

"It is all so confusing. Sometimes I feel as if I were that young girl again talking to a wonderful man I called my Noble Rescuer, and truly, I had no desire to know his real name. I was living in a wonderful fantasy. I know half the blame for this deception is my own. If I had demanded to know his actual identity, he might have confessed."

She turned as her mother entered the room scolding. "You two are causing those poor horses to wait, not to mention the young men. Are you finished dressing? I can see you are, and you both are fine." She waved her hands to encourage them to leave their bedroom. "Let us go. You know if we arrive tardy, we will certainly be refused entry. We are going to Almack's, after all."

****

They arrived as the dancing had already begun. Matthew whispered in Elisabeth's ear. "S-so many here tonight. You want to give me the first and the supper dance? S-steal a march on old Lyndon there, what hey?" She chuckled, as he meant her to do. Why could she not love a man like Matthew? He was honest, faithful and he made her laugh. Life was so very confusing. Her heart longed to belong to the duke, while her head refused to accept his apology.

In the corner sat the chaperones, her mother among them. Beside her, with her eye monitoring her young charge, Jane Hawlester, sat the duchess. She was a regal woman who occupied her chair with a very straight back and seemed years younger than Elisabeth knew her to be. Her nose, which looked noble on Roderick, was a bit too long on a female, but her hair, still mostly black, was luminous and thick. Her dresser had it piled high atop her head, Elisabeth presumed, to add height to the diminutive duchess, who had widened over the years. Her mother and Roderick's had become firm friends. She shuddered. The thought of informing the duke's mother she wished to end the engagement made her feel sick.

Matthew claimed her for his promised dance, and she determined to forget her problems and enjoy the exercise. Jane and Lyndon Peron were in the same square when the young men turned it into a sporting event, pushing their partners fiercely around the floor. Elisabeth stifling her giggles, admonished Matthew to calm down before they lost their vouchers forever. He protested saying, "S-sorry, Miss Elisabeth. You know it's the fault of that s-slow top, Lyndon. He is s-so competitive, he can't even dance without causing a race to break out. S-see, even that big fellow dancing with Sophia has entered the event."

Sophia was indeed flying around the dance floor with the huge brother of Eloise's, Edward Larkin. Her head was thrown back and she was laughing. What? Was that her serene sister causing a ruckus at Almack's? An engagement must be a wonderful thing if a person were in love with her fiancé. The thought caused the smile to disappear from Elisabeth's face and Matthew, probably detecting her mood change, twirled her around more vigorously.

They returned to the sofa which had been staked out by her group of friends. New to their entourage was a fellow named Theodore Ragsderit, a ruddy-faced young man with a rolling brogue. When asked if he was a Scot, he vigorously denied any such thing.

"People who live near the border have an accent," he explained. "I'm English, don't you know," he said with a decided Scots accent. Elisabeth liked him immediately although she cringed to recognize his naiveté.

"Pleasure to meet you, Miss Elisabeth. Misinformed. Was told you were engaged to Viscount Teasdale. Mr. Diver-Jones tells me that is an error. Sorry. Will set it about that you are *not* to be married to the viscount."

"No, I am not," Elisabeth said between clenched teeth and turned away. She wanted to protest she was engaged to the Duke of Roderick but realized how ridiculous that sounded. The truth was that she was engaged to nobody.

She wondered who was spreading the rumor she was to marry Teasdale. It could not be the viscount himself. Even he would not go that far. Would this nightmare never end? If she were a man she would call the dastardly lord out.

Sophia came up to her with a frown. "Lizzie, there are rumors flying around the room that you are not to marry Roderick, but Teasdale. Can you believe it?"

"Yes, I just heard from Ragsderit, that fellow from up North. He didn't say where he heard it from, but obviously it's a widespread *on dit*. I hope Mother doesn't hear it and fly into the bows. I could not blame her. I'm so tired of his detestable pranks, I could scream."

"Do you think it's the viscount telling everyone? Perhaps he has lost his mind?"

Elisabeth had to laugh. Sophia was so gentle she could not fathom the wickedness of a person without guessing insanity.

"Certainly it must have originated from him. Why is he so persistent? He cannot have affection for me. It must be his spirit of competition, but does he think to break an engagement in order to force me into marriage with him? It sounds outrageous, and I might even call it bizarre." Elisabeth faked a smile as her next partner came to claim her hand for a country dance.

A young man whose name escaped Elisabeth for the moment spoke to her as they passed each other in the dance. "Must felicitate you on your engagement, Miss Elisabeth. Thought you were to marry Roderick; must be mistaken. Hear now you have decided to take Teasdale." They parted as the dance called for changing partners. Elisabeth sizzled.

"Mr. Martin," Elisabeth said, finally remembering his name. "I am not now nor have I ever been engaged to the Viscount Teasdale. Please help me crush that sad rumor. How embarrassing for the viscount, since it is not true." She arranged a pleasant expression on her face, trying to unclench her teeth, determined not to allow her anger to add fuel to the situation.

"Beg pardon! Dreadful *faux pas*. A bit of a slow top all m'life, but meant no disrespect. Pray you will not relate my misunderstanding to Roderick. Crack shot. He sports the fancy, has a sweet right cross." Martin continued to babble all the way back to the sofa where her friends waited. Almost she was amused at his frantic attempts to undo what he perceived an insult to Roderick—but not to her.

She glanced over at her mother and recognized from the set look on her face that she too was receiving congratulations on her engagement to Teasdale. There was no change to the pleasant demeanor of the duchess. Perhaps she was relieved to be rid of the hoyden who was Elisabeth Barrows. Tears came to her eyes when she saw the duchess reach over and give her mother a small hug.

The two ladies stood and strolled slowly around the room, speaking to many acquaintances along the way. Eventually, they arrived at the favorite sofa of Elisabeth, Sophia, and their friends. Sophia rose from the sofa and stood chatting with her mother.

The Duchess of Roderick sank gracefully into the empty space beside Elisabeth, leaned over and whispered, "Never fear, my dear. He will not win in the end. He is a dreadful, stubborn young man, is he not?" She trilled a laugh. "Handsome to a stare, but so very absorbed in only himself.

"His parents were a pair of the most selfish young people anyone ever saw. Teasdale has no idea how wicked he really is, I suppose. Raised entirely by hired nannies and sent away to school at too early an age. Sad, really." She held hands with Elisabeth and studied her arm where a small bracelet rested over her gloves.

"I wonder how this one would look with the blue of your dress." She pulled a bracelet encircled with sapphires from her own arm and slipped it over Elisabeth's.

"Oh, my lady! It is very beautiful, but I could not…" She stopped speaking when the duchess held up a hand.

"It is not one of the family heirlooms, my dear. Never fear. You will be encumbered with those relics soon enough. This one is mine, a gift from the duke— Roderick's father, you know—on the birth of my son. I will not mention how happy it would make me if I became a grandmother. No, I said I would not mention it." She chuckled as Elisabeth ducked and hid her face with her hands.

"He loves you, you know, my dear. I think he admires your spirit. Yes, I am aware of the scam to pretend an engagement to ward off this persistent Teasdale. Your mother was forthright in informing me not to become too hopeful. You two have had a disagreement, I understand." Elisabeth could only nod the truth of it.

"Well, young people will ever scrape and fuss. If he does not please you, you certainly have my permission to cast him out of your life. Do not fret, Elisabeth. Your mother and I are in total agreement on this head, but do know I would welcome you into my family gladly. You are to visit with us soon?" Elisabeth, still too overcome for words, could only nod once more.

The duchess squeezed her hand, admired how becoming the bracelet appeared on Elisabeth's arm, rose and left with her mother. Sophia sank down beside her and laughed. "That ought to put an end to these dreadful rumors, think you, Sister?" Once more Elisabeth could only nod as Sophia held up her arm and admired the sapphire bracelet.

Elisabeth wondered did she become the new duchess, could she ever be as gracious as this mother of Roderick's? She had such admiration for this lady, and was so very thankful her mother had explained the false engagement. At least her conscience could relax on that subject.

All around the room Elisabeth could see heads turning toward her, some with a smile, others whispering behind their fans. She continued to maintain a pleasant expression, dance whenever asked, and visit with her friends. She knew patience was required and fortitude to withhold the anger she felt. The futility of releasing her fury to some unknown was more frustrating that anything. Who had started the disgusting rumors? She looked around the room but could not spot anyone she thought might be evil enough to try and harm her reputation.

"Perhaps the person who whispered it might have thought it was legitimate," Sophia offered. "If someone spoke to them before the evening started, they would have no reason to think it false." She spoke behind her fan to her sister.

"You may have figured out the puzzle, Sophie. That is certainly feasible. I cannot see anyone in this room who would be interested enough to speak that falsehood.

"So we conclude Teasdale or someone in his pay—I doubt he has very many friends—took careful aim at my reputation and started a whispering campaign. It's beginning to sound like a farce. We could take this folly onto the stage before long," she said bitterly. "You know, Sophie, after what happened two years ago, I have carefully followed all of society's rules. See how I am rewarded?"

"You have been so good, I know. None of this is to be laid at your feet. Mark tells me Teasdale causes problems wherever his eye lands. Never mind. The duchess has scotched the rumor quite thoroughly. We will hear no more of that tonight. Let us talk of pleasant things, shall we?"

On the ride home, Helen Barrows shared an amusing anecdote of the duchess before she became wife to the duke. "Youth has its problems, Lizzie, my love, and must ever struggle to achieve maturity. I doubt the viscount will ever make the change. He is too selfish to see any viewpoint but his own. We are lucky Roderick has offered to see us through this unpleasant episode. However you feel toward him, you must recognize his noble efforts to protect your reputation."

"I do, Mother. Of course I do. One of the first character traits I learned of Roderick was his willingness to sacrifice himself for others. Perhaps that is why I am so very stubborn now. He sat on a high pedestal in my mind, so the distance to fall was great. It was not his fault, I see, but my own for expectations too grand."

"He is a man, Daughter, not a saint. I think he accepts you just as you are, think you?" With that Elisabeth burst into tears.

"Why whatever has you upset now?" her mother questioned. "This is no time for you to become missish, Lizzie."

"She is feeling stressed. We talked earlier, Mother," Sophia said. "It is becoming all too much for her." Elisabeth gulped and dried her tears.

"You have found the very thing I cannot refute. Roderick, who I knew as Richard, accepted me exactly as he found me two years ago, a perfect hoyden ripe for any adventure and careless of her own reputation. It was his most endearing trait, and naïve and green as I was, I loved him for it. You remember how often and mostly fruitlessly you were trying to teach me the ways of society?"

"And now you hold him to a much higher standard than he did for you?" Helen asked. "It is causing you conflict because you realize the unfairness of your attitude. Am I correct, Daughter?" Elisabeth nodded and gulped back her tears.

"Still, I cannot overcome my disappointment that he deceived me. I try, but my heart is stubborn. It loves but does not trust. My thinking is that one without the other is but a poor substitute for the whole."

"I cannot fault you for that line of logic. You will work out your own problems, and that's as it should be. One thing only I will point out to you. How have you changed in two years? Know that you are not the only person who could see mistakes and desire to correct them. And that is all I'm going to say about that." She nodded her head and dismissed the subject.

"We are to attend the costume ball tomorrow night. Have the two of you decided on your dress?" They heard the coachman signal to the horses to slow down in preparation for stopping.

Sophia sighed. "We finally choose to execute a mite of deceit ourselves. You remember our costumes from last year? We are going to wear them, but exchange. I will be a shepherdess and Lizzie is to change to mine. She will don the sea nymph gown I wore last year. We will both be masked, so what fun to trick our friends who might remember the gowns. Do you approve, Mother?"

Helen laughed and clapped her hands. "Perfect. You are clever daughters," she said as they left the carriage and entered their townhouse.

Chapter Thirty-Three

Elisabeth was amused to see her sister dressed as a shepherdess, a gingham bonnet covering her chestnut hair and a white sequined mask disguising all but the lower half of her face. This was the one fallacy they had to overcome; one blonde and the other brunette would be too easily identified by their hair. Sophia's bonnet did the trick easily enough, but a sea nymph was a more difficult matter.

Finally Elisabeth's clever maid fashioned a cap from a silk scrap that fit tightly over her curls and trailed down her back, sparkling crystals sprinkled throughout. Over that they fashioned a golden green mask that slipped over her face, leaving only her eyes, nose, and mouth free. Finished dressing, they joined their mother in her dressing room for a test.

Helen gurgled in amusement when the sisters presented their costumes.

"I cannot tell you apart, and the familiar costumes suggest the opposite of what you are. This is a diabolical idea to say the least. You will learn each other's secrets tonight, daughters. Are you ready to share?" Both ladies flicked their fans in a coy flirt and laughed slyly with their mother.

"We have no secrets from each other fortunately, Mother," Elisabeth said folding her fan and adjusting her gloves. Her gown was wispy, closely cut muslin but with an underskirt in shades of pale green. She appeared as if she had recently surfaced from the sea. Her reticule, which Sophia had fashioned herself last year, resembled a folded pink shell as it dangled from her arm.

"Your costume is tight, Lizzie. Are you able to dance in it?" her mother asked. "I do not want you splitting a seam in an attempt."

"It could use a bit more material, but I am able to move. I do not think it will prove troublesome for this one night. I will endeavor to treat it delicately." She flicked her fan once more and made small swimming motions with her hands, setting her relatives to laughing again.

"The kitchen has sent up a small tea for us before we go. Never count on that family to have food enough for such a crowd as they invite. It will no doubt be a sad crush, as usual." Helen motioned her daughters to join her for tea and biscuits.

"Does Roderick escort us tonight?" she asked. Elisabeth shook her head.

"He sent over a note saying he would meet us at the ball. I have no clue what costume he wears. How about the captain, Sophia? Is he meeting you there as well?"

"Yes, I think they plan to surprise us with disguises. They did not see our costumes last year, so may not be as deceived as our friends. I shall pretend I do not know him even if I do. Then I will flirt with a handsome pirate as if a stranger when all the time I am aware it is Mark Estermire in my company," Sophia said, grinning.

"What if that pirate is not Mark, then what will you

do?" Elisabeth asked.

"Oh, la!" Sophia said, shaking her shepherdess staff at Elisabeth. "Surely I will recognize my own fiancé, if only by his voice."

Elisabeth assured her, but advised she be careful before she engaged in flirting. "By which I am assuming you mean like this." She opened her fan and smiled behind it to make her eyes seem laughing.

"You are too good. Lizzie. When did you perfect the art of flirting with your fan?" Elisabeth only smiled and refused to answer.

They finished their tea and called for the carriage. While a private masquerade ball was exciting, and they were looking forward to innocent fun, they were to set off on their journey to the country in the morning. Elisabeth's spirits lifted as she realized the stress of dealing with Viscount Teasdale would soon be over. She would be safe at the Duke of Roderick's estate.

*I always felt safe with my Noble Rescuer. I still do.*

The night was dry, with a moon peeking now and then from a covering of wispy, broken clouds. The line of vehicles was long, and it was a full half hour before it was their turn to leave the carriage. Helen Barrows was splendid as Cleopatra. Elisabeth swelled with pride at their beautiful mother. Angels, devils, ancient kings and queens, Shakespearean characters, sprites, and more filed past them, some greeting Sophia as Elisabeth and vice versa. The fun had begun just as they predicted. Their friends were mixing up the sisters, remembering the costumes from the year before.

Elisabeth's hand was begged permission by a giant wearing a leather vest and a mask that resembled an executioner's. She thought perhaps this was the tall brother of one of their friends, Edward Larkin, who usually danced with Sophia. He leaned down and whispered, "Hello, Miss Barrows." A twinge of conscience speared her and she whispered back, "I am Elisabeth, but it's a secret." He laughed heartily, and she was pleased she had shared the truth with him.

Sophia met with Elisabeth at the end of the dance and, still giggling, her sister related a conversation she'd had with Matthew Diver-Jones, who thought she was Elisabeth. "I fear this ruse is too wicked. Our friends are confused." Elisabeth confessed she had told the truth to one of Sophia's particular friends.

"Oh, Edward Larkin. Did I ever tell you he asked permission to pay court to me, Lizzie? I like him very well, but I refused. You know why, I presume."

"Yes," Elisabeth said and sighed. "We were bitten by some dreadful love bug when we were on a country visit." Sophia laughed and agreed she certainly had been bitten.

"Have you spotted Richard and Mark?" she asked peering around the room. Elisabeth shook her head no.

There were some creatures who did not wear a mask, but most did. Quite a few black dominoes were preferred by men. It was a formidable sight to see the black capes topped by equally menacing masks, like evil magicians. If a female elected a domino, she preferred more colorful red, blue, and occasionally pink. One spectacular gold one stood out in the crowd and Elisabeth thought perhaps it was Lady Jersey, an already flamboyant personality. Her mask was on a holder, which she allowed to slip now and then to reveal her identity.

The music drifted over the noisy crowd and a

Roman soldier bowed before her to beg a dance. Instantly, she knew it to be Lyndon Peron.

"Honored if you'll take to the floor with me, Miss Sophia," he said holding out his arm. Elisabeth nodded instead of speaking, afraid her distinctive voice would give her away. She intended to keep him wondering until at least the end of the dance. But he guessed halfway through.

"You laughed and I heard your voice, Miss Elisabeth. Always guess you. Clever trick you play on your friends," he said, admiring their ingenuity. "Slow-top cousin of mine did not guess when he danced with Miss Barrows."

"No, he did not. How chagrined he will be later, do you think?" she answered.

"He will know if you laugh or speak. Careful to keep your voice hidden when he finds you," he warned. As predicted, Matthew Diver-Jones did find her and did almost instantly guess.

"Thought you were the s-shepherdess like last year, Miss Elisabeth. Miss Barrows fooled me." He was costumed as Caesar with a white robe and a circlet of leaves on his head, but no mask. Elisabeth was amused to see a pair of trousers peeking out from underneath his white robe and a shining pair of Hessians taking to the dance floor with her. She presumed Matthew felt safer with his lower half covered.

"Why did you guess my identity so quickly," she protested. "What could give me away?"

"Bit taller. Could tell when we danced. Voice. You know anyone will guess your voice," he said.

"I can never be mysterious to my friends," she declared, teasing him with her fan. "Do you travel with us to Roderick's tomorrow?" she asked.

"Not tomorrow. S-Soon though. Familial duties, don't you know. Heard there was a race planned. Eager to enter my new mount. You s-see him yet?" he asked.

"I did not know about the race. I suppose it's only for the men," she said. "I am disappointed nothing like that can be for the women." They walked back to the corner where a glamorous Cleopatra entertained several Roman senators.

"S-Speak to Roderick, mind you. Know he'll take your wishes in consideration. Loves you. Heard. Would have asked you myself, only not reached my majority yet. Roderick is best though. Be a duchess, don't you know?" He helped her seat herself in a chair near her mother.

"If I become a duchess, will you still be my friend, Mr. Diver-Jones?" she asked, peering at him over her fan. She laughed when his face flushed rosy red, and his olive leaf circlet threatened to slip over one eye.

"Miss Elisabeth, pledge lifelong devotion," he said simply with his hand over his heart. Elisabeth believed him. He was a stalwart young man and would make an excellent husband someday. She left off teasing him.

A pirate bowed before her, his eye patch not disguising Mr. Theodore Ragsderit, sporting his new nickname. "Just call me Rags, Miss Elisabeth. Beg you will dance with me?" he asked bowing over her hand.

"How about I call you Mr. Rags?" she said. "How did you know I am Elisabeth and not my sister?"

"Heard you speaking to the Roman soldier. Know your voice now. Pretty sound." Elisabeth nodded, despairing of fooling anyone tonight. She jolted when she saw a figure, who she thought was Viscount

Teasdale. He was dressed in a black domino with a black mask, but she thought she recognized his distinctive blond hair. He was dancing with a maid who might be dressed as Rosalind. Thank goodness it was not Sophia. As she watched, he disappeared into the crowd.

She wound her way toward her sister, who was standing with several guests in costume who she assumed were their friends. The ballroom was full to overflowing, and it was difficult to navigate without stopping to visit with first one soldier or a character from the earlier century. Powdered wigs were popular items to match heavy brocade and satin gowns.

Just as she feared, a black domino appeared behind her and touched her arm. A low voice urged her onto the dance floor just as the sound of the strings proclaimed a waltz. She whirled past him and approached her sister who held out her hands welcoming her. Behind her stood another black domino, who stepped forward and took her in his arms.

Richard, she knew in a minute, had her safe. They took to the dance floor with him holding her snugly without a murmur between them. She relaxed and allowed the peace to fill her. Just for a moment, she would put aside her disappointment and enjoy a dance with the man she…well, a man she loved.

As the music wound to a close, Richard steered her toward the French windows and onto a stone patio. With an enormous chandelier filled with tiny lamps overhead and so many revelers in the room, it had become stifling hot. She breathed a cooling breath gratefully as Roderick guided her further into a garden dimly lit with lanterns.

"More comfortable, my Elisabeth?" he asked in a low voice. How could she pretend ignorance of his intentions when she welcomed them with all her heart? He ducked them behind a dense shrubbery and pulled her tightly to him.

"Pretend I am a handsome stranger, my dear. A stranger who rescued you from a frightful fate and now claims a reward." She could see the outlines of his head against the moonlight. "Remember, it was a very frightful fate, and the reward must be comparative." His lips found hers, but gently, as if he were uncertain whether she would push him away.

She lifted her head to allow him greater access to her lips. She craved the touch of his mouth on hers. He tugged at the mask until it pulled away from her face. Already he had discarded his own. His mouth came down on hers more firmly and rested there, barely moving. Pulling her firmly to his body, he groaned as his mouth began to move slowly across hers. Her pulse throbbed and strange feelings sent a shudder down her body. He gathered her close, and Elisabeth did not know who was sighing; it might be her. She felt like a victim of the desert denied water for too long. Her thirst for his mouth on hers could not be quenched. She wanted more. His hands slid down and caressed her shoulders and back, while she entangled her fingers in his hair. He pulled her firmly against him and she knew his desire. Even as her heart felt as if it would explode, a distant thought reminded her they were in public, with the chance of company at any moment. Reluctantly, she pulled away, but he tugged her back against him.

"Not yet," he murmured. "I've wanted you for so very long, sweetness."

"Roderick, we must cease this. Look where we are, for heaven's sake." He murmured something indistinguishable as his mouth moved down her neck and over one of her bare shoulders—bare? How could she resist such a delicious touch?

Suddenly Richard pulled away, then opened his domino and wrapped it around her so that she disappeared inside it completely. She gurgled with laughter as she realized his plan. Who could tell who was kissing the tall domino now? She relaxed against him, hidden inside the voluminous cape.

Richard held her close; her head nestled on his shoulder. "I've missed you so very much, Lizzie. I so want you to take me to husband. Love, do you think you could just think about it?" His hands were caressing, and she slipped her arms around his waist. He was a big man, her Richard, and she was barely able to reach around him.

Resting her forehead against his white shirt, she sniffed his fragrance. God help her, but she remembered it. She rubbed her cheek there, then placed her ear against his chest and listened for his heartbeat. It was, as she expected, beating as rapidly as her own.

"Your Grace?" she murmured, with her face still resting on his chest.

He leaned down and murmured a question, but did not release her.

"We must end this. It has no future this night, although I will confess it was a pleasant interlude." She felt him stiffen and smothered a laugh.

"Pleasant interlude! You are the mistress of understatement, are you not, Lizzie?"

He quickly found her mouth again and, when she

moaned, began to tease her with his tongue. The pleasure was intense, almost painful, and she longed for a finish to the urgency she felt. She almost swooned with pleasure and thought her knees would buckle. How much more would this man teach her about love?

Roderick gently released her and slowly allowed space to come between them.

"I'm sorry, Lizzie. You are correct. This is not the place for prolonged kissing. Can you forgive me once again? Although it pains me to ask, because I have enjoyed your closeness more than you will ever know. Tell me you also liked it?" He smoothed her gown and dropped the cape. Lizzie fought to steady her legs as he let her go.

"It was fun," she said, trying for casualness, but stumbled as she turned around to leave the garden. Roderick caught her with a soft chuckle and held her for a moment with his arms wrapped around her.

"Easy, sweetheart. Take a minute to come back to normal. Kisses will weaken the knees, you know," he said, nibbling on her ear. It was not helping, so she forced herself to move a little away.

Silently regaining her balance, she came back from where ever it was that she had flown with Richard's kisses stealing her breath away. Slowly sanity infused her brain again, and she stepped away from him.

"Stay you there, Roderick. I will find my way back in without you." With that she ducked around the shrubbery and left him in the garden. Inside, she found Sophia and heard a hilarious story about an almost kidnapping.

Chapter Thirty-Four

The entourage left town in the chilly, early hours of the morning. Helen Barrows, her two daughters, and their maid were comfortably seated inside the duke's spacious traveling carriage. The duke and Captain Mark Estermire rode outside with two outriders for protection. Half asleep still, the ladies dozed and were quiet for the initial stages, but as the day wore on, the rocking motion of the vehicle became more uncomfortable.

To divert everyone, Elisabeth insisted the tale of the almost kidnapping be explained in detail to her. Yawning, Sophia began the story with a giggle.

"You took to the floor with Roderick in his black domino. We all knew it was he because he had introduced himself to us. Mark was similarly dressed along with many other men, as you know, all masked. Those black dominoes dotted the dance floor and popped up everywhere, a favorite costume of the men. Why don't men enjoy the art of costume as we do? You can barely tell one from another, although the color of a gentleman's hair is helpful. Careful attention could distinguish one from another, but once inside the dancing, it was impossible," she continued with a slight smile on her placid face.

"Such a domino approached me begging for a dance. Mark was somewhere searching for refreshments, so I had no reason to refuse. I did not identify the gentleman, and he was a man of few words. My first clue something was amiss was the almost rough handling I was getting from this strange man. He held my hand too tight. He brushed against me on the dance floor and once clasped me around the waist. I became nervous and looked around for Mark." She paused to draw a deep breath.

"Those dratted dominoes! At that distance, Mark was exactly like every other black-caped gentleman wearing a mask, so there was no immediate rescue. I continued the set and was prepared to leave the floor to join my friends when this madman grabbed my hand and dragged me into the garden and back to a dark corner. I glimpsed a carriage waiting and knew real fear for a moment, but we paused. This gentleman had coal-black hair. I had no clue who he was or why he could possibly want to take me away from my friends and family, but I suspected that was about to happen." Elisabeth reached to squeeze Sophia's hand in sympathy, sorry now that her sister had had such an anxious time.

"Well, whoever he was, I was going no further. I stopped dead on the path and grabbed at the branch of a tree to stay where I was. Enlightenment came when the gentleman referred to me as Elisabeth. Are you full of suspicions now, my Lizzie?"

"Of course, it was Teasdale mistaking you for me, is that not correct?" She shook her head in disgust. "But Sophia, you related a dark-headed man. Teasdale has light hair. Could you not see in the garden? Was it too dark?"

"Elisabeth, when I stopped, he pulled off his mask

and then..." She broke into giggles. "You will not believe, but he wore a wig! You must admit he was a clever villain."

"What happened? Did Mark come to your rescue? How did it all come about that you were released?"

"No, I fear Mark thought I had retreated to repair my costume. He was not even searching for me at that time." She folded her hands and prepared to finish her tale.

"As we stood there in the garden, me holding onto a tree, and he pulling at my arm like—like a tug o' war at the fair, quite ridiculous, he began to tell me how we were to be married the very next morning. I think, but I'm not certain, he was trying to reassure me my reputation would remain intact.

"How very odd, was it not? How could a man kidnapping a lady reassure her of the safety of her reputation? It was not logical. Once he even apologized for the method he had to use, but said he had been forced into it."

"What were you doing all this time, my sister?" Elisabeth asked.

"Trying to untie my mask! I had it in my pea-sized brain he would let me go if only I could convince him I was not you!" She laughed again and Elisabeth chuckled with her, but her pulse had accelerated with this account of the wicked viscount endangering her beloved sister.

"As you know, my mask was tied behind my head and then my bonnet placed over it. In my excitement I tried to pull off the mask before I removed the bonnet. Of course it did not work. Until I had the brilliant thought to remove my bonnet, nothing could work."

She chuckled again.

"You will think I was frightened, but I assure you I was not. Angry, yes, but I knew he had the wrong lady all the time. What could he do when he found out? I will tell you."

"He had nudged me toward the carriage where a dim light from the street lamps revealed him to be Teasdale for certain. He smiled at me genially and gestured toward the carriage. He seemed cheerful at this point, I presume because he thought he had the prize. Imagine his face when he found out he had the wrong sister!" She clapped her hands in delight.

"Did he not become enraged? How did he handle it when your bonnet came off and then the mask?" Elisabeth thought how slim the margin that kept her free. It was only a decision to exchange costumes. Such is the quixotic nature of fate, she thought.

"It was if someone took away his breath. His face fell, and he staggered against the carriage just staring at me. 'Sophia?' he asked, as if he could not believe his eyes. He kept saying over and over, 'Sophia, not Elisabeth' until it was funny." She whooped and Elisabeth and Helen joined her in laughter.

"My heaven, what happened then?" Elisabeth asked when she was rational again. "He has a terrible temper. I'm afraid he might have hurt you."

"He slumped as if from a blow. He waved his hand at me, indicating I could flee, which I did, I can tell you. I ran as fast as I could out of there and back into the ballroom. Mark was beginning to look for me. When I told him about what happened, he ran out into the garden, but the carriage and Teasdale were already gone."

"We looked around for you, but were not worried. Roderick was with you on the dance floor, so we thought he would be protecting you from harm."

*Yes, but no one protected me from the duke and his fatal charm. It was not all his fault. I participated eagerly, and I readily admit it.* She sat in the corner of the carriage and shivered, remembering the delicious kisses Richard had given her lips, which betrayed her by craving his touches.

"Elisabeth? Are you sickening for something?" her mother asked. She leaned over to touch her daughter's forehead.

"No, Mother. Just a chill from the weather." Since the weather was sunny and dry, she felt her pulse throb and heat flush her face. How could she admit to her parent her decadent behavior with the duke? She could hardly believe it herself. The worse thing was that she longed to be with him again and…she tried to cool her blushes by thinking of something different.

With Teasdale behind her and the Duke of Roderick ahead, Elisabeth felt trapped. As the carriage rolled and dipped over the uneven roadway, she tried to sort her thoughts.

Teasdale seemed to be in the throes of some sort of obsession. It was unexplained and dangerous. He held no affection for her, so it was a mystery why he insisted upon pursuing her even after her engagement was officially announced. Her safety worried her family, so she had agreed to a false engagement with Roderick, who had conspired with her mother—odd that her mother should have sanctioned the plan, thought Elisabeth briefly before returning her thoughts to her predicament.

She loved the duke, formerly her Richard, and was susceptible to his lovemaking. *Susceptible?* She mocked her thoughts. She longed for, no craved, his touch and was drawn to him. She did not understand why she remained so set against the marriage. Was her stubbornness a sign of immaturity? Her mother pointed out how much she had changed in two years. Why did she not believe Roderick had made a mistake as well and now was sorry for it?

Deep down she thought she knew. If she accepted him back into her heart, it would leave her vulnerable, unprotected from hurt. The memory of how badly she suffered from his abrupt absence, and then the more recent revelation of his actual identity was too painful for her to accept him again. Trust was the issue, but it was not only his betrayal she feared.

She admitted longing for his touch, incredible longing, but she did not trust herself to allow the love inside again. It was too dangerous to her heart. She truly did not know if she could ever willingly love wholeheartedly again.

What did that make her? Not much different from the women of arranged liaisons who married and gave heirs to their husbands without affection. Soon they were out looking for someone to love, and many were unfaithful to their spouses. Was that something she wanted? *Unequivocally not.* As angry as she was at the duke, she did not believe he deserved a wife who could never love again. Clearly, it was her duty to refuse him. She would explain it all to him after they arrived at his estate. Then he would see how impossible this engagement really was.

The carriage came to a stop, and she peered out at

the ancient but prosperous Inn, called the Big Red Rooster, where they would spend the night. There were other travelers pulling into the courtyard with young hostlers running here and there, seemingly at random, tending the horses. They yelled cheerfully to each other and seemed to enjoy the chaos. Elisabeth did as well. The activities were healthy ones, purposeful ones, and the sight helped her leave her introspective anguish.

As she stepped down from the carriage, Richard appeared and held out his hand. She took it, enjoying the warm squeeze and the fond glances he gave her. It was exactly as she thought. She was deeply in lust with the Duke of Roderick, and there was no help for it.

****

They arrived at the duke's vast estate the next day and were settled in familiar rooms by the housekeeper. She confided that the duchess had arrived the day before and was still recovering from the trip, but that she would see them the day after.

"She sent her good wishes for your comfort, Mrs. Barrows," the housekeeper said, jangling her household keys and bustling about the room. She snapped her fingers, and two young maids came forward to assist with the unpacking of their belongings.

"Your daughters are given rooms across the corridor with a parlor between. You will be comfortable here in this corner room with a lovely view," she added, pulling back a curtain to expose the pastoral scene of the hillside dotted with grazing sheep. Helen Barrows exclaimed at the lovely view and vowed she would be happy to reside in that room.

Elisabeth and Sophia settled into their individual quarters and met soon afterward in the pretty parlor to exclaim over their special treatment.

"A vast difference when there are no rivals for the wife of the duke, eh, Lizzie?" Sophia teased, propping her feet on a soft, blue velvet stool.

"You are forgetting that the dowager duchess and our mother have been fast friends all their lives. It is more probable our different accommodations are due to that fact."

"Whatever the cause, it is a lovely arrangement. Do you think our bodies will ever stop rolling as if we were still traveling?" Sophia asked, rubbing her arms.

"It's a long way even with the overnight stop. I don't wonder at the duchess keeping to her room for a day. Why is it so delightful to have a fire even in summer?" She warmed her hands over the blaze burning cheerfully in the hearth.

Elisabeth thought she would not ride today, but she intended to visit the stables. She was that eager to meet Sweet Blaze. In her room, she was delighted to find a stack of novels, no doubt appropriate reading material selected by the duchess. Elisabeth was amused to remember the red leather book with gold binding that so scandalized the duke.

That seemed a lifetime ago, when a naive young lady poked her inquisitive nose into someplace it did not belong. Memories tumbled one over another as she wandered downstairs and out into the sunshine. The early morning fog was long gone. Inside the hazy darkness of the stables, she strolled from one stall to another looking for a familiar bay with a white blaze down its nose. She carried a small pippin begged from the housekeeper and cried out with delight when a familiar face whinnied.

Chapter Thirty-Five

"Oh, you beauty," she crooned, rubbing the young mare's face and stroking her neck. She held out the treat and laughed out loud when the velvet nose tickled her hand as the mare nibbled delicately. Tears formed in Elisabeth's eyes, though why she felt so sentimental she could not say. She clasped her arms around the mare's neck and placed her face against the warm animal. With unreserved affection, she could love this wonderful mare. Would that she could enjoy the same with its owner.

"Elisabeth, I must meet with one of my managers. Would you be pleased to ride out with me?"

She knew without turning the voice belonged to Richard. Her pulse beat a rapid tempo, but he did not attempt to touch her. Slowly, she turned around and met his eyes. He smiled at her but stood with his whip in hand already dressed for riding.

"I am severely tardy and must get about tending my business, but I would be pleased to have you for company," he said. Elisabeth nodded.

"Could you wait for a few minutes? I must change my gown. I will hurry." He gave her a genuine smile and a wink as she turned quickly away.

For the next hour, she observed the Duke of Roderick as he met and visited with first one tenant and then another. He mostly touched base and advised them to make appointments for a longer session. The visits were cordial. Roderick was apparently a well-respected landlord and, perhaps she would say, beloved, when one little girl ran up with a bouquet of flowers for him.

"You are a kind master, Roderick," she said. "The business of duke is a heavy responsibility, is it not?"

"The government required my services. Although I have an excellent agent, I have been away too long. My father and his father before him were honorable men. How could I be anything different? 'To whom much is given, much is required' was a motto in my family, a paraphrasing quote from the Bible—Luke, I believe. Are you familiar with it?" She shook her head.

"Were you not allowed a carefree youth, Your Grace? Were you never a naïve young man making ridiculous decisions and forgiven for your age?"

"Ah, well, I had careful guidance, but I must have done at some point. I am much older than you are, Elisabeth. I often wondered at myself for falling in love with so young a lady. No, don't bristle at me. I am carefully telling you the truth at all times. Do you know how first I loved you? We had not even met." He gave her a quixotic glance.

"How could that be? We met at the lily pond. I well remember flying over Sweet Blaze's head." She chuckled at the memory. "You were not in love with me then?"

"Oh, yes. Truly caught by that time. I had been watching you race James Wilkerson and knew your name by that time. You see I must confess to another ruse you know nothing about." She glared then and he gave an exaggerated cringe.

"Let me tell you the whole story and see if you are

still angry. May we stop at the lily pond and check out the ducks without you interfering with their swim?" He laughed at her pursed lips, but she nodded her head in agreement.

The duke waved at a nearby gardener who came running to hold the horses. He helped Elisabeth from the saddle, and they walked over the soft, well-mowed grounds. "Are your memories fond? You enjoyed your visit then, did you not?"

"It was a full two years ago. I was young, Roderick. Very young and had not been around men very much. Jamie…" He held up his hand to stop her.

"Jamie, now there's a good friend. I understand he refused to teach you how to kiss, did he not?" Elisabeth's mouth dropped open, and Roderick gave a shout of laughter.

"Did he tell you that? I can't believe what a scoundrel he is to gossip about me behind my back. Wait until I see him!" She stormed around as if to confront Jamie at once.

"He is a fast friend, Lizzie, and said nothing. I confess to eavesdropping that day in my library. It was not deliberate, but my wing chair hides much. It was your voice I fell in love with, my dear. You made me laugh and that beautiful, low voice of yours took hold of my heart and has not turned it loose since. I fear that in that moment I vowed it would be me who taught you to kiss."

"So you stalked me?" she asked incredulously. "What I thought was fate was instead a man taking advantage of my naiveté to make a fool of and steal kisses from a young girl?" Her fingers curled into a fist as she stared up at him with fire in her eyes.

"No, no. I planned nothing. Of course, I wanted to kiss you. What man wouldn't? And then you were so lovely atop Blaze. And so mortified in that tree! I think I felt real love that day when your foot was caught by my little owl. You stepped into his home and..." He laughed again as she felt her face growing warm and knew it was probably flushed. "You were so very adorable sitting in that tree. How could I help falling in love with you?"

"Why did you not say you heard Jamie and me?" She wandered over and sat on a bench by the pond. She knew the answer, but wanted to hear him say it.

"I would not wish to embarrass you or James. I was accidentally a witness to an endearing scene and, truly, at that time, never thought it would be a meaningful incident.

"Lizzie, sweetness, I must get back to my duties. Will you walk with me after supper? There is a man with a stack of household books I must meet with on a dusty not very nice task I had hoped to avoid for a few days. He is even now waiting for me in that very same library." They remounted and rode swiftly to the stables, afterward walking together back to the mansion.

"He is not the last manager I must deal with due to my long absence. You will want to ride with Sweet Blaze again, will you not? I would join you if I could, but I will be reconciled to you, at least, enjoying yourself.

"Will you join me after supper, Elisabeth? You have not answered."

"Perhaps, Richard. I must have time to think over this new information. I will make a decision then."

253

They parted. Elisabeth wondered about Richard's pensive expression. Did he, too, need time to think things over?

After supper, which was served in a smaller room where she was placed at his right elbow, her mother on his left, she did agree to walk out into the soft summer twilight on his arm. They kept a comfortable silence between them as he led her through the formal gardens to a small orchard off the kitchen garden.

"I played here often as a boy. Some of the village lads were my playmates, and we snitched many a green apple from these trees. There, was that enough youthful mistakes to make for you? I assure you our stomachs were very sorry later." She laughed as he leaned down to nuzzle her hair.

"I bring a message to you from my mother, Elisabeth. She would like for you to ride with her tomorrow. I leave it for her to discuss her reasons. Will you accommodate her?" Elisabeth was surprised, but she was fond of the duchess and assented quickly to the request.

"I will let her know. I believe she is set to ride around two of the clock."

Chapter Thirty-Six

"Mistress says you come to the back where she is loading her baskets," a ginger-haired maid said to her, as she descended the stairs later that day. She hurried through the long hall and made her way to the kitchen. Directions there steered her out a side door where she found a bright blue carriage outfitted with a hood, hitched to a small mare of some advanced age. The duchess directed two young boys who were loading the several baskets brought out of the kitchen by cook and a tweeny. She looked up with a smile and a wave.

Elisabeth understood she was to take a seat in the carriage and was soon joined by Her Grace. The lady dressed in a serviceable brown gown and cape with a bonnet that had seen better days. She popped a small whip in the air. The mare jerked forward and plodded slowly down the long drive.

"Ah, now we have time to visit. Nutmeg here could take a charge from one of Boney's cannons and still not increase her pace. She was once a splendid little goer, but like me, time has tamed her efforts.

"She is still a beauty. Was she a special mount for you?" Elisabeth asked, glancing sideways at the still attractive older woman.

"One of them. I had several. Shall I confess how much I have enjoyed being the wife of a great man of the land? You might suspect I have invited you to accompany me to plead for my son's happiness. That would be only partially true. I did want to introduce you to the duties of a duchess, which are many and varied. If you are considering staying in an engagement with my son, and I do hope you are, you must understand the duties you will be required to tend. I came to his father ignorant and inept, and it took considerable hard work for me to achieve the proficiency required. Fortunately my husband's mother was kind and assisted in the schooling of me. You see, Elisabeth, I wed for love and brought very little else to my marriage. Accomplishments, but no dowry, nothing at all except an enormous love for my duke. Fortunately, the foolish man required very little else." She laughed and patted Elisabeth on the hand.

"I do love Richard," Elisabeth proclaimed stoutly. "I have loved him ever since we met two years ago. That is not our problem, you see." She felt a tear roll down her cheek and rubbed it away with her glove.

"Do not fret, dear child. Please do not distress yourself. Today we are only on an excursion to become acquainted. Whatever Richard has done to make you unhappy, he is surely sorry for it now. It does not hurt for an important man to grovel for a spell, do you think?" She chuckled and popped her tiny whip again. The mare picked up speed but settled down soon afterward into her slow plod.

The duchess pulled beside the gated yard of a thatched cottage. Several young children ran out speaking in high-pitched voices a dialect foreign to Elisabeth. She tilted her head in a puzzled manner trying to hear one word with clarity.

"Do not bother to try. One of our young men

served as a soldier and came home with this wife and their children. It could be French, but then I suspect Spanish. It is so garbled it could be neither. Never mind. We are here to visit the mother who has produced yet another happy sibling for these children. Would you help me with that basket with the red cloth?" Together, they tugged the basket and placed it on the kitchen table.

A young, pretty woman came forward holding a tiny babe in her arms. She, too, spoke the indecipherable language, but with gestures and nods, they managed to converse with her. One word came through clear.

"Thank you," the woman said. She offered the babe to the duchess, who took it in her arms and admired the red scrunched-up face. It was sleeping but woke and yawned widely. Elisabeth was instantly enchanted and held out her arms where the duchess willingly deposited the minute bundle. She caressed the infant's cheek with the tip of her finger and it hungrily sought the touch with a nuzzle, smacking his tiny lips.

"Oh, I think he needs you." She transferred the bundle to the smiling mother who snuggled it against her chest. They said their goodbyes and left in the blue cart, the mare plodding once more.

"Now we are on a more unpleasant errand. Should you prefer to stay in the cart? There is an old woman in her last days, and she is not always eager for visitors. Once she was a wonderful nanny, but retired years ago. She has no family to care for her, but we assign one or another of the young girls to take a turn. The sharpness of her tongue makes them glad to leave."

"Was she nanny to Roderick?" Elisabeth asked

curious.

"Sort of, but not really. Already her joints were failing her, which is what makes her so cross now. We put her in charge of younger and more agile nannies which she carefully trained. It made for a smooth transition for the boy. Richard visits her now and then. He's probably already stopped by to say hello since he's been home."

They were welcomed at the door by a young girl in a gingham gown. She smiled as if in great relief. The duchess went immediately into the cottage and spoke quietly to the patient. With the young maid, Elisabeth assisted in emptying the basket of both medicines and food.

"How is she feeling today?" Elisabeth asked. The young girl shrugged her shoulders.

"Nawt much better, missus. Her joints hurt her somethin' terrible. This medicine will help." She lifted a small bottle the duchess had included from her own stillroom.

Soon the duchess was saying goodbye, and they rejoined the mare on the many errands yet to come. Elisabeth had helped on her father's estate before he died, but it had been a few years since she was required to tend the families of farmers. She was learning from the duchess.

They made the rounds for two hours until all the baskets were delivered, and they finally turned Nutmeg toward home. Elisabeth's head was whirling with the names of the many tenants and their children, understanding she had met only a small portion of Roderick's people. It was a great thing to be in charge of such a large property. She could see the division of duties overlapped between the duke and his mother. Clearly a duchess was an important person to this estate.

"Your Grace?" Elisabeth asked as they wound their way back up the long, straight driveway toward the mansion. The good lady turned toward her with eyebrows raised.

"Should I become a duchess some day, I mean if ever…?"

"Yes, dear, I understand. Go on."

"How could I learn all this? The stillroom alone is a formidable task." She wrung her hands in anxiety. Even if she could convince her heart, she doubted she was up to the requirements of wife to a duke.

The duchess trilled a laugh. "Never fear. My staff could operate this place for years and never miss me. They would rally around you as well. I just wanted you to have a glimpse of some of the good you can do—it is my presence as much as the baskets that Richard's people appreciate. Try and enjoy yourself during your visit here, Elisabeth. That is all that is required of you at this point."

"It appears we have company," she said waving at someone in a carriage which had just pulled up.

The invitations from the Duke of Roderick had been accepted as carriage after carriage pulled in front of the mansion depositing family after family. Up the driveway raced three horses abreast, their riders whooping. Elisabeth recognized James Wilkerson, Matthew Diver-Jones, and Lyndon Peron, who seemed to be out in front by a nose. They rode directly for the stables, leaving a cloud of dust behind them. Elisabeth was relieved to see her friends and took to heart the duchess's last words. She was there to have fun and enjoy herself. There was a certain mare with a white blaze that had been neglected for too long. Tomorrow, she would join the riders.

She left the blue cart and the gracious lady who drove it and went directly inside. There she found several of her friends already conversing with Sophia. Jane Hawlester came in with Eloise Larkin, with whom she had been visiting. The ladies were served tea while they waited for their luggage to be situated and rooms assigned.

"I vow, but it is a long drive," Eloise said. "My bones are still shaking."

"We shall have such fun, you will see," Jane promised.

Chapter Thirty-Seven

Roderick had many small excursions planned as entertainment for his guests. Captain Mark Estermire arrived with several young men in tow to complete the guest list. There was talk of a shooting sport planned for the young gentlemen. The ladies were to visit the village for shopping. They were delighted to find ribbons and gloves, and two enterprising ladies discovered a talented milliner and bought trimming for their hats. The local inn served steaming mugs of tea with a popular apple pastry. The young ladies agreed it was a charming village. Elisabeth was amused by their innocent excitement. Had she ever been so green?

In the afternoons, archery was popular with both sexes. It was one of the familiar pastimes in which both Elisabeth and Sophia were proficient. Sophia managed to put all challengers to shame by not only hitting the bull's-eye, but once splitting the arrow stuck in it. Great whoops of approval rose at this incredible feat, while Sophia managed a modest mien.

The duke put his stables at his guests' disposal as well. Next morning very early, Elisabeth, dressed once more in her red riding habit, entered the stables. A groom met her there with Sweet Blaze already saddled and waiting. Roderick, on his monster black, was pacing around outside. She joined him without a word, and they dropped the reins to allow both mounts to shake the fidgets out with a swift run.

Elisabeth was exhilarated to be riding freely once more. If she was not to have her Richard, then Roderick's horses must be a winning second favorite, she thought. She ventured to say to him just that as they paused upon the hill underneath the oak tree. The view below was one of peaceful, bucolic beauty.

"I would win you no matter how, my sweet. If it is my high steppers you love, then so be it. Marry me to ride your sweet mare then?" She grinned at him and patted Sweet Blaze. It was a hard ride up the hill, but she had been up for it.

"There's a bridle trail around through the wood, near a tree with a hollow in it. Should you like to try it? It ends at an old ruin and part of a stream you will recognize."

She nodded and they were off, ambling along the pleasant warmth. The ride by the woods was cool and refreshing, but they did not stop there. When they broke out of the shadows, Elisabeth spotted the ruins on the side of a small hill. There they dismounted to take their horses to the stream for a drink.

Elisabeth pulled handfuls of dried grasses and rubbed her sweating mare down as the horse nibbled succulent green grass near the stream. Roderick performed a similar service to his black, but tied him to a shrub within reach of the water. He came over and tied Elisabeth's as well. The horses were content enough to graze and drink within the shade of a young oak. The duke reached for her hand and led her toward the ruin.

"I intend to kiss you, my Elisabeth. I warn you, in case you would prefer to flee."

She looked up at him but said not a word. She suspected he knew how susceptible she was to his caresses. He pulled her tightly against his hard body. There he paused to gaze deeply into her eyes.

"My longing for you knows no depths. I think of you all the time, my love. Say we may marry, before I anticipate the ceremony and make you mine." He leaned down and took control of her mouth with a fierceness of hunger. She met his kisses with an eagerness of her own, hearing his groans as he felt her passion. He stood back and nudged her into the shadows of the old castle.

She heard herself moaning and calling his name as she slid slowly to the grassy meadow beneath them. He dropped with her and cradled her in his arms tenderly. Their mouths fused as their bodies entangled with a sweet passion. Elisabeth eagerly gave over her will to the exquisite moves of her tutor. She murmured his name over and over as waves of pleasure rolled over her.

A wonderful peace entered her consciousness, and she felt as if she floated above their heads. Finally, she relaxed and closed her eyes almost on the verge of sleep. Roderick settled her in his arms and relaxed as well.

"Did you like that, Elisabeth?" he asked in a sultry voice. "You are a passionate lady, did you know?" But Elisabeth heard him only from a distance. As she recovered, she remained in a languid condition but understood an urgent need to rise.

"Roderick? Was what you did something married couples do? Is it sinful, do you think?" She heard his chest rumble and knew he was amused at her question.

She sat up and he reluctantly removed his hands from around her.

"Tell me, Your Grace. Should that have waited for a marriage ceremony?" she insisted. He lay on his back in the grass gazing at the sky with a smile on his face.

"Well," he said sitting up and facing her. "You cannot provide an heir with what we did, but probably your mother would have suggested we should have waited for the minister. Are you angry with me?" He pulled straw from her hair and touched her cheek with one finger.

"I don't think I am. How could I feel anger after that?" She smiled at him and then they both burst into laughter reaching and hugging each other.

When they emerged some twenty minutes later, Elisabeth's hair was in urgent need of repair. Richard did his best, but he proved unskilled as a ladies' maid.

"I am afraid you will be required to pretend to another fall, my love," said Richard, grinning at her.

"I will develop a reputation as a clumsy lout," retorted Elisabeth. "And when I think of all my care these last two years to adhere to society's rules, only to disappear into what I'm sure must be the whole countryside's trysting place."

"But my mother said that you should become more familiar with the estate, my love." They both laughed and returned to their horses.

Chapter Thirty-Eight

Days drifted lazily into one another as Roderick's houseguests enjoyed their visit. Sophia and Elisabeth took on all challengers at archery, but soon they were noted as the "unbeatables" and could not find a game. Jane and Eloise worked to gain expertise but, so far, were easily overcome. There were many small riding parties exploring here and there, and some had discovered the old ruins. Jane teased for a picnic when the weather was dry. Roderick, with a glance at Elisabeth agreed. She ducked her head with a secret smile, not daring to look at the duke.

They still met in the early mornings, but in company having agreed to avoid a repeat of what happened between them at the ruins. "I cannot trust myself, Elisabeth. I love you too much to risk your reputation. We will exhibit more self-control, what think you?" She agreed, and they avoided solitary rides for several days.

Elisabeth sat in the garden alone one afternoon, watching honeybees work on the blossoms, while butterflies flitted here and there, and a small red-breasted robin tweeted over her head. Such peace as she had not felt in a while settled over her. She heard the crunch of the gravel on one of the paths and steeled herself for company. Roderick rounded the corner and came to her, holding out his hands.

She grasped his while he pulled her to him and kissed her softly on the mouth.

"I cannot fathom my garden without you in it, Elisabeth. I am aware I broke your heart even as I did not realize I had, but now I understand and I am so very sorry. I am in dreadful danger of having my own broken as well. Will you agree to pity me, wed me, and allow me to make lifelong love to you, my darling? I pledge on my life you will never regret it a day." He took advantage of the seclusion provided by the fragrant rose bower in which Elisabeth had been sitting to pull her more firmly to him and cover her face in kisses.

"If I marry you only for your kisses, will you settle for that?" she asked only half-way teasing, and then laughed out loud for the surprise on his face. "I am saying yes, Richard."

He whooped and grabbed her around the waist and swung her around and around. She cried out for him to put her down, but he cradled her in his lap, taking possession of the garden bench.

"I will work to earn your love, but if you are satisfied with other things for now, I will call for a special license, what think you? I want you completely, my Elisabeth. If you like what happens between us so far, you will be very happy to learn what comes next." He grinned and kissed her on her cheek.

"My mother and your own will be scandalized, but many of our friends are present. I agree. Send for a special license and let us complete the deed very soon." She trailed a finger down his chest, wriggling it to creep inside his shirt. He groaned and placed a hard kiss on her open mouth. He stood and set her on her feet.

"We are having a dance party tonight, a good time to announce the date of our wedding, think you?" She nodded her head. Truth, she was looking forward to the wedding night to find out what the duke had yet to teach her. He had turned out to be a remarkable tutor. What she had learned so far was pretty exciting, and she gave a small shudder of delight at the thought of more of his kisses. She doubted anything could be more exciting. Of course, she knew there was more to learn. Babies did not come from the antics they had enjoyed so far.

"I am leaving you now and going to my mother. She will want to be prepared for the announcement tonight, if that is agreeable to you. Do you go to your own mother and sister?" She nodded yes with a smile, imaging her mother's reaction.

****

Sophia squealed and her mother, contrary to Elisabeth's expectations, uttered "Thank goodness" in response to the announcement that the engagement was not only a real one, but that the wedding was imminent. Seeing her daughter's surprise at this calm acceptance of the arrangements, her mother raised her eyebrows.

"Did you think, my dear, that I would have consented to Roderick's ridiculous plan to 'save' you from Teasdale, without first being very sure that the duke was essential to your future happiness? Her Grace and I have had our heads together these many weeks, I assure you."

"I won't pry into what made you change your mind. Was it that sweet mare you are so fond of?" Sophia asked. "I knew the duke would win you over if only he could get you near his horses." She ducked the

267

pillow thrown at her head and ran from the room laughing.

"I know you have not allowed a horse, even a very nice one, to change your mind, Lizzie, my dear. Marriage is for a lifetime, and you must be certain." She kissed her daughter on the forehead.

"I am certain, Mother. I've known it for a while, but my stubbornness would not allow me to admit it. I've always loved him. I had a problem trusting my heart to him the second time, but I'm reconciled he's a good and honorable man. He will never leave me again." Her mother embraced her and wiped a tear from her eye.

"Besides, I rather like the thought that I could be a duchess. It sounds like a formidable job, but, as you know, I must have an outlet for my energy. I know I must work at it to become proficient, just like the duchess said. In the end, I imagine I will be content." She received another smile of approval.

"Oh, and then there's all his wonderful horses." She too ran laughing from the room, leaving her mother smiling and preparing to pen a note to Her Grace. It was time to put in place the plans for the wedding that had occupied them on many a quiet morning. Elisabeth's godmother and her Aunt Anna would be arriving soon, along with a few of the duke's connections.

****

That night there was an air of anticipation, as word spread throughout the household there would soon be a new duchess. Elisabeth dressed with care wearing a newly designed gown of white lace over pink satin. Her blonde curls were held back by pins with sparkling pink crystals. A knock on the door was answered by her maid and her future mother-in-law entered. Elisabeth looked up with surprise.

"Is everything all right?" she asked, feeling some alarm. Was something wrong with Roderick?

"Yes, dear. I have brought you a little something to wear tonight if you care to." She opened a jewel case and pulled out a three-tier strand of rare pink pearls. "These are always given to the brides in the family. There is a bracelet and a tiara to match. Do you care to try them on?" She smiled when Elisabeth's eyes filled with tears.

"Yes, how perfectly lovely. They are beautiful. Thank you so much." Had her mother known all this time? She had been so set on helping her choose the exact shade of pink for this gown.

"They are yours after tonight, dear. There are many more sets should you care to learn about them. We will meet someday soon, and I will turn the keys over to you." She leaned over to embrace Elisabeth. "I am pleased you have decided to take that scapegrace of a son of mine. He will never make a mistake like that again, I assure you. You have led him a proper, merry chase."

She walked arm in arm with Elisabeth down the stairs and into the ballroom. Inside, she nodded to Roderick and Helen Barrows. The gathered crowd quieted, anticipating an important announcement. Elisabeth noticed servants hanging at the doors listening. All the guests were assembled, save those family connections who, her mother had assured her, would be arriving within a few days.

"My dear friends, I am happy to announce that Miss Barrows and I have decided to move our wedding forward. We ask you all to be our guests for the ceremony here today week." As the guests applauded, Roderick signaled to the musicians, reached for his future bride, and took to the floor in a waltz.

"I see Mother has graced you with the bride's pearls. Awake on every suit, our mothers! Those pearls are lovely on you, but not half as beautiful as my passionate Elisabeth," he whispered in her hair, brushing her cheek with his. "You are a lovely lady, my Elisabeth. Passionate and lovely." She pinched him on the shoulder.

"Behave. Both our parents are watching, not to mention the entire house party and what…some invited guests as well?" He twirled her around and around until she was dizzy. Other couples took to the floor, Sophia with her Mark, both grinning over at them.

The night ended with Elisabeth exhausted but too happy and excited to sleep. She wondered why it had taken her so long to trust her heart to the one she loved, but perhaps it was exactly the right amount of time. The duchess said she should not forgive her son too soon. Elisabeth tested her heart and found it open again to both her Richard and the Duke of Roderick. He would always be her Noble Rescuer, in her private thoughts, but really, there was so much more to the duke than a few shared kisses in the garden. How glad she was the wedding would take place soon.

Epilogue

(For the reader curious to discover, or who perhaps has already guessed, why the Viscount chased so hard and long after Elisabeth Barrows.)

A mile away in an old cottage, tucked into the edge of a wood once owned by some ancient duke, Ronald Harrison and Viscount Teasdale huddled over a poorly lit fire. They had been there for a week waiting for an opportunity to kidnap Elisabeth Barrows. Teasdale had the special license, and Harrison had found a rector who liked his rum too much and was willing to officiate in spite of an unwilling bride. A rough goon entered the cabin and dumped an armful of freshly cut wood near the fireplace.

"Nawt company goin' home now. His Grace be married by the end of the week. Celebrations and big banquets with the village invited. Goin', milord?"

Teasdale swore loud and long. He knew now he had lost, not only Elisabeth Barrows, but his grays, his possessions, and his allowance for the foreseeable future. All would be sold or pledged to pay off the insane wager he made with Lord Silvertip. It would wipe him out. His father would never support such foolishness, as he would not mince words calling it. Teasdale must rusticate or…rusticate.

Teasdale wondered not for the first time what he

was doing hanging around with such an unsavory dolt like Harrison. Really, the man was missing a few bits of his brain. He turned to speak to Ronald Harrison but found the man packing up to leave.

"No sense in hanging around now. Roderick won't come off his estate until he has a couple of heirs. Might try for him then." Harrison left the room leaving Teasdale sitting there with his mouth hanging open. Soon he, too, packed up his gear and left the ancient cabin.

## A word about the author...

Emma Lane lives in Western NY on a few acres where she spends many hours gardening. Besides a love for regency romances, she also writes cozy mysteries under the pen name Janis Lane. Visit her at www.emmajlane.com

Thank you for purchasing
this publication of The Wild Rose Press, Inc.

If you enjoyed the story, we would appreciate your
letting others know by leaving a review.

For other wonderful stories,
please visit our on-line bookstore at
www.thewildrosepress.com.

For questions or more information
contact us at
info@thewildrosepress.com.

The Wild Rose Press, Inc.
www.thewildrosepress.com

Stay current with The Wild Rose Press, Inc.

Like us on Facebook

https://www.facebook.com/TheWildRosePress

And Follow us on Twitter
https://twitter.com/WildRosePress